THE HOUSE'S MONEY

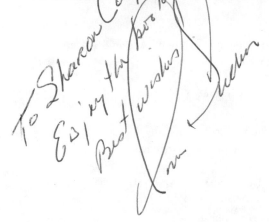

OWEN SULLIVAN

AUTHORITY
PUBLISHING

The House's Money
By Owen Sullivan

1. FIC000000 - Fiction / General 2. FIC 002000 - Fiction / Action & Adventure
3. FIC 020000 Fiction / Men's Adventure

ISBN: 978-1-935953-35-7

Cover design by David Flanagan
Interior design by Stephanie Martindale

Printed in the United States of America

Authority Publishing
11230 Gold Express Dr. #310-413
Gold River, CA 95670
800-877-1097
www.AuthorityPublishing.com

To Genevieve with love and gratitude.

ACKNOWLEDGEMENTS

I would like to thank Andrea Hurst of Andrea Hurst & Associates for taking on an unknown author and guiding him with patience; Stephanie Chandler and Amberly Finarelli at Authority Publishing, who helped me negotiate the publishing maze; Jessica Schmitz and David Flanagan at Misfits for their combined creative marketing and advertising genius; and Genevieve Sullivan, my loving wife, for her encouragement, input, and invaluable insight. I couldn't have done this project without all of your help. Thank you.

ONE

Matt maneuvered his old Honda up the circular drive of the Olympic Club, where it sputtered to a stop in the valet line. The place met all his expectations. White columns bathed in light graced a massive entry staircase, set off by acres of rolling emerald lawn that made up the world-renowned golf course.

He watched valets running up to drivers and speeding off with Mercedes', Rolls-Royces, and Jaguars. "Damn, I should have taken a cab."

Rubbing his sweaty palms on freshly ironed dress slacks, he looked around for a valet. "Come on, hurry up," he muttered to himself.

A woman in a glittering cocktail gown stepped out of a Lexus in front of him, laughing with a male companion while tossing a shawl over her bare shoulder like a character in a pinot noir commercial. Nervously, he felt the breast pocket of his coat, fingering the outline of the formal invitation.

Once again, he ran through his plans for the evening. The event had been on his calendar for months. Hours of research and effort had landed him the invite, with a little help from the dozen roses he'd sent the director's secretary. When he learned from his buddy Drew, that Franklin Smith was looking for a new trader for its mortgage-backed securities and that the head of the department, John Ramsey, would be attending tonight's event, his one objective had been to obtain seating at his table. Nothing was to be left to chance.

Finally, a man in uniform ran up to the driver's side with the requisite haste and self-deprecation of his position.

"Keys in the car?" the valet asked as he opened the door with a white-gloved hand.

Matt nodded. "Thanks."

He straightened his scarlet tie, thinking how well it worked against his charcoal suit, and then proceeded up the marble stairway to carved oak doors. His heart beat so hard it threatened to push right through his chest. He took a deep breath to rein himself in. The Olympic Club was a landmark of San Francisco. The powerful had walked its halls—Donald Trump, Warren Buffet, Bill Gates, Presidents Eisenhower, Kennedy, and Clinton all had been honored guests, and now he, Matt, was about to embark through those doors.

He walked through the expansive entry that was lined with oil paintings of famous athletes: Jack Nicklaus, Arnold Palmer, Tiger Woods, and Joe Namath shared the space with luminaries of modern sports. A pang of regret surfaced, accompanied by the ever-present dull ache in his left knee. He squashed the memory of sitting in the emergency room, still in his quarterback jersey, in excruciating pain. Matt Whiteside, golden boy, dethroned by one untimely tackle. I am on target now, he reminded himself. Today, my ten-year plan for success moves into full gear.

Refocused, he continued down the paneled hall to the large ballroom. "It's show time." Guarding the entry, five attractive young women sat behind a mahogany table. Matt moved to the front of the line at placard U-Z. A flashily dressed brunette met his eyes and a light flush rose from her neck to her cheeks.

"Hello. Your name, please?" she asked, smiling.

He raised his voice to be heard over the laughter and conversation resonating off the high ceilings. "Matt Whiteside."

She shuffled through a small box, her dark curls falling softly over her face. "Ah yes, here you are, Mr. Whiteside. If you lean forward, I'll put this corsage on your coat for you."

She took her time pinning the flower to his coat. "I really like your tie."

"Thanks," he said, wondering how much she'd like it if she knew he'd gotten it from the 75% off rack at Macy's. "Can you tell me where I could find my table?"

"Do you have your invitation?" she asked.

The question caught him for a moment, and he had to fumble through his pockets. He handed her the invitation.

"You're at table 34, near the front." She pointed toward the dining room. "Will your wife be attending? I can give you a wrist corsage to take with you," she said, her sparkling eyes never leaving his.

"No." Matt smiled. "My status is single." He paused. "If I'm lucky you could save me a dance later." There was some of that old spirit.

She smiled back, biting her bottom lip. "Oh, I see. Yes certainly, a dance would be nice, Matt."

"That would be wonderful..." he looked at her name tag "Karen. It's nice to meet you."

Matt meandered through streamers and balloons, past tables with elaborate flower arrangements. The men wore precision-cut jackets and silk ties. The women were in designer gowns, the light sparkling brilliantly as it danced off their diamonds. Money—all of them were swimming in it, and happy to show it off.

Matt arrived at his table and recognized Mr. Ramsey deep in conversation with an attractive middle-aged woman, probably his wife. There was a seat open next to Mr. Ramsey...bingo! As Matt pulled up a chair, the man beside him extended his hand.

"John Ramsey," he said, giving Matt's hand a firm shake. Heavy gray eyebrows stood out against his tanned face, and deep-set lines around his eyes and mouth suggested he laughed more than he frowned.

"Matt Whiteside."

"Pleasure. This is my wife, Ann."

Ann Ramsey was an auburn-haired beauty, with high cheekbones and eyes that implied she knew more than she said. She quickly touched her fingertips to Matt's outstretched damp palms.

"So nice to meet you both."

Matt resisted the urge to adjust his tie. So far, so good. Ann was giving him the once-over with her eyes. "It's my first time here," Matt continued, although by now he felt he had made that fact pretty obvious. "My boss had a prior engagement and offered for me to attend in her place. I'm happy to represent the company." It was a small exaggeration, as she had offered him an invitation—just not to this event. The clandestine maneuvers that had secured his invitation would have made James Bond proud.

"We've been coming to this event for over fifteen years," Ramsey said, scanning the room with an expression of bored familiarity. "The money goes to a good cause and the membership is a nice company benefit. What firm do you work for, Matt?"

Matt took a sip from the ice water in front of him, trying to seem relaxed. "I work for Sun Systems in San Jose. They manufacture silicone chips for most of the major computer firms."

"What's your position with them?" Ramsey asked, raising his eyebrows in apparent genuine interest.

"I'm in charge of their pension plan. I oversee the investing and distributions of the employees' retirement program."

"You seem young for so much responsibility."

Matt shrugged. "I'm twenty-eight," he said, trying to make it sound neither defensive, nor like he was bragging. He knew that most people would kill to have his position and salary at his age. But Matt wanted to trade in his Honda, coasting along in a fifty-five zone on a road to nowhere, for a Ferrari on the autobahn with no speed limit. Franklin Smith was the autobahn.

"Your firm is a client of ours at Franklin Smith. We're a hedge fund and I'm in charge of the West Coast mortgage-backed securities division."

"Yes," Matt said, nodding. "We do invest with your firm. I have to say, I like working with your people." He looked at Ann Ramsey in an effort to include her in the conversation.

Ramsey smiled at the compliment and took a sip from his scotch. "Thank you."

"Mortgage-backed securities are a hot-ticket item these days, aren't they?"

"They are now. I don't know if you were in the business in the late '90s, but at the time the darling investment of the hedge funds was the stock of the dot-com companies. When the bubble burst, the hedge funds needed another source of steady income, so they turned to mortgage-backed securities. How did you get started with Sun Systems?" Ramsey asked.

"I started in 1998, and just when I got settled, the dot-com bubble burst. That was an interesting year in many ways."

Matt smiled as he spoke, remembering those wild months when he still hadn't fully comprehended that his athletic career had ended and he was going to be just another employee at a boring firm. Ramsey seemed to be reminiscing as well, staring at the table as though he were looking through it into the past. He came back quickly enough—not a man to lose his composure, Matt noted. Ramsey leaned back in his chair, his tuxedo lapel slipping to reveal white suspenders. "You must have been fresh out of college, Matt. I still remember those days well."

They talked about college—exams, professors, fraternities, hazing rituals, and the lack thereof. Ramsey recollected horrors his frat house buddies had inflicted on him with a good-natured tone reserved for prized times long past. Through fits of laughter, Matt could see the man missed those days, holding them up like a kind of golden age when college pranks were the things of legends, not the watered down escapades of this new generation.

Ramsey shook his head. "Ah, well. You mentioned college ball. Ever play?"

"Actually, I had a football scholarship at Santa Clara University. I played quarterback there, but blew my knee out badly my junior year. I transferred to San Jose State and finished there."

Ramsey leaned forward, nodding in appreciation. "I played basketball at Stanford, right up until graduation in '72. I started working for Franklin Smith in 1977 and have been there ever since. Never could convince Mrs. Ramsey to let me back into playing. I miss it like hell."

Mrs. Ramsey had joined a couple of friends and now returned to their table, flushed with laughter and possibly the wine. The healthy glow and sparkle in her eyes made her look younger, and a stray lock of hair added a girlish charm to her appearance. She cupped the wine glass in her palm and relaxed back in her chair, giving Matt a look of approval, much to his surprise.

"So, where is your significant other?" she asked. "I can't believe a handsome young man like you would be unattached."

Matt felt his face burn and smiled, caught off-guard by her forwardness. "I'm not dating anyone right now. I uh, keep looking for the right one, but so far she's eluded me." Besides, he didn't have time for a woman. The memory of Kathy Ann, with her long blonde hair, surfaced. Awkwardly, she'd asked how he was doing after his surgery, and when he could only look down at his knee, where the fresh cast was already beginning to itch, she'd said with a flip of her wrist, "I just don't see you being the next Joe Montana or anything now." She dumped him right after that. No, women were not part of his plan.

"Well, I doubt if you'll be on the market long." Mrs. Ramsey smiled at him. She glanced around the room. "From what I gather, there are a lot of ladies here who are hoping you'll ask them to dance later. I'm sure you'll be busy."

She suddenly snapped her fingers, making Matt jump. She turned to her husband and said, "Paul Newman. Matt looks just like a young Paul Newman except with hair mousse. I was trying to explain it to Harriet..."

Ann Ramsey's voice was drowned out by other guests approaching the table. By now, the table for eight had filled up and introductions were being made all around. Ramsey leaned in to Matt and handed him his business card.

"I think you're a smart, energetic young man and I'd like you to call me. We can discuss opportunities at Franklin Smith." He winked. "I think it would be worth your while."

Matt took the card, his heart pounding, and nervously stuck it in his pocket. "Thank you, I'd love to talk about a position."

This had almost been too easy. What was today, Saturday? He'd call Ramsey on Monday. No, Tuesday. That would show he was interested, and that he kept his word, but that he wasn't too eager.

The conversations blurred as he felt heady with excitement, a different kind than when he had arrived. It appeared that his future was getting brighter by the minute.

Two

For the next three days, Matt was on edge. One moment he was looking online at lofts with marble countertops and killer views, dreaming about a high-paying job, and the next he was buried in work at Sun Systems, hoping it would end soon.

He checked his calendar. Tuesday, time to make the call. Taking an early lunch break, he headed to his car and carefully dialed the number on the business card. Ramsey answered on the second ring, sounding impatient.

"Mr. Ramsey? It's Matt Whiteside." Silence. "We met at the Olympic Club's benefit on Friday?"

Dead silence. "Oh yes! Matt Whiteside." Ramsey's tone was instantly friendly. How are you?"

"Good, good. I was just following up on the uh, the opening at your firm you mentioned."

"Right, right." He sounded distracted and said something in a muffled tone to someone in the background. "Matt, can you make it here today? In the next hour or so?"

Now?! Matt calculated in his brain. One-hour lunch break. One hour to get to San Francisco, plus one hour back and the time spent talking with Ramsey. He'd need to get the rest of the day off. But how?

"Sure, not a problem," Matt said.

"Great! See you in an hour. I'm on the twenty-seventh floor of the Embarcadero Building Number Four," Ramsey said as if it was an afterthought.

Matt made his excuses back at the office and ran for the garage. Stunned, he sat immobile for thirty seconds before turning the key and revving the engine.

He breezed through the city. Another light made, he thought, praise to the traffic gods. The bridge traffic was light, relatively speaking, and the fog didn't blanket the streets in smothering gray. He turned into the parking garage at Embarcadero Number Four, found a space immediately, noted the stall number, and then sprinted to the escalator. He exited at the second floor, and paused a second to look at the hustle and bustle around him—secretaries, attorneys, financial planners, all in a hurry to get somewhere. The clicking of high heels and leather shoes on the terrazzo floor echoed around the plaza. He was in the heart of things now, standing in the middle of commerce and money; dollars and yen were in flux, the euro not far behind. I belong here, he almost said out loud.

He proceeded through the double glass doors and approached the security desk. One guard sat watching a row of television monitors, and a second guard was answering questions from five different people. Matt eyed his watch as his position in line moved slowly to the front.

Finally, Matt stood in front of the guard stand. He leaned in. "Matt Whiteside—I'm here to see John Ramsey at Franklin Smith."

"Thank you, Mr. Whiteside." The guard punched some letters on the computer and after a second looked up and handed Matt a badge. Matt thanked him and headed toward the elevators to the twenty-seventh floor.

He checked in with the receptionist.

"Please fill out this application, Mr. Whiteside," she said, handing him a clipboard and company pen. An application? This must be the job interview…today. His heart rate quickened as he filled in school dates and work histories.

He began fidgeting with the navy Brooks Brothers suit he'd worn. At least he'd had a good Perry Ellis shirt hanging freshly cleaned in the car and had the sense to wear a blue and red Polo tie—not the polar bear one his buddy, Drew, had given him for his birthday a year ago. After several minutes, the receptionist called to him. "Mr. Ramsey is waiting for you."

"Thanks," Matt said, following the angle of her pen to a closed door. He hesitated for a second, wondering if he should knock, and then pulled the handle and walked in.

John Ramsey was at his desk, hanging up from a phone call. He stood to greet Matt.

"Matt, it's good to see you," he said, shaking Matt's hand. "Thanks for coming on such short notice."

"It's was no problem, sir. Thank you for taking the time to talk to me. Here's my application." If Mr. Ramsey only knew the grief he was going to get from Sun.

"Call me John," he said, heading for the door. "I want you to meet Stuart Gibson." Matt followed Ramsey out of his office, down the hallway, and into a luxurious conference room. A long, rectangular glass table was surrounded by twenty plush leather chairs. "Have a seat, Matt."

A heavyset man entered, his tie loose, shirt a bit wrinkled, and hair disheveled. Matt knew all about Stuart; he was the largest trader for Franklin Smith and had made close to five million dollars last year. Matt also knew he was a top player in the financial game.

"I'd like to introduce you to Stuart Gibson, one of Franklin's star traders," Ramsey said.

Matt reached out his hand. "Nice to meet you, Mr. Gibson."

"Likewise, Matt."

They took seats at the conference table—Matt on one side, John and Stuart on the other. The manager looked over Matt's application. Matt felt his mouth go dry. He hadn't brought anything for an interview, and he felt isolated by the sheer length of the table and the silence. Perspiration beads broke out under his collar as the two men scrutinized his application.

Ramsey finally looked up. "Matt, I've told Stuart all about you. Since he's the one you'll be working under if we feel you are the person for this job, I thought he would have some questions for you."

"Sure, Stuart, fire away."

"I see you graduated from San Jose State, Matt."

"That's correct."

"You started at Santa Clara and then it appears there was a year and a half gap before you returned to school. What happened?"

The guy didn't miss anything. "I was on a football scholarship at Santa Clara, but during my junior year I got hurt and lost my scholarship. Santa Clara is a pretty pricey school, so I dropped out for a year, and worked and saved enough to finish my degree at San Jose."

Stuart jotted notes down, while Ramsey, a bit grim in the face, nodded in sympathy. He hadn't told Ramsey how bad his knee was damaged, and he guessed the fellow sportsman knew what the end of a career would mean to a young man. He felt a twinge of shame that his parents hadn't been able to afford to pay the tab for his last year at Santa Clara. They were working people, but didn't have a lot to show for it. He wanted them to be proud of his success and for Kathy Ann to hear about it and regret that she had dumped him.

"You graduated with a B.S. degree in business administration with a major in finance. What was your grade point average?"

Matt snapped back to attention. "I ended up with a 3.8 grade point average overall."

Matt watched Stuart scan the job history portion of his résumé that admittedly was a bit sparse. "How did you find your position at Sun Systems?"

Matt sat forward in his chair. "One of my professors was a real mentor to me and knew I was looking to enter the financial business market. He heard about the position and with his excellent recommendation, I was offered the job. After a few years, I was offered a promotion based on my performance reviews and, I believe, my strong work ethic."

Stuart raised his eyebrows at Matt. The bags under his eyes made him look a little like a basset hound. "Glad to hear it. We demand that kind of rigorous attention at Franklin Smith. What are your goals? Why do you want to work here?"

Matt sat at attention, kept his eyes straight on Stuart. He'd rehearsed this quickly in the car. "I want to work at a firm where I will be challenged, and rewarded when I meet that challenge. I did some research on Franklin Smith and found it is a solid, well-respected firm with a reputation for being fair and generous to its employees. Franklin Smith is one of the best in the business, and I want to be part of its team."

Stuart was straight-faced throughout the interview. His tone was business, though his questions extended into the personal. Matt couldn't decide whether his answers were right or wrong, and it unnerved him to not be able to read the game.

After several more grueling questions, Ramsey finished up the interview with the basics.

"Do you smoke?"

"No, sir, never have."

"How about drugs? Would you object to taking a drug test?"

"Anytime you want, I'll take a drug test."

"Have you ever been arrested? The policy of this firm is that if an employee is ever arrested for anything, it is cause for immediate suspension without pay and dismissal if convicted."

"No, I've never been arrested and I don't intend to be in the future."

Ramsey smiled. Matt realized it could have sounded like a joke, which could be bad, or good.

Stuart turned to Ramsey. "I think I'm done with this young man, unless you have any further questions?"

Ramsey stood up and extended his hand. "Thanks, Matt, you'll hear from us soon."

"Thank you both for your time."

As Matt headed for the lobby level exit, an attractive young woman in a tight skirt and high heels headed right at him on a collision course. She was trying to balance an easel, a whiteboard, and an armload of boxes and was losing the struggle. A pencil was poised above her ear, and a large curl of brown hair slipped from her otherwise tidy ponytail.

Matt could see disaster in her near future and possibly his if he didn't move quickly. He rushed toward her, watching the boxes shift and almost tumble before he stretched for them and helped her steady the load. The sudden aid seemed to catch her by surprise, but she righted herself quickly and laughed in embarrassment.

"Thanks," she said, her lips parting to reveal a dazzling smile. "Apparently, multi-tasking is overrated."

Matt returned her smile. "No worries. Where are you heading? Could I help you?"

"Oh, thank you." Matt took the boxes from her. "I'm heading to the twenty-second floor to help a friend with a presentation. I'm Stephanie by the way," she stuck her hand out from under the easel.

He shook it quickly before she resumed her grip on the items. "Matt Whiteside. Nice to meet you, Stephanie," he said, keeping up with her pace as she started for the elevator. At the next floor, they were pushed together by the swarm of people piling into the car. The doors hissed closed. Matt leaned closer to Stephanie. "So what floor do you work on?"

"I work in Sacramento. I'm going back in the morning."

"Really? My parents live in Sacramento. I visit them all the time." Why did he say that? She didn't care how often he saw his parents. She stared straight ahead as if she hadn't heard anything. They stopped at her floor and Matt followed Stephanie into an office reception area. She set the board and easel on the floor and Matt did the same with the boxes.

"I can't thank you enough for your help," she said, gathering her stray hair back into the smooth ponytail. "I really appreciate it."

"My pleasure."

They stood in awkward silence until Matt abruptly turned to the elevator. Come on, just do it, he thought. You just aced an interview, after all.

He turned and saw Stephanie starting to walk away. Time slowed just enough for Matt to see that he was about to miss the moment. He was riding high that day, even if he was nervous, so why not?

"Hey, Stephanie," he called out. She turned toward him, her polite expression replaced by the inquisitive sparkle in her eyes. He caught up with her and moved in close. She didn't seem to mind.

"Do you have a card? I'd like to call you next time I'm coming to Sacramento. If it's okay with you."

He couldn't gauge her reaction as she pulled a card out of her purse. His heart was racing now, as if he were running down the field with the ball in his hand. "Here you go, Matt. That has all my numbers." She handed him the card.

Matt studied the card for a second. Stephanie Bernard. "You're a real estate appraiser? Interesting."

She nodded and was about to say something when a well-dressed man in a brown suit came around the corner. "Stephanie, you made it!" he said. "Come in when you're done." He was shorter than Matt and looked a couple years older. He stared at Matt a second, then walked away.

"Duty calls," Stephanie said. She raised a hand. "Thanks again, Matt."

"You're welcome," he said as he watched her retreating figure.

He flicked her card against his fingers, grinning like a fool. Now if his excitement didn't keep him awake at night, Stephanie Bernard sure would. Full of the need to share the day's events, he flipped open his cell phone.

"Hey, Drew, it's Matt. I'm in the city. Got time for a beer after work?"

"What's up, Matt? You sound like you just won the lotto."

Matt looked at his watch. 4:30 already. His boss at Sun was going to kill him. "Let's meet at the 13 Views Bar. I'll fill you in when I see you."

Matt sat at the bar enjoying the marvelous floor-to-ceiling view of the San Francisco Bay. This city had always held wonder for him, but now he was seeing it in a different light, changing from an untouchable fantasy to a tantalizing possibility. He could very well live here, work here, make a home here.

The bar wasn't busy—the small clusters of patrons drank with controlled urgency, as though they, too, were pushing their break times too far.

The bartender, a lean man with an easy stance, walked over to him and smiled. He wore an impeccably starched white shirt under an even more impeccable white starched jacket, the ensemble perfect but for the slightly tilted clip-on black bow tie at his throat. "Can I get you a drink?"

"I'll take a Newcastle, please."

"You got it."

Matt turned to the window, watching as the city slowly disappeared in the foggy dusk. Ghost lights through clouds made it seem both eerie and wonderful.

The bartender handed Matt a beer and followed his gaze. "That fog out there covers everything like a cold, wet blanket. But on a sunny day, I would say there are fewer sights as picturesque as that. You can see not only Alcatraz, but just a little west is the Golden Gate Bridge and Sausalito."

Matt stared, lost in the gray. In his peripheral vision, he caught sight of Drew rapidly approaching. Drew shot Matt a mischievous grin and slid into his seat, never breaking his gait. He snapped his fingers and gave Matt the "dueling guns" move, pointing and using his thumbs as hammers. "What's up, pal?"

Drew, an athletic, six-two lady killer with hazel eyes and a neatly trimmed haircut, pulled out a barstool. Impeccably dressed in a gray Calvin Klein suit with a light-blue shirt, he loosened his paisley tie. His face was tanned from many hours on the golf course, but could just have easily been from a movie set. He motioned to the bartender. "Hey Billy, how you doin'?"

"Fine, fine, you? What'll you have, the usual?"

Drew nodded an affirmative. "If I was doing any better, I'd have to be two people." Drew was the epitome of the saying that you catch more flies with honey.

A television in the corner of the bar flickered as stock prices crawled across the bottom from the day's Dow Jones. Drew nodded to a couple of secretaries. "Those cuties work at a law firm on the twentieth floor."

He turned to Matt in rapt attention, resting his arm on the counter. "So, what's up, my man?"

"It's been quite a day—a last-minute job interview with Mr. Ramsey himself." Matt filled Drew in on a few details.

"Sounds like you killed it," Drew said.

Matt shrugged, a tense smile on his face. "Hope so. I can't thank you enough for telling me about the opening at Franklin Smith. I used all the info you gave me and did my best to impress. But still, I just don't know. I couldn't read either John or Stuart. They grilled me for almost two hours and wanted to know my whole life story."

Drew patted Matt on the shoulder. "Don't feel bad; they weren't just picking on you. Happens all the time with these high-profile, prestigious jobs. These guys want to make sure they don't make a mistake. It's all super high-pressure bull. When something goes wrong, everyone scrambles to find a stick and a head to put on it. They're just making sure you won't be the cause of them ending up on that stick." A couple of men in business suits pulled out the seats next to Drew and sat down at the bar. It was beginning to fill up with the after-work crowd, and the tinkling of ice cubes in glasses along with multiple conversations brought the noise level up a notch.

"I understand, but it doesn't make my stomach churn any less. I can taste this, Drew. I was meant for this job." Matt hunched over his drink.

"Cheer up. You're applying for a job. You didn't just get fired. You're still employed."

"Drew, were you stressed when you landed your position at Hartford Financial?"

"It was a different situation back then. When I was hired, I started at the very bottom of the company doing grunt work." Drew sipped his beer. "You were still at State doing keg stands, but in the real world the growth was insane. Anyway, they needed bodies and started promoting from within. I just rode the growth of our fund right up. Now here I am, trading mortgage-backed securities with the big boys and riding high on the wave."

"I miss those keg stands sometimes."

Drew burst out in bellowing laughter. "Yeah, I bet you do."

Heels clicked on the tile floor across the room near the hotel entry as harried executives hustled back and forth across the lobby. Drew nursed his second beer as he filled Matt in on the latest buzz.

"Let me tell you, it's a jungle out there. The single-family-home market is on fire, and the hedge funds are fighting like demons for those mortgage-backed securities."

Matt could taste the opportunity this presented for him. "I'd sure like to go to work in this jungle. I know it would be exciting."

"Hang in there. I'm guessing you did better than you think. If I were a betting man, I'd think you'll get that job." He took a swig of his drink. "Let's move on to a lighter subject. Are you dating any hotties? What's the scoop?"

Matt took off his coat and hung it on the back of his bar stool. "No scoop, I'm still flying solo. But that may change. I met a girl today after my interview, really cute."

Drew elbowed him and gave a thumbs-up as he drank. "Who is she?"

"She's a real estate appraiser from Sacramento. I helped her carry some packages, and I just felt it—something clicked. She was beautiful and had this smile…man. I got her digits."

"Well, look who's a big winner. Yeah! Better get your game back on. You've been out of practice. I would hate for the lovely girl to be disappointed."

Matt threw a peanut and watched it bounce off of Drew's jacket, then down to the plush carpeted floor. "I'm serious, man. Hey, just because I don't sleep with every woman I make eye contact with like someone I know, doesn't mean I don't have what it takes. It just hasn't been right for me."

Drew took a sip from the bottle as they both grinned. "You're a hopeless romantic, you know that, man? You've got to stop reading those Harlequin novels and watching the Lifetime Channel. If I had a sister, Matt, I'd want her to date you. I could trust you to do the right thing. As a matter of fact, I know I could trust you."

Matt slid off the barstool and picked up his jacket. "I'm heading back to hit the gym, then home to crash. I need to figure out what my excuse for being gone all afternoon is going to be."

"Well, good luck to you, Matt. You know I'm pullin' for you. I'll take care of the tab. Call me the minute you get word, and keep your head up."

THREE

Matt moved through the office like a ghost, shuffling papers back and forth from one pile to the next, after enduring his supervisor's chastisement for missing half a day's work.

The first day after the interview he checked his cell phone every five minutes, making sure the battery worked and that the ring volume was at the highest setting. By the second day, he was convinced they had chosen someone else. It was that stupid comment he had made about not having been arrested before. He began to feel foolish—why should this work out? Every time he had confidence about something he'd accomplished, it crumbled in his hands.

Standing in his kitchen that evening, Matt was punching slits in his microwave dinner when his cell phone suddenly vibrated and rang, almost causing him to drop the knife.

He fumbled for the phone, snapping it open and saying, "Hello" with more intensity than he'd intended.

"Hello, Matt. It's John Ramsey. Are you free to talk?"

"Sure, Mr. Ramsey. I was just getting ready to eat." Idiot. Not something a man possibly offering him a job would want to hear.

"Oh, no problem, Matt, I'll be quick. Stuart really liked your interview, said you had the right attitude. We'd like to offer you a position with

Franklin Smith as an assistant trader of mortgage-backed securities. You would start at a base salary of ninety thousand dollars per year as we discussed, with a full benefits package and an annual bonus based on the volume your group generates."

"Oh. Wow," Matt said. Then, as silence ensued on the other end, he stammered, "I mean, yes, Mr. Ramsey, I accept. I'm excited about coming to work with you." His mind raced. "Is it all right if I start two weeks from tomorrow? I want to give Sun Systems some notice. I mean, they've been very fair to me, after all."

"Two weeks will be fine, Matt. I would expect nothing less from you. Congratulations, and welcome to Franklin Smith."

"Thank you so much, Mr. Ramsey...John."

Matt hung up the phone and let out a yell. He danced Tom Cruise/ *Risky Business* style from the kitchen to the living room, and speed-dialed home.

"Mom, you're not going to believe it. I got the job!"

"Oh Mattie, congratulations! I had no doubt that you would get it. We're so proud of you. Hold on, let me get your dad. He's out in the back yard." Matt could hear his mother's excited voice as she hurried outside. "Stan, Stan, come talk to Mattie. He got the job at Franklin Smith."

He heard the phone crackle as it shifted on the other end. He thought about what he would purchase first—a new car or a new condo, or should he help his parents out? Money changes things.

"Matt, this is incredible news," his father said in his deep baritone. "You should be proud of yourself."

"I start two weeks from tomorrow," he said, catching his breath. He wasn't sure if it was from the frenetic dancing or the rush.

"Well, go out and celebrate. You deserve it. Your sister will be happy to hear the news. We'll be sure to tell her."

"Thanks, Dad. I'll be home on Friday, so we can do it together."

"Great, Matt, we'll see you then."

Matt hung up, and immediately dialed Drew. Drew answered on the third ring with his requisite, "Wassup?"

"I got the job!" Matt yelled into the phone.

"Awesome! Way to go. See, I told you, Matt. Don't sell yourself so short. You've got a lot to offer. I'll bet you'll really do well at this job."

"Totally. It's my time now, man."

The next morning Matt stood outside the office of Diane Amory, his boss at Sun Systems, waiting to break the news to her. He'd always liked Diane, which made what he had to do that much harder. He lightly rapped on the door. Diane looked up from her computer.

"Diane. Can I have a word with you?"

"Of course."

Matt took a seat and felt the room getting smaller by the second. "What's on your mind?" Diane asked.

"I hate to do this, but I'm giving you my two weeks' notice. I've accepted an offer to work at Franklin Smith."

"Oh wow, I'm sorry to hear that." She took off her glasses and leaned back in her chair with a disappointed look.

He felt a pang of guilt. There was a lot he disliked at Sun, but it would be tough leaving the old gang. Diane shifted a bit and sat up in her chair, professional as always. "You have been a very good and loyal employee. Is there a chance we could make you an offer to keep you here?"

"I don't think so, Diane. I've enjoyed working here, but I feel my career lies elsewhere. Thank you, though, for all your support."

"Well," she said stiffly as she stood and extended her hand, "this sounds like a wonderful opportunity for you. Are you leaving immediately or do we get a couple weeks out of you?"

"I planned to stay and leave in two weeks, if that works for you."

"I wish you would stay longer, but that will work. Congratulations. Don't forget about us. Check in once in a while."

Matt stood up. "I will do that. Thank you for giving me the chance you did."

Matt headed back to his office, the guilt building. Diane did give him a great boost to his career, but he had to think of his ten-year plan.

Oh sure, he'd miss this place and the people here, but not that much. Sun Systems could not take him where he wanted to go. Part two of the plan—a high-paying job with room to grow—was falling right into place, and he wasn't about to let a guilty conscience derail that.

Later that day as he packed a few boxes, he thought of Stephanie. He'd made a date with her this weekend. He hardly knew her, but she had been edging around his thoughts more and more. He vowed to himself to take it slow and steady. Besides, he had plans, and a woman might complicate them.

Four

Sunset Mortgage was located on one of the busiest streets in Car-michael. Broker Janet Waller sat at her desk, gazing out the large office window at the bustling Fair Oaks Plaza across the street. An attractive raven-haired woman, she had sealed countless deals with her mesmerizing, fiery green eyes. Her gaze idly shifted to the office wall and focused on numerous framed awards and certificates displayed there. A slow grin spread across her face as she realized she owed most of those to her relationship with Whitney Homes and especially to Taylor Whitney. It was hard work to play both him and her customers. Nothing was handed to her, all of it earned in blood.

She idly picked up the schedule for Taylor's private jet. Soon, she'd be on her way to Hawaii, one of the perks of this relationship. She sat back in her chair, remembering her first meeting with Taylor.

It had been a Saturday in 2002 at the grand opening of a Whitney Homes housing project in Bakersfield. She'd been to the company's main office many times in Granite Bay, a city just northeast of Sacramento known for its money and exclusivity. Photos of Taylor Whitney, the owner, were plastered all over the lobby walls of the office, and she'd had no trouble recognizing him when he walked in. About five-ten, Taylor was a balding, pudgy man in his mid-fifties. He wasn't ugly, but he wasn't the "leading actor" type she preferred. She was sitting in the sales office going through lending quotes when Taylor arrived with an entourage of people. He waved them off, smiled at her, sat down in front of her desk, and introduced himself.

"Hi, I'm Taylor Whitney, owner of Whitney Homes."

"Janet Waller; I own Sunset Mortgage. I've heard a lot about you, Mr. Whitney." Janet stood to shake his hand. She looked out the window toward the new home next door. "Your models are gorgeous."

"Thank you. Call me Taylor." He stared at her, never looking at his houses. "You know, I've heard about you, too. You're in charge of my account at Sunset."

"Yes, that's me. I hope you're satisfied with the service I've provided. You're such a great client; I instruct my staff to go the extra mile for you."

"Well, I expect nothing less, and so far I haven't heard any complaints. Your job is safe...for now." He smiled at her and she watched for the body changes.

They were there, all the signs of his interest. The hand on the chin, the eyes wandering from her face to her chest. Adjusting her seat, she straightened up. She always made sure the "girls" were on display for times like these, and she noted he did not try to hide his stare. He was either supremely confident, crude, or a heavy dose of both.

"Are you sure you're old enough to own a mortgage company?" he asked.

"Thank you, Taylor, I'm flattered," she said, leaning on one hip. "I'm a few years over thirty. That's old enough, I think." She smiled and blushed, playing up the flattered female angle. "I'm glad you're happy with us. If there's anything else I can do, please don't hesitate to ask."

He stared at her a moment. "Are you staying in Bakersfield tonight?"

"Yes, I'm at the Red Lion Inn on Ming Avenue. I fly out of here tomorrow morning."

"Good. Would you have dinner with me tonight at the Tam O'Shanter?" Taylor fumbled with some papers on the desk. "I'd like to hear about some of, uh, your programs."

Janet had heard about the Tam O'Shanter, one of the best steak houses in the area. "That would be great. I'd love to walk you through everything we can do for you and your buyers."

"Great. I'll see you at seven-thirty."

Dinner was innocent. She was no dummy and knew there might be an ulterior motive, but Taylor talked mostly about his favorite subject: Taylor. Janet bided her time, looking interested as he droned on and on. Letting him talk allowed her to determine that he was wealthy—certainly more so than other men she'd had in similar situations. She also had plenty of time to exercise her old standbys: slowly eating the cherry from her Tom Collins as she kept eye contact with him, crossing and re-crossing her toned legs, touching her face, and laughing delightedly at his stupid jokes. There were roadblocks, unfortunately. He was married, for one. But she'd had other affairs with married men. He also sweated. She didn't like men who sweated.

Come on, girl, you know what this could mean if you just buckle down, she thought, trying not to look at the fat drop of perspiration running down the side of his head toward his ear. She ran her hand through her hair, careful to give it an extra flip for a tousled look, and focused on the $2,000 suit he was wearing instead.

After dinner they moved to the bar. "What time do you leave in the morning?" Taylor asked as he held her chair for her.

"My plane leaves at ten-thirty for Sacramento." She sat down with a coy look at him.

"Mind if I ask you a personal question?" His hand, still on the back of her chair, grazed her shoulder lightly.

"Sure."

"I have to admit, I've been checking and I don't see a ring on your finger. No man been lucky enough to snare you yet, huh?" He chuckled like a movie mobster as he sat down across from her.

"Nope," she said, keeping her voice open and airy as she slowly crossed her legs, almost too slowly and too revealing. No need to bring up her failed engagement, or the memory of her fiancé pulling the plug on their wedding less than a month before the event. With a force borne of much practice, she stopped the tears from welling, ignored the hurt in the pit of her stomach, and re-focused on the task at hand. Work had saved her in the past; it would save her now. It was something she could control and conquer—just as she could control and conquer this man.

Taylor leaned back, smiled, and nodded. Janet was relieved to see he hadn't noticed the shift in her emotions. "I was just curious. Have you ever been told you look like Teri Hatcher from *Desperate Housewives*?"

She hadn't. "I've been told that a few times."

"I have an idea. Why don't we go dancing at the Hilton?" Taylor lifted up his wine glass and took a sip without removing his eyes from her face.

This was good. He wanted her—and soon. Time to leave him hanging. It would take her a little time to mentally prepare for his sweaty form grunting on top of her. She frowned in pouty disappointment.

"Oh, that sounds like so much fun," she said, looking at her watch. "But I'm afraid I just have so much to prepare for tomorrow—including your files, I might add." She looked at him, pretending to consider. "I'll tell you what." She leaned in close to him, touching his forearm lightly. "I'm always looking for a good reason to go to lunch or have an after-work cocktail. Why don't you give me a call one of these days."

His face lit up like a teenage boy's before a big meal. "That sounds great. As a matter of fact, I'll do one better." He leaned over and caressed her hand. "I've got a yacht anchored just outside of Crawdad's Cantina on the Sacramento River. We can take it out for an afternoon and play in the sun."

"I'd love that," Janet purred. She stood up and smoothed her skirt. "Thank you for the dinner."

"Time to drive you back to your hotel, then," he said, struggling to his feet. He left a tip in cash so large she would've known he was new money if she had just met him this minute. They walked out together, Taylor sticking close to her side.

A valet pulled up in front of the restaurant and hopped out, holding the passenger door open. "Nice car," Janet said as she slid into the seat of the Lincoln Continental.

He took his seat. "I tried to find a Ferrari or a Bentley, but apparently there's no demand for them in Bakersfield. If it wasn't for my houses, I would never step foot in this town."

He drove up to the Red Lion entrance, got out, and opened the door for her. Janet leaned toward him and whispered, "Thank you for the wonderful evening." She sashayed away slowly, knowing he watched her every step toward the hotel. Oh yes,

Taylor Whitney was hungry for her, but not quite starving…yet. She would change that and soon.

And now here she was, two years later, sitting in her office, flipping the jet schedule between her fingers. This little affair was about to pay off big.

Her daydream was interrupted by a soft knock on the door.

"Miss Waller?" Her assistant, Carol, stood in the doorway. Pretty girl, Janet thought. She didn't usually hire pretty girls as she didn't like the competition, but she'd been desperate to find someone quickly after she fired her last assistant and hadn't had time to be choosy.

"Yes?" Janet kept her tone supercilious. Younger women peeved her, especially good-looking younger women.

"I have a fax here for you from Whitney Homes. It looks like an itinerary. It says the old one has changed," Carol said.

"Let me see it," Janet said, irritated.

Carol handed her the paper, then stood awkwardly with her hands folded before her. "Hawaii must be beautiful this time of year," she said.

Janet let out an exasperated puff of breath. "Yep, it is." She kicked off her shoes and put her stockinged feet on the desk, turning slightly from Carol. "You can go now," she said, waving her hand dismissively.

Janet packed up her things and drove home. She laid the new schedule on the buffet by the door. Just enough time left to take a long soak in the tub and change before the limo arrived.

Dressed and ready, she checked her watch. It was eleven-thirty in the morning. The driver was seven minutes late. She would have to mention this to Taylor. The doorbell rang and interrupted her building rage. A burly black man in a chauffeur's uniform stood before her.

"Ms. Waller? I'm Robert and I'm here to give you a ride to the airport."

"Of course. You're late. The bags are behind the door."

After putting the bags in the trunk and closing the car door behind her, the driver finally got in and started the car. Janet pulled out a compact and sucked in her breath at the sight of the dark bags under her eyes. Leave it to Taylor to plan this rendezvous for the busiest time of the month. She fished in her purse for her concealer.

"Going to be a nice day," said the driver.

"Uh huh,"

"Supposed to get to seventy-five degrees in the—"

"Look, could we just keep it quiet?" Her rummaging grew more frantic. She must have left the concealer on her vanity. Damn it all. And this weather-happy driver wasn't helping. She wasn't here to pass his time more quickly.

"Yes, ma'am."

She cringed. When had "miss"—or heck, even "hottie"—changed to "ma'am"?

They drove in silence to the airport tarmac where Taylor's plane, a sleek white jet with a blue stripe and the Whitney Homes logo on the tail, stood parked. Two uniformed pilots stood by the plane's steps. The older one, a silver-haired, distinguished-looking man, stepped forward as Janet got out of the car.

"I'm Captain Bishop and this is my co-pilot, Captain Rogers." Rogers, younger and much better-looking than Bishop, nodded and tipped his cap to Janet. "We'll be flying you to Hawaii today."

Janet nodded.

"We'll be flying in a Citation Sovereign Model 680," Captain Bishop said. "Very fast, able to fly at a speed of up to 458 knots with a range of 2,600 miles."

"Great, I'll be sure to remember that if I ever need another plane." Janet gave him a cold, bored look. The two men, obviously irritated, motioned for her to enter the plane. As she ducked through the small doorway into the craft, she breathed in the smell of leather and brass polish—the scents of money and power. She sat down on one of the four high-back seats, placing her bag on a card table.

"That chair can swivel 180 degrees and recline to almost full prone position," came Captain Bishop's voice behind her. He pointed to a stereo system bolted to a cabinet. "We've got a Bose stereo system with surround sound and over 150 channels for your listening pleasure. As you can see, there's plenty of room for you to stretch out. Make yourself comfortable. Any questions, Ms. Waller?"

"The liquor cabinet is…?"

He looked startled, and she fought the urge to defend her early morning beverage choice.

"Of course," he said slowly and, like a seasoned flight attendant, indicated with a thumb and two fingers a wooden cabinet toward the front of the plane.

"Thank you."

The captain nodded and walked toward the cockpit without another word, shutting the door with a snap.

The flight would take just under five and a half hours. The weather was calm, the skies clear, and Janet was relaxing into her second vodka martini and the swelling symphonic sounds of Chopin when the hot-looking co-pilot came down the aisle to her.

"Is everything all right, Ms. Waller? Can I get you anything?"

Janet kicked her pumps off and pushed the seat back into an almost horizontal position. Her skirt was hiked halfway up her thighs, and she remembered she wasn't wearing panties. Hmm, she thought. He is kinda cute. In other circumstances, I would take him up on his offer. Maybe another time. She wondered who had brought the Chopin CD on board. It certainly wasn't Taylor's style. Was it his wife? She shook the idea from her head and gave Rogers a thin smile, letting the alcohol's warmth course through her.

"No, I'm all right. Check back in about thirty minutes and I'll let you make me a martini."

The co-pilot touched his cap—more men should do that, Janet thought—and went back to the cockpit.

When the plane landed in Maui, Janet walked down the jet's stairway right to a waiting white limo. Tall palm trees swayed in the tropical breeze. The weather was warm, but not uncomfortable, and a flock of colorful parrots squawked noisily in a nearby magnolia tree. The driver, a short Hawaiian man, introduced himself as Kaola, and opened the car door. Without a word, Janet got in. She was nursing another martini when they entered the driveway to the Four Seasons Hotel in Wailea.

Driving past acres of freshly mowed lawn, lush gardens, and exotic waterfalls, the driver brought the limo into the porte-cochere. A uniformed bell captain opened the door and helped the driver with the luggage. Janet asked the bellman, "Which way is the lobby and check-in?"

He pointed to a pair of large glass doors. "Through those doors to your left, ma'am." He hadn't finished his sentence before Janet was through the entry. She left him with her luggage.

Large vases of colorful flower arrangements filled with hibiscus, birds of paradise, and lilies lined the expansive two-story-lobby entry. The lobby extended onto a veranda overlooking the main pool, which was a bundle of activity with tourists escaping the mainland's freezing winter weather. A constant ocean breeze permeated the area, picking up the scents from the gardens surrounding the pool and channeling them throughout the lobby.

At the front desk, Janet waved at a young clerk with a beautiful complexion and dark eyes, dressed in traditional Hawaiian garb. "I'm Janet Waller. I have a room reserved."

The woman checked her computer. "Yes, here it is, Ms. Waller." She scanned a confirmation sheet. "Could I swipe a credit card to cover any incidentals you might want to buy during your stay with us?" she asked innocently.

Janet took off her sunglasses, feeling an ache forming at her temples. She needed a massage. And this little twit was not helping. "I will not give you my credit card," she said with a cold smile. "I am a guest of Taylor Whitney. Surely you know that name"—she looked at the girl's nametag—"Kalea?"

The clerk's eyes widened. "I'm sorry, ma'am," she said, her face turning red as she shuffled through papers on her desk, "but it's company policy."

The ache in Janet's temples began to throb. "Get me your manager, please," she said, rubbing her forehead in slow, small circles. As the clerk began to formulate a reply, Janet snapped, "Now! That wasn't a request."

The clerk went around a wall behind her and came back with her supervisor. A short, portly man wearing a Hawaiian shirt and thick glasses greeted Janet.

"Hello, Ms. Waller, I'm Mark Billings," he said brightly. "I understand you don't want to leave a credit card."

"That's right. I know Taylor Whitney is a good client of this hotel and I'm sure he won't be pleased if I am put out by your policies."

Billings nodded his head in recognition. "Mr. Taylor is indeed a good client. We want to please his guests as best we can." He turned to the clerk and said, "Please get Ms. Waller her key. We wouldn't want her stay to get off to a bad start."

Janet sighed. "I'm afraid you're a little too late on that one," she said as she took the key from his hands.

"I'm so sorry, Ms. Waller. I do hope the rest of your stay with us is a pleasant one."

Janet nodded and walked to the elevators. She smiled and thought, Sometimes you have to let people know who's in charge. She exited on the twenty-first floor and found room 2150 at the end of the corridor. The door opened into an extensive suite with a wall of windows and a panoramic view of the ocean. A king-sized bed sat in the middle, with a map of the Hawaiian Islands framed behind it. A small, round table sat next to the sliding door with a silver bowl of fresh pineapple, mangos, and oranges. An antique vase of fresh orchids on the credenza across from the bed permeated the room with their sweet scent. Janet threw open the sliding glass door and stepped out onto a huge balcony that ran the length of the room. She stood still for a minute soaking it all in. In the distance, a catamaran was sailing across the ocean. Surfers sat idly on their boards waiting for the next series of big waves. The breeze was cool and fresh. Now this was more like it. She would remember to pay Taylor back for his hospitality.

A knock on the door broke her train of thought. She opened the door to a young bellman. "Where would you like these bags, ma'am?"

Janet pointed to the bed.

He did as instructed. "Do you need anything else, ma'am?"

"No, thank you. Here." She held out a dollar. The bellman looked at the dollar, gave her a look, and mumbled something to himself as he left the room. She fixed herself a drink and saluted the great blue Pacific Ocean just yards from her deck. Seven days in heaven. Or seven days in hell, if she thought about Taylor and his insatiable needs. But she wouldn't focus on that now. After this drink and a massage, she would think about it. Maybe it'd even be fun. She took a gulp. It was all a game anyway, right?

FIVE

Taylor Whitney stood on his balcony overlooking the pristine white Maui beach, drinking a rum and Coke. A cool breeze swept up off the water—salt with a hint of something floral. He closed his eyes and smiled, letting the wind move past him. He turned to the open sliding door and yelled, "Guy, get out here, you have to see this. It's beautiful."

Guy Beasley turned from the golf match on TV and ambled out onto the deck.

"It sure is a great setting, Taylor. You're a lucky man."

"This view of the ocean is priceless, Guy. I don't care what anybody says—Wailea is the most beautiful place on the islands. And I'm four minutes away from the Four Seasons Resort and the famous bar, along with all the ladies who haunt there." He gave Guy his signature lecherous look.

"It's a great piece of real estate, Taylor. This place is impressive."

Taylor gazed toward the luxury resort a half-mile up the beach. Lounge chairs in tidy rows covered the sand from the hotel to the water. About half the chairs were occupied by hotel guests lying listlessly on white towels, as waiters in bright blue and yellow Hawaiian shirts scurried back and forth carrying trays of drinks. Brazen seagulls strutted between chairs looking for a morsel or an unattended plate.

Their feathered companions jostled on the seawall leading to the resort entrance, squawking and bickering.

"Noisy birds," Taylor muttered. "I hate those ugly pests. Nothing ruins a nice day at the beach like that squawking."

Taylor looked at the diving scavengers; their constant grating calls annoying him. For a moment, he was back at The Oasis, listening to his father and his cronies arguing about which team was better in the pre-season. Mindless, stupid-talking, old, fat men hunched over in the dark lights of that seedy bar. He snapped himself out of it. "It's good to be king. I wonder what the poor people are doing."

Guy chuckled and turned back inside. He slumped down on the smooth leather couch and went back to watching the match. "They're probably mowing the lawn out on the golf course you played on today, or shining those golf shoes you left in front of your locker."

Taylor fixed himself another drink. "As much as I like this place, I've been looking at a building lot that came onto the market and I might just buy it. I can get it for eight million—a steal, really, once you see the view. I saw this incredible mansion that sits above the beach in Kaanapali, custom and modern. You can tell by just looking at the setup that they dumped millions into it. It blows everything away, and that's what I want to build." Taylor glanced at the tall ceiling with thick planking, then over to the far wall, where a bookcase sat full of pictures and Hawaiian artifacts. There were framed photos of him at various vacation spots. This was a nice place, worth every penny he had put into it, but it was time to move up. He thought of the seagulls squawking and the image of his father and The Oasis, and swallowed hard. Only the best for Taylor, remember?

"What wrong with this place?" Guy asked, leaning his head back on the couch and throwing his arms up wide. "Didn't you just spend a million and a half fixing it up? Why would you want to spend that kind of money on a second home? You can't beat the view here and the location is fantastic, Mr. 'Four Minutes Away From the Bar.'"

Taylor walked over and sat down on a second couch, a twin to the one Guy was occupying. He leaned back and took a sip while searching for a good answer.

"Simply because this house isn't the best. Not by a long shot, Guy. It's good…not perfect. I want everyone who visits, who walks by, to know that my house is the best on the island. Besides, this place was built by that lead guitarist for Deep Velvet.

Considering the amount of drugs the guy ingested, I'm sure the residue has permeated the walls. It's too old, Guy; I need something new, spectacular, not a thirty-year-old relic."

Guy got up from the couch, walked behind the bar, and grabbed a beer out of the refrigerator. "Look, Taylor, why don't you settle down with this place and not be foolish. Your old man did okay. Started from nothing, built one or two homes a year, and never spent money on big-ticket items. Since you took over the business, you're big-time now, but you need to think ahead. You can't keep borrowing money to play. You'll kill your business."

"Thanks for the lecture, Guy." Taylor was quiet for a moment. He remembered his father all right, but not how Guy did. Bad days and long hours had turned the already bitter and angry man into a terror. At three in the morning, Taylor would be rousted up for some unnamed crime, forced to stand outside in the cold. To his old man, Taylor hovered between disappointing heir and worthless punk. The only way Taylor could tell the difference was by the severity of the beating.

Taylor had his own ideas about how the business should be run, felt it in his gut. His instincts were sharp; he didn't follow the old school—didn't feel working harder was the best way when working smarter earned bigger dollars. His old man was as ignorant as the sea gulls on the beach. Coming up with new ways to humiliate his boy in front of the goons was his father's favorite form of entertainment.

"Well, screw them all now, Guy. You're right: I am big-time, and the old man and his cronies are all dead or dying in retirement homes, poisoned by their careers and chemicals. Who's laughing now?" Taylor took a slow drink, waiting for a reaction.

Guy's body went rigid. He shook his hand at Taylor in a karate-chop motion. "You won't be having the last laugh," he said in dead seriousness. "I know as an accountant I have always been a little conservative for your taste, but you know what your problem is? You don't listen, not to anyone—not to your friends, not to me. You have to listen to your guys sometimes, bud; you pay your top brass well. They didn't get those big degrees because they are stupid."

Guy sat back on the couch, turning his eyes from Taylor and hitting the remote to change channels.

"Screw them. They don't know their ass from third base. They haven't built what I've built, Guy. They aren't out there in the trenches, making the deals and working the dealers. My track record speaks for itself. I don't need a bunch of uppity college grads telling me how to run my business. I don't need numbers; I've got the nerve and the results to back it up. Why do you care how I run my company, anyway? It doesn't affect you."

Guy laid the remote on the glass table. "Because we go a long way back, Taylor, and I consider you a friend. I always respected your father, too. I don't want to see you run his business, now yours, into the ground. Besides," he said with a wink, "I need a patsy to play golf with, and you're it."

Taylor sat up and moved back to the bar, wiping it down. "Well, don't worry about me. I'm untouchable." He'd had this conversation before. His board of directors didn't like the moves he made, but they didn't dare say it in public, not with the money coming in. Greedy rat turds, all of them, with their degrees framed and spit-shined on their walls. Taylor knew they must hate bowing down to a high school dropout, and he lived to see them squirm.

Guy returned to the couch and focused his attention on a money market show. "I read an article in the *Wall Street Journal* yesterday that said the housing bubble could burst any time—there's just no way this market can continue doubling the way it has for the last few years. Eventually, inflation will price all the buyers out, and there won't be anyone who can afford a house."

Taylor bellowed a loud "Hah," which echoed through the mansion. "I don't read any of that garbage. Those desk jockeys don't know jack about the housing market. It's always the same with them; the sky is always about to fall. When the market's up, they chew their nails and worry about how it will fall any second. Reading any of those business publications is a waste of time."

Taylor glanced at the TV as the news anchor rattled off numbers from the stock market, giving the day's closing Dow. He took a big swig of his rum and Coke, sucking air through his teeth and glaring with contempt at the smart-mouthed analysts.

"What do they know? Really, I mean that—what would they know about the real estate market in Northern California? Are they in it? Are they buying and selling like I am? Hell no, 'cause if they were, they wouldn't be on that damn show in their hundred-dollar suits from Men's Wearhouse. They would be sitting in their mansions in the Hamptons giving it to their immigrant maids. I have fifteen active subdivisions all over California, and my finger is closer to the pulse than any of those so-called experts."

He gazed out at the calm Pacific Ocean. "This market will last at least another five years at this pace, and when it slows down I'll still be solid and active. You know why?"

Guy smirked at him. "Enlighten me."

"Because everyone wants to live in sunny California, where the summers never end and Hollywood is five minutes down the interstate. All of them want a big, wonderful house, and Whitney Homes will be there to deliver. I'll build more than six hundred homes this year and make over sixty million dollars." Taylor stood up and stood in front of a large mirror that hung over a massive brick fireplace. He adjusted his white golf shirt and peered at the large bookcase that ran from the floor to the ten-foot ceiling, behind him across the room.

Guy shook his head. "You better hope you're right, because you're going to need to make more than sixty mil the way you spend money. Speaking of sales, how are Whitney Homes selling these last few weeks?"

"No idea; it's called vacation for a reason. My people are informed that for two weeks, I'm not to be disturbed. Course, that doesn't stop my controller from bugging the living daylights out of me by email. I end up deleting most of it. The world isn't coming to an end in two weeks. I work to pay for their sports cars; they can at least leave me the hell alone for a while. Anyway, I'll be talking to them on Monday as I need them to wire some money." Taylor refreshed his drink and came back to the couch, but decided on the recliner instead.

Guy tossed him the remote. "See if you can find something."

Taylor aimed the remote at the TV and hit the off button. "I almost forgot. I need to call Artie Tennelli to place a bet on the college basketball championship game."

"Who are you taking, U Conn or Georgia Tech?"

"I'm putting five hundred thousand on Georgia Tech."

Guy sat up. "On a college basketball game? Are you nuts?"

Taylor shrugged. "It gets me comped when I go to Vegas and stay at the Bellagio. They send their limo to pick me up at the airport. They'd fly me there in their plane if I didn't have my own."

"Those fellows in Vegas didn't build giant casinos because they lose money. That type of gambling will catch up with you someday."

"You're such a worrier, Guy. Typical bean counter." Taylor picked up the sports section of the newspaper lying on the maple coffee table. "It's under control. Besides, I rarely lose."

"So who's this Artie Tennelli?"

"He's my bookie. I met him in Cabo a few years ago. I was tired of penny ante betting—too low and it didn't satisfy me. Artie was able to get me the big scores, bigger lines than the casinos had the balls for. He's able to cover it, and he loves me."

"How does he cover what the casinos can't?"

"Obviously in with the mob or the cartels, whatever greasy immigrant is in power right now."

Guy turned a shade of white reserved for bleached sheets. "Mob connec—Taylor, what are you thinking? Are you sure about this?"

"Relax, Guy, I only bet with the guy once in a while. He's harmless."

"There's no such thing as a harmless mobster, Taylor."

"I've got it handled. Grow some balls, would you?"

Guy shook his head. After several minutes of tense, awkward silence, Guy spoke again in a lighter tone. He adjusted the stained-glass Tiffany lamp standing next to his chair toward him. "I saw your wife a couple days ago, lugging a big suitcase to the garage."

"I sent her back to the mainland. I'm flying in my loan-officer friend. I'm putting her up at the Four Seasons for a couple of days."

"Not what's-her-name...Janet? I thought you broke that off awhile back. You know you're going get caught, just like you did with your first wife."

Taylor laughed, his gut rolling. His first wife, Angela, had long turned from sexy and demure to annoying and bitchy by the time he started his affair with Monica. One afternoon, after finishing "lunch" at Monica's apartment in Sacramento, he walked out to the parking lot to get his Ferrari and found the parking space occupied by a different car—Angela's Mercedes.

"I loved it when she switched her car for mine. Always did want more than she had." He shook his head. "That was a sharp piece of work. Too bad I couldn't stand her anymore, 'cause that was funny. The three years of attorney fees and the twenty million I had to shell out, not so much. But I had Monica to slide right in and take her place, both in the bed and in my wallet. Who said a good woman is hard to find?" Taylor took a sip from his drink.

"Good grief, Taylor. How many times are you going to repeat that story? I've heard it ten times and it's not getting any funnier. You're not the brightest when it comes to women, as much as you think you are."

Taylor flipped Guy the bird. "It was pure bad luck that I got caught. This time it's different. I'm planning my affairs out now. I learn quick, especially when it costs me too much. Besides, Janet is one nasty vixen and sex with Monica is almost non-existent."

Guy sighed. "So you're flying Janet Waller here. You're either crazy or have no clue."

Taylor raised his glass to Guy. "I'll take crazy."

Six

Matt entered the dining room with its familiar waxed blonde maple table. "Anyone home?" he yelled to no one in particular. China and crystal glasses displayed in a hutch threw rainbow prisms against the beige walls.

Matt's dad walked into the entry and gave Matt a big hug. "You're home."

"I see you dressed up for the occasion," Matt chided, eyeing his dad's jeans and golf shirt from Northwest Industries, where he had worked for the last fifteen years as a project manager. "Looking good, Dad. A new haircut and a real tan."

"That's the perks of overseeing outside construction work. You look office-white as ever," his dad kidded.

"Well, look who's here just in time for dinner." Matt's mother, Barbara, brought salad and lasagna in and set them on the dining room table. She brushed a lock of her chestnut hair out of her face, hair that was tied up in the back but was slowly coming unraveled after working another long shift as a checker at Richardson's Supermarket. "Congratulations, Mattie," she said, sweeping him into a hug.

With soft skin and cheery blue eyes, his mom looked much younger than a woman closing in on fifty. She still had on a pair of slacks from work with a short-sleeved white shirt and the Richardson's logo stitched across her right shirt pocket. She brought in bread and a pitcher of lemonade, and then finally sat down to join them.

Stan said grace. "Thank you, Lord, for this good food, for blessing our family, and for Matt's new job." He looked up with a grin. "Dig in."

Matt savored his mom's home-cooked lasagna. As usual, his sister's dog, a Chihuahua-mini-Doberman mix named Markus, sat patiently at his feet, hoping Matt might make a mistake that he could capitalize on.

"Mattie, you won't believe what we found out," Barbara said as she passed him a bowl of freshly baked rolls. "I told you the Johnsons sold their house, which is similar to ours, for two hundred fifty thousand dollars. We couldn't believe it!"

Matt helped himself to a second roll and smothered it in butter.

"Your dad and I talked about it and we're thinking about doing the same thing and getting a newer home, something more modern."

Matt put his fork down and stared at his dad. "You sure about this?"

"Yeah, we already started looking around for a new place and we found the perfect subdivision in Antelope, built by Whitney Homes," Stan answered.

Barbara chimed in, "We found one that we both fell in love with. We wanted to tell you first, but we had to make up our minds quickly. We signed up because they were having a lottery to select who can buy one of the first twenty houses being released."

Matt almost choked on his food. "A lottery for the privilege of buying a house?"

Stan shook his head. "It's happening a lot lately. Everybody wants in on this real estate boom. Sixty other people were crammed into one of the models, vying for the first twenty lots."

"Oh Mattie, you should see how they decorated the models. I could haul all my clothes and move in just as they are, and think I went to heaven. I'm sorry, Stan, I didn't mean to interrupt, go on."

Matt stared at his parents. He could not remember the last time they looked so excited. "So what happened next?"

"So we're standing in the middle of this room, and they start pulling names out of this wire cage that they keep spinning around and around. Lo and behold, the seventh name called is ours. We can't believe it." Stan leaned back in his chair and waved his arms in a circular motion. "We started screaming like schoolgirls and jumping up and down until we realized there were other people who hadn't been called and were getting annoyed at us, so we went back to the sales office and completed our paperwork."

"And we got the lot we wanted," Barbara said. "It's about a half-acre and has two gorgeous old oak trees on it. We've been out to the lot every night this week making plans."

"That's exciting, guys. I'd like to take a look at the model you're buying and your lot. It's about time you did something for yourselves. You've sacrificed enough for Sis and me."

Barbara stood up and walked to the kitchen counter. She picked up a couple of Whitney Homes brochures off the counter and handed them to Matt. "Here's a corporate brochure—they've won awards throughout the fifty years they've been in business."

Matt nodded approvingly as he scanned the brochure. "Impressive." He set it down and went back to work on his now cooling lasagna. "Sounds like a good deal, Dad. Will they start construction soon?"

Stan held his plate across the table. "Barb, could you spoon me a little more? The estimate they gave us was four months and we'll be moved in."

Barbara clapped her hands and bounced in her chair. "I just can't wait. We need to do a few things around here before we list it, but the market is so frenzied, the realtors we've spoken with think this will sell in a weekend."

"What about your loan to finance the new house? Do you know who you're getting your loan through yet? Maybe Drew knows them."

"Whitney has a preferred lender named Sunset Mortgage," Stan said. "I believe they do all of Whitney's new loans. We met with the owner. She seemed real knowledgeable—a bit stiff and cold, but very knowledgeable. She had us pre-qualified in about an hour. It was all pretty painless."

Barbara got up and took Matt's dish. "Enough about us. Tell us about this young lady you have a date with tomorrow."

Matt stood up. "Here, Mom, let me help. As usual, your food was awesome. It's a good thing I don't live here anymore—I'd gain twenty pounds in a week and she wouldn't want to date me."

Matt followed his mom into the kitchen and helped stack the dishes. "I met Stephanie Bernard last week right after my interview with John Ramsey. She seems very nice, intelligent, and is extremely attractive, and she lives right here in Sac-town. She's an appraiser. She was at St. Francis when I was at Jesuit."

"I wonder if she's John Bernard's daughter," Stan said. "I knew him from Rotary and from St. Mel's Church. He died of cancer about eighteen years ago. How old is Stephanie?"

Matt shrugged. "I'm not sure. She looks to be in her early twenties."

"I'll bet that's his daughter. There aren't too many Bernards who attended St. Francis. She must have been real young when he died. He was a nice man."

Markus announced his presence with a squeaky bark. Matt leaned down and stroked his ears and Markus reacted by immediately kicking his tail into overdrive. "Hey there, little doggie. Let's see if we can find you a treat." Matt opened the refrigerator and found a hot dog. He tore it in half and held it above Markus, who was spinning excitedly underneath. "Okay, Markus, time to shine. Sit. Now lie down, that's it. Now roll over." Markus executed each command to perfection and Matt tossed him the treat.

"Matt, that dog is so spoiled. He's impossible to deal with after you leave, you know. It takes us two weeks to get him back to normal."

Matt took a sip of his beer and smiled. "I'm just getting back at you before you have a chance to spoil your grandchildren."

"So Matt, are you ready for your new position?"

"I don't think the reality of getting this job has hit me. Just going to the financial district in downtown San Francisco gives me chills."

"It'll hit you soon enough when your first deadline is missed or you don't hit a quarterly projection," Stan said. "I'm amazed that you wanted to move on from Sun Systems. If it had been me, I would have been happy to retire there."

Matt leaned down and picked up Markus, who eagerly licked his face as he held him. "Going with Franklin Smith gives me a chance to be a real player in the finance world. I want to be a player."

"I'm sure you know what you're looking for, son, but be careful what you wish for."

That evening, Matt thought about seeing Stephanie. Heck, he was up in Sac—why not? He was scheduled see her tomorrow, why not tonight as well? He excused himself and wandered into the family room where he dialed the number and she answered on the first ring. Within minutes, he was heading out the door to meet her.

Stephanie was late. Matt glanced at his watch. Ten past seven. He wouldn't have pegged her for the fashionably late type—or even the change-a-million-times-before-deciding-on-an-outfit type, but then again, he really didn't know her.

An uncomfortable tightening in his stomach made him get up from the rustic wooden bench. What was he doing here, anyway? He'd asked her out on a whim, on this, a Friday night—couldn't even wait for Saturday. He thought again about how sexy she looked when they first met, in a skirt and heels, holding that easel. He was really starting to think of her a lot and they hadn't even been on a date. That couldn't be good.

"Matt!" He whipped around, nearly tripping over the bench he'd just been sitting on. Stephanie rushed toward him in an obvious state of anxiety. Her ponytail bounced behind her as she grasped with two hands the purse slung over her shoulder. She stopped abruptly when she came to the bench.

"I'm so sorry!" Stephanie said, clapping a hand to her forehead. She was in tight jeans and a black tank top.

Matt smiled at her. Wow, he thought. She looks as good in those jeans as she did in that skirt I first saw her in.

"I got lost because I've never been here," she gestured at the historical buildings. "Then, when I thought to call you, I realized I didn't have your number. You called my work number and I didn't copy your cell down from there, and I'm just so sorry—"

"Don't even worry about it," Matt said and reached out to squeeze her arm. Stephanie looked down at it. What the heck am I doing? he thought. He quickly retracted his hand, but Stephanie's look told him that she hadn't really minded. A rush flowed through his body. Just calm down, man, she's just a girl. She didn't stand you up, and she's just a girl.

So why was his heart thumping like he'd run up and down the stairs of his apartment ten times?

"Since it's your first time to Old Sacramento, why don't I give you the tour?"

They strolled past the Wells Fargo Museum and Pony Express statue, past the Spuds shop that smelled like canola oil and potatoes, and the candy store with barrels full of colorful taffy.

Stephanie pulled out her sunglasses as they walked along the boardwalk lining the Sacramento River. The smell of railroad ties and rope hung in the warm spring air. A few fishermen with poles and a group of loud, laughing teenagers passed them by; other than that, it was peaceful. A yacht glided through the water toward the yellow Tower Bridge, and Matt stopped, gesturing to a bench overlooking the water.

Matt focused on the yacht where he could just make out two couples as they sat drinking wine on the fly bridge. "This place is a total tourist trap, but it's fun." He leaned back on the bench, stretching his arm out over its back; his fingertips were inches from her skin.

Stephanie followed his glance out to the river. "Wouldn't that be great?" she sighed, as the rear of the yacht disappeared around a bend in the river.

"It will be great," Matt replied and felt embarrassed when Stephanie laughed. But it was an open and honest laugh, one that told him that she was really listening—not the kind that so many other girls put on, self-conscious little-girl laughs that they thought made them sound cute.

"I like your determination," Stephanie said. "How can you be so confident about that?"

Matt shrugged. He couldn't sound too earnest about what he was about to say or she really would laugh at him. "It's sort of part of this ten-year plan I have…"

"You mean like your guidance counselor tells you to do in high school? I've never met anyone else who's actually done one, too!"

Too? Good—he wasn't such a freak, apparently. "Exactly. Not that I was paying too much attention to my counselor in high school."

Stephanie crossed her arms over her chest. "So…? Tell me."

"Ah, you know…find a good upwardly mobile job, finish paying off student loans and debt, save for a down payment on a house, nice car, nice watch, sock away money for retirement and vacations—"

"And a yacht."

"And a yacht, naturally." He grinned, realizing that nowhere in his list was there room for a girl—or a woman—or a relationship of any kind. Was there any wiggle room? Or was this just temptation…

"Come on," he said, standing up. He jerked his head toward the little main street. "If you've never been on a horse and buggy ride, I'd say it's about high time you did."

Stephanie stood up quickly. "Sounds good to me, partner, as long as you get me back early. I have to work tomorrow."

"I'll get you home early, but only if you tell me all about your ten-year plan," he said as they walked back toward the shops. She seemed relieved that he had changed the subject of work.

Matt was impressed with the small, well-maintained homes lining the quaint street where Stephanie lived. He drove up to a light-blue house with white shutters surrounded by rose bushes. Walking up the brick walkway, he couldn't help but think how much the house reminded him of his grandmother's home. He knocked softly on the door and within seconds, Stephanie greeted him.

"Hi Matt, it's nice to see you again. Are we ready?"

Matt held the door of his dark-blue 320I BMW as she slid into the passenger seat. He couldn't help but notice her breasts through her low-buttoned shirt as she got in. Stephanie rubbed the leather interior with her hand. "Nice ride, by the way. I love your car. It almost feels like you're driving on air."

"Thanks. I just bought it."

"I bet you can't wait to start your job. It sounds exciting."

Matt turned up the stereo a notch. "I am ready to start. I'm sure it will be intense, but I'll be learning a ton."

The Beatles' "Let It Be" came on the radio. Stephanie stared at it for a second. "That was my father's favorite group. Every time I hear one of their songs it reminds me of him."

"Was your dad's name John?"

She turned to him, eyes widened. "Yes, it was. How did you know?"

"My dad mentioned he knew him. He spoke very highly of him."

Stephanie stared down at her hands. "He died when I was eight. I miss him terribly."

"I'm sorry." Matt moved up to valet parking at Il Fornaio restaurant and escorted Stephanie to the front door.

At an intimate candlelit table next to a window overlooking the State Capitol building, Stephanie noticed Matt couldn't take his eyes off of her and felt herself blush. Matt noticed and turned his eyes to the menu. She's as attractive as I remember, he thought. I better be careful.

Over dinner, they continued their conversation from the previous night, talking about how their paths had probably crossed dozens of times while they were growing up.

Around 12:30 a.m., Matt pulled up to the curb at Stephanie's house and ran around the car to open her door. She stepped out and reached for his hand as they walked to the door. "Matt, I had a wonderful time tonight. Thank you."

"You're welcome, Stephanie. I had a great time, too."

She looked down into her purse and fumbled for her keys. Matt touched her waist and moved in closer for a kiss. His lips were soft and welcoming. She kept his gaze for a long moment. "Thanks again, Matt. That was nice." She slipped the key in the door and stepped inside. "I hope we see each other soon. Good night."

Matt turned after the door shut and headed to his car. He tossed the keys up and down in the air. Whistling to himself, he climbed in and drove off.

SEVEN

On a clear, crisp Monday morning, Matt walked through the garage at the Embarcadero Building, and as was his habit now, took the escalator to the second floor. He looked at his watch. Only 6:45. He veered left and entered the Posh Bagel, where a young man with curly hair stood making a latte at the counter.

"Hey John," Matt said, "how are your studies coming over there at Cal? You still pulling straight A's?"

The young man looked up and smiled. "So far, so good. I made the dean's list again this quarter."

"You're my hero. The only way I would have gotten near a dean's list is if he'd dropped it on me. Keep up the good work, man."

John looked up at Matt, handing him his order. "How's the world of high finance? You still buyin' every mortgage in town?"

Matt drew out his wallet. "Yeah, I'm trying to corner the market. Here you go. Keep the change."

After getting off the elevator, Matt entered Franklin's office, waved at the receptionist, who was busy with the phones but managed a wave back, and walked into his office. At his window, through the bright sunlight, he could see the Bay Bridge in the distance, packed with commuters trying to get into the city. He turned and glanced at his diploma from San Jose State, which he had hung on the wall alongside some old prints of wildlife scenes. It had been a wild beginning at this place. He was finally settling into his new job, and had completed his first sale. Matt thought he had an understanding of securities, but after the first few weeks at Franklin Smith, he knew he had a lot to learn.

I need to get rid of those prints and bring in some of my own, or better yet, buy new ones, he thought. I've been here almost five months, long enough to make it my own.

Matt had just logged on to his computer when Pete Ramsey, the boss's nephew by marriage, stuck his head in the doorway. He looked a little anxious, which was unlike him. He had seniority on Matt, but Matt wasn't sure what to make of Pete, and that made him uneasy.

"Hey, Matt, there's a call for all senior management at ten a.m. in the conference room. It's from corporate in New York. Everybody needs to be there."

"No problem, Pete." That seemed a bit odd. In the time he'd been with Franklin Smith, they had never had a conference call from the corporate office. Something must be up. He opened his e-mail, saw a note from John Ramsey, and read it quickly. "Please see me when you get in this morning." Matt jumped up and bolted out the door. He rapped on John's office door.

"Hey, Matt, come on in. I wanted to chat with you before we take that conference call." John, dressed as usual in a smart suit, gestured toward a chair.

Matt sat down quickly. He nervously rubbed his hands together.

"I was talking to the head of security last night, and he tells me you haven't left your office before midnight for the last two weeks." John picked up a legal pad and jotted some notes. "I saw that you closed the United Bank deal late last week. Congratulations."

Matt cleared his throat. "Thank you. It took a bit more time than I expected."

"I'm proud of you." John leaned forward and looked over the top of his eyeglasses. "Keep up the good work. You could go somewhere in this company."

Matt couldn't contain his smile. "Thanks, I'll do my best."

John glanced at his watch. "We'd best head to the conference room."

The phone rang precisely at 10:00 a.m. John answered on speaker. "Hello?"

"San Francisco?" a soft female voice inquired.

"We're here."

"Denver?"

"Here."

"Atlanta?"

"Here."

"Seattle?"

"Here."

"Minneapolis?"

"Here."

"They're all ready, Mr. Blackstone," reported the soft female voice.

John Blackstone was the impressive CEO of Franklin Smith. A Harvard graduate, he'd worked for Smith Barney before moving to Franklin. His management style was direct and blunt, always to the point. He was a man with a mission—Matt could relate to that, but his reputation of chewing up and spitting out senior managers was legendary.

Every trader in the conference room leaned forward toward the speaker, pens at the ready. A nervous tension hung in the room.

Blackstone started out with his usual style. "I'm calling you people from our corporate offices and I've got a couple of traders on my end listening in. As you know, we're almost into the second quarter of 2004, and we've had banner quarters up 'til now. I've received some calls from pension fund managers lately that have been pretty disturbing. You are probably aware of reports that came out last week showing a spike in delinquencies on real estate mortgages, and they're sending shock waves through the industry. Many of our major clients are pension fund directors and portfolio managers for large corporations."

Matt watched John, who was vigorously writing notes. Pete was leaning back in his chair, tapping a pencil on the conference table, looking bored. Papers could be heard rustling through the speaker phone as if someone was looking over notes.

Blackstone continued, "They're concerned about how much of our portfolio is in mortgage-backed securities and, of those, how many are secured with subprime loans. They worry we might be taking on too many risky subprime loans. Now, I know that's a lot of garbage and that they're using these reports to cherry-pick our products. However, I want every manager here to make sure we're purchasing as many prime loans as possible. Understood?"

Matt chewed nervously on the end of his pen. The request seemed to be suggesting they cut back on purchasing loans and that would hurt the office's bottom line. Damn, it could affect his bonus, too. He glanced around the room looking for signs to see if the other traders shared his concerns. They all looked as if they were in a solemn poker game and had no expression on their faces.

"Mr. Blackstone, this is Bob Smith from Minneapolis. How can we determine what is subprime and what isn't? We buy these loans bundled together and it would be almost impossible to determine every loan's status. "

"Good question, Smith. Most of the time you can tell the loan type by the lender, or the loan itself. Williams Credit, Santa Clara Investments, Worldwide Funding all generally put out subprime loans. That means no income qualifiers, stated income, and similar loans. All risky."

Blackstone coughed. "If our investor clients think we are too heavily invested in subprime loans, they could cause a run on the company and put us in a dire liquidity condition. I don't want that to happen. They need to be reassured that we're not making risky investments, no more than fifteen percent subprime. Any questions?"

There was a long pause.

"Before I sign off, Ramsey, is your trader Whiteside there with you?"

Matt sat up straight. He leaned in toward the phone. "Yes, yes, sir, I'm here."

"Congratulations on that United Bank deal. That will make your numbers out there in San Francisco look great for the quarter."

"Thank you, sir," Matt said nervously.

"Okay, is there anything else?" He paused a few seconds. "Good, get busy." Click.

Matt turned to John. "How are we going to comply with Mr. Blackstone's request? I'm working on a package with Santa Clara Investments, and I'm guessing at least thirty percent of those loans are subprime. Do I go back and renegotiate? Take all the subprimes out?"

"You'll have to be creative. You obviously can't buy that package as it stands. I would suggest getting Santa Clara to reduce the number of subprime loans and give them a better deal in return. From this point on, throttle back on those purchases."

John flipped the pages of his notepad over. "Good job, Matt. I knew you'd get attention from New York. As Blackstone said, your work made our numbers for the quarter look good."

Matt smiled. "Thanks. I hope to duplicate those numbers this quarter."

Pete interrupted, "Why do we care if these loans go bad? Isn't that loan service's problem? Besides, we end up selling them off to Freddie Mac and Fannie Mae and get a big fee. After that, it's not our problem."

John stared at Pete, shook his head, and got up and left the room.

Pete turned to Matt. "What, did I say something wrong? I mean, every trader in this company, and others, knows we're buying bad loans. We just need to sell them off before they go sour. Bleed off the fees and do it again."

"What about the people who have been put into these houses they can't afford? What happens to them?" Matt asked.

"Who cares? Once these deals close and I make my money, I could give a rat's ass what happens to them." Pete stood up with his folder in hand. "I'm in this to make money, not worry about whether or not some bozo can afford his home. Besides, as long as the market stays hot, no one should get hurt. As long as Freddie Mac and Fannie Mae keep buying up our loans, this market will continue. Everyone knows this is what goes on, and could care less about the borrowers."

Matt shrugged. He went back to his office, mulling over the two big loan packages he had pending, both with bundles of subprime loans. Somehow, he needed to talk his clients into switching the subprime loans out for regular loans. They wouldn't be happy. It would mean a lot of work and those deals were ready to close. He hoped they wouldn't just cancel. He thought about what Pete said. Did every trader take the same position and help put people in houses they were never going to afford, all to make a lot of money? He thought about his parents, whose new house was almost completed, and a chill went down his spine. Did John really know about all this?

He dialed his cell phone. "Hey, Drew, you're buying loan packages similar to mine. Does every trader in this business care about anything other than the bottom line? I mean, I'm getting the impression that everyone here is ruthless."

"Welcome to Wall Street, Matt. Pretty much everyone I know here is strictly business. If you're referring to the fact that we're buying loans and encouraging lending to people who have no business buying a home, most here take the attitude that it's not their problem. I wrestle with that question myself. I know that sooner than later there's going to be a day when the market changes, and a lot of people's lives will be affected."

"I'm glad I'm not the only one with a conscience. Making money is great, but making money at the expense of others doesn't sit well with me."

"If you assume that most people who work on Wall Street have no morals, you won't ever get disappointed. But I wouldn't worry. The market is still strong enough to bail out most of the bigger risk-takers. We just don't want to get caught holding the bag when all the loans go south."

"I hope so, Drew." Matt could see the first crack in his ten-year plan. He hoped it would not turn into a full-fledged earthquake. Matt shuffled some papers. "Gotta go. Work calls. Let's hook up in a couple of hours."

"How about six o'clock at the Rusty Pelican?"

"I'll see you there."

Matt leaned back in his chair and looked out over the San Francisco Bay. This view will never get old, he thought. I've got to push myself harder and make more deals come together. My plan needs to happen.

At 6:00 Matt arrived at the entrance to Pier 39. A disheveled man with a wispy beard and soiled hat sat on a planter, playing his guitar. Matt could see a few coins sprinkled about in an open guitar case. He listened to the music for a second, plucked two dollars out of his pocket, and dropped them in the guitar case. The man nodded appreciatively and continued playing. Matt continued down the wharf until he found the Rusty Pelican. He moved a bar stool out from the rustic bar and eyed the room. To his left was a large window overlooking the bay. The Bay Bridge was visible, as was his office tower a couple hundred yards away. The bar was dark with framed pictures of past celebrities who had been there. Model clipper ships sitting above a large mirror lined the back of the bar.

Matt turned and looked out onto the bay, watching a Coast Guard cutter cruise between Alcatraz and the mainland.

Drew came up from behind Matt and squeezed his shoulder. "Hey, Matt my boy. How ya doin'?" He spoke to the bartender. "Hey, could you snag a Corona for me, and a Coors Light for him, please?"

"You got it."

Drew did a slow survey of the crowd. "Hmm, there are a few good lookers here today, but I guess you're not interested."

Matt ignored him.

"Okay, buddy, I get the hint. So how goes the high finance biz? Did you get those mortgage packages cleaned up?"

"Pretty much. Once I figured out what price the sellers were willing to take, it went fast. You weren't lying: Money talks. I'm amazed how these loan officers can take someone who's basically a deadbeat and with a few tweaks make him into a decent borrower."

A tall man in a plaid shirt and old jeans put money in the jukebox and pressed a series of numbers. The jukebox jumped to life with the sounds of the Doobie Brothers. Matt tapped his fingers on the bar to the beat.

Drew sipped on his beer. "Yeah, it really isn't that tough," he said. "You have to wonder how these borrowers will handle all that debt. I mean, if you really dig into these files, there are people paying out thousands of dollars more a month than they are bringing in. I saw one file today where the house had closed and the borrower was approved on a stated income application."

"My parents are going through the process. Their new house is almost finished. Should I be worried?"

"I'm sure your parents are fine—they have real jobs and real income. But this one was different. This loan application stated that between the husband and wife, they were making close to two hundred and fifty thousand dollars annually. But there was no verification of that income, only what the borrowers stated on the loan application. They had a Mercedes, a Suburban, and about fifty thousand dollars in credit card debt. But if you did a little research, you could see they don't come close to making two hundred and fifty thousand."

"How did you find out they don't make that kind of money?"

"I looked at their checking account. They only list one account showing direct deposits every two weeks, one for $3,456, and one for $2,855. That's about $6,200 a month take-home. When you look at their savings history and see they aren't socking away any significant savings, where is all their money they say they're making? The answer is they don't make it."

Matt plucked a handful of pretzels from a bowl on the bar. "Why would they put themselves in a position to fail? If you know you can't keep up a payment over a long period of time, why would you take on the debt?"

"I'll tell you why. The banks and mortgage companies are in a major dogfight to put as much money out on the street as quickly as possible. They offer ridiculously low teaser starter rates, which is just what they are, teasers. They offer six months at one percent interest only, and then it jumps to five and a half percent for a year and a half, and again after two years to seven percent, and finally to eight-point-eight percent after four years. The problem comes when they qualify the borrowers at the one percent rate." Drew paused and eyed a woman who had just taken a seat at the bar.

Matt reeled him back. "Let me help you out before you get into trouble. Can't you see that big wedding ring on her hand?"

"Hadn't really gotten to her hands yet."

Matt sipped his beer. "What kind of people fall for these scams?"

"The mentality of the borrowers is that they'll take that low rate for a year or so, let their house go up in value, and then refinance or sell the house while putting a few bucks in the bank, or in some cases, buy new toys. It all works great as long as the housing market stays hot."

Matt held up an appetizer menu and perused it. "What happens if the market doesn't stay hot? Can it keep rising like it has been the last couple of years?"

"That's a good question. Most experts think the market will stay strong through 2007. They say it will correct itself sometime in the near future, but the correction will be gradual and easy."

Matt waved the bartender over to take his order. "Chicken wings and another beer, please."

The bartender nodded. "Sure thing."

"That's what I like to hear," Matt said to Drew. "Five years of this market and I can retire and do something like invest in real estate. That's where the big money is. It's all part of my ten-year plan, which is coming along nicely. I've got to admit, though, the job pressure is intense. If I don't sell those packaged mortgages Friday, Ramsey's not going to be happy. I just got a pat on the back for a deal I did last month, but that won't matter if I don't perform."

Drew patted him on the shoulder. "That's why they pay you the big bucks. You put up with a tough job and you get the reward. Enough business; it's happy hour. How about the lovely Miss Stephanie? How long have you been seeing her now?"

"About five months. When you meet her, you better be on your best behavior. Try not to embarrass me."

Drew threw his hands up in mock defense. "Please. I wouldn't think of doing something so preposterous. Do you have a picture of her?"

Matt snapped his fingers. "As a matter of fact, I do." He fished around in his breast pocket and pulled out a photograph. "I meant to put it in a frame I've got lying around my office."

Drew reached for the photo and looked at it. "Hey, I've seen this babe. She was here in this building a few weeks ago. I remember her because she was so stunning and had a great smile. Fortunately for you, I didn't get a chance to meet her." He handed the photo back to Matt.

"Stephanie was here? A few weeks ago? I wonder why she didn't let me know." Matt stared out at the San Francisco Bay as a large tanker made its way toward the Golden Gate Bridge. Great, he thought, another Kathy Ann. That's what I get for not staying focused on my goals.

Matt put the menu he was holding back down on the bar. "You know, I'm thinking of shopping for a condo. I make enough money, and I need a write-off. I may as well cash in on this hot market, too."

"There's nothing wrong with that logic. Just don't buy something beyond your means. Mortgage brokers will have no problem helping you get into a place that's more than you should afford, but there'll be a day when the market corrects itself, and you don't want to be in over your head."

"I'll remember that advice, Drew, thanks."

Through the large mirror at the back of the bar, Matt saw Pete Ramsey walking toward them. He nudged Drew and nodded in Pete's direction. "See that guy over there? He's John Ramsey's nephew. He works in the office next to mine. Something about him weirds me out."

Drew looked in Pete's direction. "He looks harmless to me."

Pete stopped at a table where two women were talking. They seemed startled at being interrupted.

"He thinks he's a real ladies' man," Matt said. "He's constantly hitting on our poor receptionist."

"He sure is a scrawny dude. Ichabod Crane comes to mind. Nice comb-over."

Matt laughed. "He's married and has two kids. I don't know what it is, but I almost feel like I have to go take a shower after being in the same room with him."

EIGHT

Relaxing on the couch in her floral sundress, Stephanie mindlessly turned the pages of the latest Nora Roberts novel. She curled up to make room for the furry black cat purring contentedly beside her. Stephanie put the book aside and spoke softly to the cat.

"Smokey, I wish my life could be as uncomplicated as this book. Happily married to a handsome, wonderful man, working on starting a family. Hopefully someday?" The cat raised his head and yawned. Matt had hinted a few weeks ago about dinner at his parents' house soon. Now, that seemed like a big step, and tonight was the night. She looked down at the cat, stroking his neck. "I'm really falling for this guy, Smokey. I guess I'd better watch myself. I'm supposed to be a professional and keep my personal life separate."

Her cell phone rang. Stephanie glanced at the clock. Who was calling so late on a Saturday? She checked the caller ID. "Oh, great, Janet Waller. Just what I need—another appraisal lesson from her."

She set the cat aside and answered. "Hello?"

"Hello, Stephanie. Did you receive those comparable sales figures I sent you to help justify the sales price we achieved?"

"I did get them, thank you. The problem is your comparables are not in the Portraits Subdivision as is the subject property. They're about five miles away. I've been having trouble finding a comparable in the subdivision similar to your sale."

"You're not going to find a similar sale because this house is the highest-priced sale in the area to date. There are no comparables."

Stephanie raised her voice. "It sounds like you're at a party, Janet."

"I'm at an outdoor restaurant at the Four Seasons in Hawaii."

"Wow, June in Hawaii...must be nice."

"It is."

"Well, I can't appraise the house up to your price. If it was a thousand more, or even fifteen hundred, I could stretch it, but seventy thousand dollars is out of line."

"That's crap," Janet retorted. "I need you to use my comparables and get this appraisal done by Wednesday. This loan is scheduled to close next Friday. If you can't make it happen, I'm sure your boss, Mr. Burns, will be happy to hear from Taylor Whitney, and he can explain how, in the hottest real estate market in the century, you can't find seventy thousand dollars in value."

"I'll look again for you, but if the value isn't there, I'm not going to increase the appraisal. If you want to call Mr. Burns, be my guest. I have no problem justifying my position."

"Raise the appraisal by seventy thousand, or I'm going directly to Taylor Whitney. Bye."

Stephanie hung up. "Jeez, she's such a witch." She got up from the couch and paced the floor, trying to calm down and put her thoughts in order. I bet you'd flip if you knew I had dinner with your assistant Carol last night, and she gushed information like a broken fire hose. And your nice partnership with Taylor Whitney...a lot of people would like to know all about that, too.

Stephanie slowed her pace. Janet was not the only one deceiving people, and she was feeling a bit guilty herself. When Justin Miller, Worldwide's high-powered attorney, had made her an offer, she never guessed she would be falling for someone involved in the investigation. It was fate she had run into Matt, boxes in hand, just when she was sealing the deal with Worldwide Funding.

Worldwide had been burned by a large number of phony loans from Sunset Mortgage and Whitney Homes. Justin's plan was to get someone on the inside to figure out where these loans were being generated and by whom. That's where she came in, and dealing with Janet Waller was a big part of the nightmare this job was turning into. Justin had gotten her the job as an appraiser at Burns and Finch to get her closer to the action. She was getting close, all right, but she was finding there were a lot of big fish in this pond.

She heard a knock on the door and rushed to open it. There was Matt with an armload of red roses and a big grin.

"Matt! You are too sweet. They're beautiful, thank you so much. Here, let me put them in a vase." She took the flowers from Matt and turned to the kitchen. "Oh, these flowers smell wonderful." She leaned her face in and took a deep breath.

"I'm glad you like them."

After putting the flowers in a vase, she set it on the kitchen counter. "Hey, I didn't greet you properly."

Matt came to her and she threw her arms around his neck. He pulled her close and kissed her on the lips.

"There, much better. I sometimes forget my manners."

Matt laughed. "As long as you make up for it like this, I hope you forget them often."

Matt looked down at a framed photo he'd spotted on the counter of a man with two boys. Leaning over, he looked more closely at the picture. "Isn't that the man you were helping with the presentation in San Francisco when I first met you, and the one you visited recently?"

"Yeah, those are the Miller twins with their daddy. I baby-sit them about once a month. They are so precious."

"The father looks young. Where's the mother?"

"Justin is a year or two older than you. The mom died in a car accident when the twins were two. Raising the boys by himself has been tough on him."

"Wow, that's tough. They are a good-looking family."

"Well, are we ready?" she asked.

"I'm all set." Matt opened the front door for Stephanie.

"I'm looking forward to meeting your parents. They sound really nice."

"Well, I think they are, but I'm prejudiced." Stephanie put her arm through his and walked down the walkway toward the street. "Did I tell you they are buying a new Whitney Homes house out in Antelope?"

Stephanie stiffened.

"How are things at work?" Matt asked. "I imagine you've been busy."

"Matt, you can't believe how frenzied it is. Housing prices are shooting up at a record pace and everybody wants to get a piece of the action. People are refinancing their homes so they can take that money and buy more homes. It's nuts."

"Well, keep 'em coming, because my firm is buying as many mortgage-backed securities as we can get our hands on."

Stephanie rubbed his arm. Matt looked over at her and squeezed her hand. "Are you ready for a wonderful meal?"

"Yes, I haven't eaten much all day—too much work stress. I've got this bulldog of a loan officer giving me grief over an appraisal."

"My work has been hectic, too. I rarely get home before eight and I've been working a lot of weekends. It will level out one of these days, and we'll find more time for each other."

The ride to Matt's parents' house took only minutes from Stephanie's home. Matt kept looking over at her, and she hoped he wouldn't notice how nervous she was tonight.

Matt pulled into the driveway of a neatly landscaped, older home in a quaint neighborhood. All the surrounding houses had manicured lawns with well-cared-for flower gardens. Large, mature trees lined the street. He stopped at a house with a blue and yellow C&B real estate sign hanging in the front yard. A red "Sold" notice was placed on top of the sign.

Barbara greeted them, warmly embracing Matt with a big hug. She let go of Matt and smiled at Stephanie. Matt drew Stephanie closer. "Mom, this is Stephanie Bernard."

They shook hands. "Stephanie, it is so nice to meet you. Matt has told us a lot about you."

Stan had gotten out of his reclining chair in the family room and stood in the entry, dressed in a blue golf shirt and a pair of dark slacks. "Hello, Stephanie, I'm the dad. Welcome."

"Nice to meet you, Stan, thanks."

Matt turned and looked at his sister, who had just rounded the corner. "Stephanie, this is my little sis, Michelle."

A petite, perky blonde with her hair in a ponytail extended her hand. "Nice to meet you, Stephanie. I can see why Matt is all atwitter about you."   Stephanie blushed. "Thank you, Michelle."

Barbara guided Stephanie out from the entry into the kitchen area. "Can I get you something to drink?"

"Barbara, I would love a glass of water."

Matt followed. "Hey, Mom, I was telling Stephanie you guys are buying a new home. Whitney Homes is the builder, right?"

Barbara filled a glass with ice from the refrigerator and answered without looking up, "Yes, they're just finishing it up. We're scheduled to move in two weeks. This house sold quickly and is supposed to close at the same time."

"Are you by chance using Sunset Mortgage to do your loan?" Stephanie asked.

"Yes, I understand they're Whitney's preferred lender. If we use them, we get twenty-five hundred dollars credited toward our closing costs. Stan, what's the name of the loan officer who pre-qualified us? Janet something?"

Stan entered the kitchen. "Waller, Janet Waller."

"That's right, Janet Waller. Do you know her?"

Stephanie took a gulp of water. Oh my, she thought, this is getting sticky. "Yes…I do know Janet. I do a lot of appraisals for Sunset Mortgage." She took another sip.

Stan joined the conversation. "Our house is in Antelope—the Portraits subdivision, lot 12."

Stephanie nodded. "I know the subdivision and may have even appraised your house. I've been working on that subdivision with Janet. She sent me a sale on a lot right across the street from your new house, but it was, let's just say substantially higher than the comps."

Stan looked at Barbara. "The same house sold for a lot more than ours? I hope it goes through. That's great for us. She was very professional, very to-the-point. This is only the second house we've bought in our lives, so we don't know much about all the financing programs. We have to trust Janet, but she seems to know her stuff."

Stephanie smiled slightly. Oh, she knows her stuff, all right. She knows how to put people in loans they can't possibly afford or worse.

"Are you familiar with Whitney Homes? Are they well-built?" Stan asked.

Stephanie wanted to excuse herself and just run. Why of all builders in Sacramento did these people have to buy a Whitney Home and use Janet Waller? She couldn't believe she heard herself saying, "I hear they build good homes."

"Do you know the owner, Taylor Whitney?"

"I've never met him, but he has a reputation of being pretty arrogant and likes expensive toys."

Barbara laughed. "Well, we're as excited about this house as we can be. We go out to the lot at least twice a week. But enough about that. Matt, why don't you show Stephanie around the place, and I'll get dinner ready. I'll only be a couple of minutes."

Matt took Stephanie's hand and walked her into the family room. She observed how tidy and neat everything was, homey and warm. There was a Thomas Kincaid painting on one wall, and a portrait of the entire Whiteside family, including their dog, hung above the fireplace. An elegant bookshelf with porcelain figurines and framed family photographs covered another wall. Michelle opened the sliding door and in bounded a fat little black-and-brown dog. He ran up to Matt at full speed, squealing and jumping. When Matt bent down, the dog rolled onto his back, exposing his stomach.

"This is Markus," Matt said. "I gave him to Michelle five years ago for her birthday." He rubbed Markus' belly and the dog's tail kicked into high gear.

"Oh, he's a cutie. What kind of dog is he?"

"He's a Chihuahua-mini-Doberman mix. We call him a Rattweiller."

Stephanie giggled. "A Rattweiller, that's good."

"That's him. Come see my old bedroom."

Stephanie eyed the neat and tidy room with posters of athletes on the wall. A football sat on a desk by the bed, and a shelf was filled with trophies and team photos. She leaned a little closer to the trophies and read the inscriptions.

"Team captain, most valuable player, wow."

He leaned over to kiss her but was interrupted by Barbara calling from the kitchen.

"Okay everybody, dinner is served. Come to the dining room."

Matt finished his quick kiss, and then led Stephanie to the dining room.

After everyone was settled, Stan said a short prayer, and then Barbara started dishing up the dinner. "I hope you like rigatoni. I love this recipe. It comes from Biba's Italian Restaurant downtown."

"I love any pasta, Barbara. I'm a foodie. Matt took me to there a couple of weeks ago. It was delicious."

Stan filled his plate. "Matt tells us you went to school here at St. Francis High School."

"Yes, I did. I was four years behind Matt. We knew all the Jesuit boys, so it's ironic we met after college. How did you and Barbara meet?" asked Stephanie.

Stan glanced at Barbara. "We met almost thirty years ago at a mutual friend's wedding. I had just gotten out of the service after serving a tour in Vietnam and a buddy I knew from high school introduced us. I thought she was the best-looking woman I'd ever seen." He smiled at Barbara. "Still do."

Barbara's eyes lit up and she smiled. "Thanks, Stan, you're pretty handsome yourself."

Stephanie looked down at the table for a moment. "My father served in Vietnam. I was pretty young and I don't remember him talking too much about it." She looked back up.

Stan put his fork down and raised an eyebrow. "Your father and I were in the same Rotary Club. He was a very nice man."

Stephanie smiled at Stan. "Thank you for saying that. Matt mentioned you knew him." She could feel her heart tugging at the memory. If her dad were alive, he'd be a lot like Stan. Suddenly, she stiffened up. "I feel something licking me under the table!"

Michelle and Matt yelled in unison, "Markus!" Matt pushed back from the table, went to the sliding door to where Markus had beaten a hasty retreat, and let him out. He shook his head as he came back to the table. "He must like your perfume."

They all laughed.

"So how is the appraisal business, Stephanie?" Stan asked.

"It's pretty busy. I can't keep up with the work. Matt asked me to come to the Bay Area a couple weeks ago, but I was too busy." Not to mention she had to review about fifteen files had Justin sent over from Sunset Mortgage. The deeper she got into this case the more complex it became. Stephanie still hadn't figured out who was involved from Whitney Homes, but she felt she was getting close. Since she was here anyway, she might as well ask Barbara and Stan a few questions. "How was your experience with Janet? Did she explain everything well?"

Stan shrugged. "Well, she walked us through the process and put us in a low-rate loan. She told us we could refinance in a year and get a better deal. It all seemed to make sense."

Stephanie played with her pasta. Oh, it made sense, all right. Janet was trying to manipulate the market and was probably putting these people in a loan they wouldn't be able to afford in a couple years. Janet didn't care; she made her fees.

If they could just wait a couple months, this will all be exposed, Stephanie thought.

Stan looked at Barbara. "We're so excited. We're moving in a couple of weeks."

Stephanie swallowed hard and sipped her water.

"I enjoyed meeting your parents," Stephanie said as she watched the traffic through the passenger window on the ride home. "So your dad was in Vietnam, just like mine."

Matt relaxed his grip on the wheel. "Yeah, he won a Purple Heart and a Silver Star, for bravery."

"Really," Stephanie said.

"His platoon fell into a firefight and my dad and his best friend were hit with shrapnel. My dad took the hit in his shoulder, but his buddy was hit in the head. My dad carried him half a mile to a field hospital for help. Unfortunately, his buddy didn't make it. My dad's shoulder was badly injured and he still has limited use of his right arm. He doesn't like to talk about it much. He thinks he might have been exposed to Agent Orange in Vietnam. He has respiratory problems."

Stephanie faced Matt. "I know about Agent Orange. Dad's doctors were convinced his cancer was related to exposure to it. My mother still hasn't forgiven the Army."

"I don't know what I'd do if something like that happened to Dad. Both he and Mom have worked really hard to get where they are. They've sacrificed a lot for my sister and me. I'm happy they're finally able to enjoy the fruits of their labor with this new house. Part of my ten-year plan is to help them get a vacation home in Lake Tahoe."

"Along with your yacht?" she asked. Matt turned to her and grinned. She stared at the glove box in front of her as they drove. *Do I warn Matt about his parents' purchase?* she thought. *Their deal is probably fine and I'm worrying over nothing.*

She had a job to do, too.

She placed her hand over Matt's. "So, how are things going at work?"

"I love it. It's definitely intense and all business. I never realized how bottom-line-oriented Wall Street is. I like almost everyone in my office, except there's one trader that I'm uncomfortable with." Matt turned the car around a corner.

"Really? What's his name?"

"Pete Ramsey, my boss's nephew. He doesn't seem to have ethics or scruples. It's difficult to pinpoint anything specific, but he is just different."

Stephanie stared straight ahead. Hmmm, Pete Ramsey, she thought. If he's our source, I need to find a connection between him, Whitney, and Janet.

After parking, Matt walked Stephanie to her door and waited patiently as she fumbled through her purse for the keys.

"You're going back to your parents' tonight, right?"

"Yeah, I am."

She leaned closer. "Are you expected home at any particular time?"

"Do you mean do I have a curfew? No, I'm an adult, and they treat me as one. I don't like to stay out too late, though. I don't want my mom to worry."

She clutched his hand and pulled him inside. "Why don't you come in for a little while? I won't keep you out too late, I promise."

She wrapped her arms around his neck and kissed him eagerly. His hands gripped her waist and held her close. Her hands slid down his chest and fingered the buttons on his shirt. A voice in her head yelled loud and clear, Don't go there, Stephanie—this won't end well. Mixing business with pleasure is a bad idea.

Forcing these thoughts from her mind, she unbuttoned his shirt and ran her fingers down his chest. Keeping eye contact, she reached down and gave his belt buckle a sharp tug, releasing the clasp. She placed her fingers into the top of his trousers and backed him toward her bedroom.

NINE

Sitting on the couch, a steaming cup of coffee in her hand, Stephanie flipped the legal pad she was holding onto the coffee table in front of her and leaned back. Her hair was pulled back in a ponytail, and she wore a white T-shirt with a huge Minnie Mouse logo on it, and light-blue pajama bottoms. Petting her cat and holding him close, thoughts about Matt and what she had felt the night before left her head spinning. Her whole body glowed in a way she'd never experienced before. It bothered her that she had had to lie to Matt about her real reason for her visits to San Francisco. Certainly, he would think it was a complete betrayal—her helping with an investigation of his firm. How long could she put up this façade?

The sun beamed through the kitchen window and lit up the room with its radiance. The roses Matt had given her were sitting in a clear crystal vase and had opened up during the night. Stephanie poured herself more coffee, bent down to smell the roses, came up smiling, and sat down at the kitchen breakfast bar. She picked up her cell phone and dialed a number. A male voice answered, "Hello?"

"Hi Justin, it's Stephanie. Is it okay to call you on a Sunday?"

"Hey, Steph, of course—I'm at the office."

"How's the view from the twenty-second floor of the Embarcadero Building?"

"Spectacular. It's a beautiful day. Boats are cruising all over the bay. I just had a few loose ends to tie up. So what have you found?"

"So far, Janet seems to be getting the bulk of her new homes sales from Whitney Homes." She took a sip of the coffee. "The prices these homes are selling for range anywhere from fifty thousand to seventy-five thousand dollars higher than the same house that the general public is buying. I don't know how she's getting these sales, but obviously it's someone inside Whitney, possibly Taylor Whitney himself. She's funneled all these sales to Worldwide for funding. Every loan is a no-income qualifier with one hundred percent of the inflated purchase price financed. I don't know who the beneficiary of these sales is yet, but I think I'm getting close. What did you find out?"

"Worldwide has bought nearly every loan Sunset is making because we've been successful in selling all of them to Franklin Smith and a few other hedge funds. We think someone at Franklin is in on the deal because the majority of the loans have been laid off to Freddie Mac quickly. The loans Worldwide didn't sell off quickly enough were the ones that went bad. Oh, I almost forgot to mention, we have determined that your friend, Matt, is not involved."

Stephanie closed her eyes and took in a deep breath. Thank goodness! That would have been awful, dating a person of interest in a fraud case. She stood up, stretched, and walked outside to find the paper. "What about Hartford Financial and Drew Mathews? Are they involved?"

"No, there's no evidence they're doing anything other than normal business transactions. The only reason this is starting to come to light is Franklin Smith has been cutting back on their purchases from us and we've been forced to hold onto these loans longer than normal. That's when we discovered the borrowers never made a payment and couldn't be found. If Franklin had kept buying our loans and reselling to Freddie Mac, we would never have known about this scam. Do you think you could possibly get into Janet's office and copy some documents? We need to know who else is behind this and how she's getting these loans approved and funded. We also want to know if we're the only lender targeted."

"Jeez, Justin. I didn't know."

"Just try. I don't want you to get caught—we don't want a Watergate on our hands. That would be bad PR for the bank."

"For the bank! What about me?"

Justin laughed. "How about your friend Matt? Do you think you could pump him for information without letting on what you're up to?"

"I not sure, Justin. I'll have to think about it. I like the guy and the last thing I want to do is put our relationship in jeopardy. I feel guilty enough about deceiving him."

"Well, see what you can find and get back to me before you try anything. You could pretend to buy a Whitney Home and get in that way. I don't know, give it some thought. You're doing a great job, Stephanie. We should be wrapping this up in a couple of months, and then you can go back to your regular job of spying on cheating husbands."

"Right now that kind of investigation sounds really good. Hey, say hello to the twins for me. I want to see them soon."

"I'll do that. You take care."

She put the phone beside her on the couch. "Come here, little cat," she said softly, holding him up underneath his front shoulders. She brought his nose to hers. The cat gave her a sleepy look. "Smokey, Matt is a problem for me. I worry I'll slip up and he'll learn the truth. Then what?" She set the cat back down on the couch and continued to pet him. One glitch continued to trouble her…Drew. He was a sharp guy and she got the feeling when she met him that he was not buying everything she said. She yawned. She'd think about it tomorrow.

TEN

Taylor Whitney sat at Cattle Baron's with his wife, Monica. He leaned over the long cherry wood bar. "Give me a rum and Coke, and she'll have a margarita, no salt." The bartender nodded and went to make the order.

Monica ran her hand across the top of the bar seductively. "This thing is so smooth. I love the color of the wood." She surveyed the crowd. "What a nice gathering, Taylor. I don't think I've seen so many important people in one place for a long time. Sheriff Turner definitely knows how to celebrate his re-election." She adjusted her diamond necklace, then stroked her ruffled white blouse. "There has to be over three hundred people here. Seems all of Sacramento society turned out."

Taylor raised his voice to be heard over the noise of the crowd. "Well, Ron can thank me for this one. He wouldn't be sheriff without me. I donated twenty thousand dollars to his campaign."

"Were you worried Sheriff Turner may have to help you get out of trouble someday?" She looked at him with a smirk.

Taylor ignored the dig. "Not at all. I just like to be a part of these events so I can show all these fools here that I have what they want: money."

Monica admired the jewelry on her arm. "I love my new diamond bracelet. Thank you again." She kissed him on the cheek.

"For fifteen thousand dollars, you better love it." He glared at her. He pulled a handkerchief out of his breast pocket and dabbed the sweat from his face.

The bartender placed their drinks on the bar.

Monica did a slow burn. "Why must you always tell me what everything costs? I know it's expensive."

A curvy waitress came up to them with a tray of appetizers. "Would you like to try the salmon mousse with lemon and dill?" she asked, smiling sweetly at Taylor as she held the tray in front of him.

Taylor picked up a cracker. "I'll try one." His eyes slowly crawled down her face to her chest, paused a second, slid past her waist, and then back up again. He was mentally unfastening her bra when Monica's elbow to his ribs brought him back to reality. He spat some of the cracker out and started coughing, then grabbed a napkin from the bar and wiped his mouth.

"You pig," Monica hissed. "Did you not remember I'm standing right here?"

"Hello, Taylor and Monica. How are you two tonight?"

Preston Carson, a local builder-developer, was standing right beside them. Monica let her eyes wander over the tall, well-built man.

"Hi, Preston, how's it going?" Taylor said, stifling a cough.

Monica's demeanor changed immediately. She cooed, "Preston." She extended her hand out and fingered his coat. "I love this suit, and your blue striped tie."

"Thanks."

Taylor ignored the obvious flirtation. "Hey, Preston, you have to see my new yacht. It's a monster, a first-class beauty—built by Hampton Yachts, 52 feet long, and powered by two 260-horsepower Yanmar diesel engines. Gorgeous, and sleeps eight."

"Yes," Monica said as she stroked Preston's arm. "You should come out with us sometime for a little trip down the river."

"Thanks for the invite. I might take you up on the offer sometime. Are you two just back from Palm Springs?"

"Yeah, we were there. I bought a place on the fifteenth hole at the Big Horn Country Club. Don't worry, Preston, you can't afford it," Taylor said sarcastically.

Preston laughed. "You're probably right. But we'll never find out because I'm too cheap to think about spending that kind of money for a golf club membership. It almost kills me paying fifty bucks a round at Turkey Creek."

A waitress came up offering a shrimp appetizer. Preston shook his head. "No thanks."

Taylor plucked a shrimp off the tray and stuffed it in his mouth. "Come on, I wouldn't play that course if you paid me. It's so low-rent I wouldn't be caught dead on it. I did shoot a smooth eighty-nine at Big Horn, though. My swing is just starting to come back."

"I'm impressed, Taylor. I didn't know you were such a good golfer. How are your subdivision sales going?"

"We should sell six hundred homes this year. Even though it's just October, 2004 is already my biggest year ever."

"Really? I've read many economists are predicting a major correction. Aren't you concerned about over-building?" Preston asked. "Every major builder I've spoken with plans to cut back on new starts next year."

"Preston, when are you going to learn? These big corporate builders aren't very bright. They can't react to the local market like I can. It's like they're trying to steer a huge cruise ship; they move slower and slower." Taylor leaned over the bar and motioned to the bartender. "What do executives in New York know about the California real estate market? I'll tell you what they know: zero. They only know what they read in the *Wall Street Journal,* and the writers for the Journal don't know anything, either. Trust me, I've been doing this for thirty-five years and know what I'm doing."

Preston shifted his position slightly, forcing Monica to drop the hand resting on his arm. "Are you seeing any changes in dealing with the banks? It looks as if they're starting to be more cautious."

"My banks love me. They know there are twenty other banks just begging for my business, and if they give me any grief, I'll get rid of them." The bartender placed fresh drinks in front of Taylor. Taylor lifted up his drink and looked across the room. "Duty calls, Preston. There's Sheriff Turner and I need to say hello."

Taylor and Monica rose to circulate the room. As she passed Preston, she gave his butt a flirtatious squeeze. Startled, he jumped. She smiled at him with her eyes as she followed Taylor to where the sheriff was holding court.

After about an hour, Monica tugged on Taylor's sleeve. She whispered, "Taylor, we've been hobnobbing for over three hours. It's time to get out of here—I'm bored."

Taylor looked around the room and nodded. "Okay, I'm ready. Let's get the car." The weather outside had turned nasty and a driving rain was coming down. Taylor handed a ticket to the valet attendant. "Be careful with my car," he told the young man. "It's a Bentley. The minimum cost to fix dents is twenty-five thousand dollars. Your daddy couldn't afford to pay that."

The attendant gulped and his eyes grew large as the numbers rattled around in his head. "Okay, sir, I'll be very careful." When he went outside, his umbrella was almost blown out of his hands as he nervously headed to the parking lot in search of Taylor's Bentley.

Monica turned to Taylor and said, "What a nice young man. You'd better tip him well."

"I'll give him something, but I'm not going to spoil him. He needs to learn there is no such thing as easy money. I don't just hand out money for nothing. People have to earn it."

"That's the truth," Monica mumbled, adjusting her bracelet. "I certainly earn mine."

A minute or so later, the attendant pulled up to the curb and hopped out. Dripping wet, he held his umbrella up to shield Monica and Taylor from the driving rain. As he held the door for Taylor, he said, "I was very careful with your car and didn't touch a thing, sir."

Taylor slid into the driver's seat and flipped the stereo on. John Mellencamp's "Pink Houses" drifted out of the Bose speakers. "Congratulations," he said as he counted out a two-dollar tip in a grand gesture right in Monica's view. The attendant could see the wad of hundred-dollar bills he yanked the bills from. "Can't say I'm not generous," he said with a sneer.

They had only driven a mile when Monica spoke. "So who are you screwing now, Taylor? Anybody I know? I hear the whispers from people around us. I'm not stupid. Who is she?" Her voice was low but steely.

"Don't be ridiculous, Monica. I'm not messing around. Why do you repeatedly accuse me of being unfaithful? I've been concentrating on golf and business and haven't had time for anything. Why don't you focus on something else for a change? Didn't I just buy that bracelet? Doesn't that show I care?"

"No, it shows me that you're up to no good." She forcefully turned the stereo off. "When you start throwing big money my way, there's a reason for it. Remember, I was the one you were having an affair with while you were married to Angela. I remember how you showered her with gifts when she was suspicious. You're not fooling me."

"Wait a minute. I'm not the one who had to have that bracelet. You were. I bought it because you wanted it."

Monica's voice rose. "Taylor, you only spend money on yourself. The only reason you bought that bracelet was to shut me up. You figure that as long as I can keep buying myself expensive things, I'll let you do what you like. Well, here's a news flash for you: I won't roll over and play dead while you go screwing another woman—or for that matter, *women*. Keep in mind I have the number of Angela's attorney, Mary McDougal. Remember her? She took you to the woodshed once, and she'd be happy to do it again."

Taylor yelled back, trying to be heard, "I'm not doing a damned thing. If you keep pushing me, you might just get your wish and be free of me. I'm not afraid of anyone, including you or that attorney. Don't threaten me. You ought to be happy with what you have and remember where you came from. If it wasn't for me, you'd still be cutting hair at the Grand Salon making twelve bucks an hour."

"Screw you, Taylor, throwing that up in my face again. I'm not ashamed I was a hairdresser. I wasn't born with a silver spoon in my mouth and my daddy didn't die and leave me his multi-million-dollar business when I was twenty-eight, like yours did. I worked hard for my money and am damn proud of it. And yes, you have elevated my social standing, but don't equate hairdresser to moron. I know what I'm entitled to, so you better think twice with both of your heads if you know what's good for you."

Taylor turned up the radio to tune her out and hit the gas. The guard at the entrance to their subdivision recognized Taylor's Bentley, and opened the iron gate. Taylor checked out his car window at the guard as he passed. "Whatever the association pays that ignoramus is too much. All he ever does is sit there all day reading the sports section and comics."

"What else is he supposed to do? He's stuck in that booth. Why don't you try it for a week and see how you do?"

They took a left at the second street and drove up to the entrance of their home.

"Look at this house," Taylor gloated, leaning his beefy arms on the steering wheel. "This is why I'm so successful. I made sure my driveway was long and curved and a hundred and fifty feet from the street, with hand-stamped concrete. That blue grass came from Kentucky, and the pond and waterfall are right out of the brochure from the Maui Hyatt. Everything is top shelf, first class. Isn't that enough to make you happy?"

"Are you crazy? I know where you bought this stuff and what you paid for it. I was with you when you built this house, remember? You keep telling me, and everyone else within earshot, what it cost. Money isn't everything."

Taylor drove past the front door and pressed the remote to open the middle garage door. Halfway into the garage, he stopped. "The Ferrari needs washing; so does the Porsche, and the Hummer. When you see

Manuel tomorrow, have him take care of it. Oh, I guess you can have him wash your Mercedes if you want."

Monica opened the car door and leaned back in. "Why don't you tell him yourself, jerk? Make sure you remind him how much those cars cost and how many *pesos* it will cost him to repair any scratches he makes." She stepped out and slammed the door. She marched into the house through the garage, leaving Taylor sitting in the car, its engine still running.

He waited for a minute in silence, watching the windshield wipers go back and forth in a steady rhythm, then backed the Bentley out of the garage and shot back down the driveway. He sped through the entry gate, ignoring the guard, turned left onto Auburn-Folsom Road, and headed toward Sacramento. He picked up his cell phone and dialed a number. A female voice answered. "Hello?"

"Want some company?"

ELEVEN

The party was still going strong to celebrate the sheriff's victory. Preston sipped his drink as he watched Taylor and Monica leave the restaurant. "I thought they'd never leave," he said under his breath. In one of the corners of Cattle Baron's, a photographer had set up a backdrop for various dignitaries to take a photo with Sheriff Turner. Preston had waited in line about a minute when his turn came up. They shook hands. "Congratulations on the re-election, Ron. I can sleep well knowing you're in charge of our streets."

Ron laughed at him. He was out of uniform in a dark double-breasted suit with a dark-green tie. "Preston, it's good to see you, and thanks for your help. I saw you earlier talking to Taylor Whitney and his wife. Did he tell you he'll build six hundred more homes than you this year?"

Preston raised a brow. "I thought he said it was closer to seven hundred."

"That guy is something else. How is business for you? The housing market is sure hot right now. You must be making a killing."

"Yeah, Ron, it is, but it will cool off one of these days. It can't keep going up and up forever. The trick is to get out before it falls."

"Who the heck knows when that will be?" the sheriff said. "I was thinking about upgrading our house—we've been in it for over fifteen years. What do you think?"

"I don't see why not. It seems as good a time as any to fix up a house. You could only increase its value."

The photographer had them squeeze together, told them to smile, and snapped a picture. They shook hands again and Ron asked, "Are you playing in my golf tourney next month? I'd like to speak with you more when there are fewer people. I hope you're bringing that great wife of yours to the dinner."

"I'm playing and I'll see you there."

"All right, bud, take care."

Preston left the sheriff and retrieved his raincoat from the coat-check. At the entrance, he handed his valet ticket to an attendant. Looking out the door, he said to the valet, "I wouldn't want your job today. You're earning your wages."

The kid, whose dark hair was completely soaked and dripping into his eyes, smiled. "It's only bad for a minute or so, and then I get to drive cool cars."

"I like your attitude, young man. What's your name?"

"Seth, sir." The attendant ran off into the rain to retrieve Preston's car. Two minutes later, a black Suburban showed up at the curb. The attendant hopped out, ran to the door with his umbrella, and escorted Preston to the front seat of his car. Preston pulled out a ten-dollar bill and handed it to him.

"Here you go, Seth. Thanks for the service."

"Anytime, sir, thanks." He shut the door and waved as Preston drove off into the dark, rainy night.

Preston picked up his cell phone and dialed home.

"Hello?" Karen's vibrant voice warmed him.

He dropped his voice a notch. "What are you wearing?"

"Just a smile, my love, only a smile."

"Great, I'm leaving the party and will be home soon."

As Preston drove, he thought of the conversation he'd had with Taylor. Taylor was delusional. The weekly *Ryness Report* tracked new home sales in the area. Every builder in town reported to it, and every builder in town subscribed to it. There were no secrets in the industry.

Whitney's sales had been average this year, just like everyone else's. Now he was planning to double his volume from last year by building more homes on speculation?

He switched the radio to a country station. George Jones' rich voice filled the car. Taylor was gambling in a huge way that the market would continue to stay hot. If his gamble was wrong, he would be adding more to his standing inventory and could end up wallowing in a huge mountain of debt.

Preston thought about how Monica had grabbed his butt. What was that all about? What a pair of squirrels she and Taylor are, he said to himself. They deserve each other.

He stopped his car at the guard shack. Recognizing Preston's vehicle, the guard opened the gate as Preston rolled down his window.

"Hey, Andy, how are you doing today?"

Andy stuck his head out the window of the shack. "I'm doin' fine, Mr. Carson, just fine. How're you, sir?"

"I'm okay, but I don't have to be outside in this miserable weather. Is the heat working in your building there? There was a problem with it last year."

"It seems to be working all right, Mr. Carson. I'm warm."

"Okay, Andy. Good to see you. Have a good night." He drove through the gate. Two minutes later, he entered the house. Karen was sitting at the kitchen table reading a newspaper. She had her hair up in a bun and was wearing a dark skirt with a blue blouse. Her high heels were lying next to her feet.

She looked up. "Hi there, good-looking. Why don't you start a fire and we can whip up something to eat?"

"Hey, I thought you were naked."

"Ha, ha—psyched you out. You snooze, you lose."

"Oh well, another time," Preston said. "Does the paper have anything profound to say today?"

"Only that housing prices increased twenty-seven percent over last year. Amazing market."

"This year has definitely been good for me, and it's only October," Preston said. He opened the hall closet and hung up his coat. "I sure hope 2005 will be as good, but I have my doubts."

"What makes you think next year will be different?"

"I don't know when it will be, whether it's next year or the year after, but at some point this market will stall out. There's no way we can continue to increase prices twenty-seven percent a year and not price people out of the market. The past years it's been like a feeding frenzy. "

Preston picked up some wood next to the fireplace and laid the pieces in a stack. Seventies music, pouring from a satellite station and beaming in through the television, played "Reeling in the Years." He hummed along with Steely Dan.

"This market will cool off and just like musical chairs, when the music stops some people won't be able to find a seat. I don't want to be one of those people."

"What are you going to do?" Karen asked. She came over and sat down on the couch.

"I'll finish out the subdivisions I've started, which should be about thirty-five homes, and I'll sell off my remaining vacant lots. They would have kept me busy for the next couple of years, but I'm going to finish what I've got and watch from the sidelines for awhile. I may miss out on a big payday, but if I'm right I won't get into a major bind when I can't sell my homes." He leaned into the fireplace and lit the gas log lighter.

Karen lifted a magazine off the coffee table and perused it. "That's probably not a bad way to go. Better to be safe than sorry. Besides, you've been working so hard these last few years; you could use a break."

"Yeah, I could slow down for awhile. Are we still going to the Hyatt for New Year's Eve?"

"Yes, I bought tickets last week. It should be fun. Dinner is being catered by the four-star restaurant in the Hyatt, Mia Belle's. Then there's music and dancing until two." Karen's soft face lit up at the thought. Preston loved seeing her happy. She looked like the pretty girl he had married thirty years ago. He sat down beside her on the couch and drew her toward him.

Karen laid her hand on his sleeve. "How was Sheriff Turner's event?"

"Nice, a lot of dignitaries. Everyone asked where you were and I explained you had a prior commitment." Preston rose, took the poker, and shifted the logs. The flames rose higher and the comfortable smell of wood smoke drifted toward him.

When Billy Joel's "Piano Man" came on, Preston snatched the TV remote from the coffee table and turned up the volume. "I love this tune. Anyway, I got to talking to Taylor Whitney—you know, the builder I've told you about. Taylor thinks he knows more than any person around. This coming from a guy who barely finished high school, and spends ninety percent of his time chasing golf balls or skirts."

"Does his wife know about his womanizing?"

"Who knows? Taylor was having an affair with her when he was married to his first wife, so it shouldn't come as any big surprise. If she does get wind of him fooling around, I think she'll cause problems. I hear she has a nasty temper, and before she met Taylor, she had her brother beat up a boyfriend she thought was cheating on her. Hurt the guy pretty bad. It was all over the news a few years back."

"That's terrible! Does Taylor know about it?"

"Probably not. He's too busy talking to listen to anybody else. He never gets tired of talking about his favorite subject: himself."

Preston stood in front of the fireplace where the fire was roaring. "What does his wife look like?" Karen asked.

"She's good-looking in a Hollywood kind of way. Petite, five-foot-four; a nice figure. She has long, dirty-blonde hair. She wears her hair really big, like those '80s glam rock singers, and a lot of makeup. Long, dark, false eyelashes; lots of blue metallic eye shadow. She's has the Tammy Faye Baker starter kit."

"Taylor sounds like a real jerk."

"He is that and more."

TWELVE

Fair Oaks Boulevard was quiet on the late Monday night. Normally a major thoroughfare during the day, only a few cars traveled the street, mostly diners who had chosen Morton's or Ruth's Chris in the Pavilions shopping center.

A small light shone down on the open filing cabinet, small enough to illuminate the subject two feet in front of it, but not bright enough for anyone walking on the sidewalk to notice. Stephanie held the pin light in her mouth as she carefully fingered each file in the top cabinet located outside Janet Waller's office. She gently lifted out a file, flipped it open, skimmed its contents, and then set it on a stack on the floor.

In a squat behind a desk, Janet's assistant Carol nervously watched out the window, eyeing the empty parking lot in front of their office. The lights from the parking lot radiated a soft, eerie glow into the office.

"Stephanie, how long are you going to take?" she whispered anxiously, not taking her eyes off the parking lot. "I'm dying in here. I know the cops are gonna show up any minute and we'll be hauled off to jail."

Stephanie spoke softly through her clenched teeth without looking over. "Hush, Carol, relax. You know Janet's in Hawaii and isn't returning for a couple of days. No one will notice us unless they hear you talking." She nodded her head toward the stack of files. "Here, do something useful. Make a copy of every one of those files and be sure you return each document to the exact position they were in before."

Carol crawled over to the file cabinets. Looking all around, she stood up, quickly snatched the files, and then dropped back down on her hands and knees. "I don't like this, Steph. Are you sure this isn't illegal? I mean, we're here dressed in black like a couple of ninjas."

Stephanie turned her head and the penlight shined directly on Carol, who shielded her eyes. "Let me worry about that. Hurry up and copy those files and we can get out of here." She turned back to the file cabinet, checked a name on a list she had in front of her, and pulled open another file. "I don't get this," she mumbled. "I thought all Janet's loans were with First Pacific Title. But the files I'm pulling are with New Federal Title. I've never heard of them, and where are the certified closing statements?"

She thumbed through a file and looked over the loan application— Carlos Mendoza, 222 Del Paso Boulevard #201, Sacramento.

Two-twenty-two Del Paso Boulevard. Why does that sound familiar? she thought.

She put the file down and opened another file she had looked at previously. Juan Gonzales, 222 Del Paso Boulevard, #104. That couldn't be a coincidence. She looked in a third file. Manuel Garcia, 222 Del Paso Boulevard, #208.

Car lights swept the office and Stephanie hit the floor, her heart racing. Carol shrieked and started to cry. Stephanie crawled over to her. "Sshhhh. If you make any noise you'll be heard. Be quiet."

"I'll try, but I'm so scared."

"I am, too, but stay still and we can leave in a minute." The two of them huddled by the copy machine for two long minutes. Nothing. "Stay here. I'm going to see if I can see anything out Janet's office."

"Oookay. You are so brave."

Stephanie crawled through the hallway to the window that looked out over the parking lot and across to Fair Oaks Boulevard. No, I'm not brave, she thought. I'm just stupid.

She felt as if her heart were about to leap out of her chest. Her next conversation with Justin wouldn't be pretty.

She slowly lifted her head up to the window sill. The lights from the parking lot crept across her face. Directly in front of the office sat what looked like a new Mercedes-Benz. She dropped her head, then after a few seconds of silence raised it carefully, inch by inch. She could still hear Carol whimpering softly in the hallway. There appeared to be two people in the car embracing. They slid slowly down the front seat out of sight. The car began to rock back and forth and to gather momentum. Stephanie lowered her head and leaned against the wall, her breath coming slower. I can't believe it, she thought. There are a hundred offices along this street and these two dummies have to get amorous here.

She crawled back to Carol and whispered, "It's okay. It's just a couple getting it on in the parking lot."

Carol's eyes widened. "Really? Could you see them doing it?"

"Don't be a pervert. If I wanted to see porn I'd rent a movie. Copy those files quickly and let's get out of here—I don't want to push our luck."

Stephanie couldn't resist. She picked out one last file: Whiteside.

The next morning, Stephanie was at her desk reviewing the copied files. She had calmed down and decided she wouldn't quit on Justin yet, but she reserved the right to give him a piece of her mind. After two hours of poring through everything, she dialed the phone. Justin answered on the second ring.

"Hello, Justin, it's Stephanie."

"Stephanie, good to hear from you. What did you find?"

"I found that I'm not good at being a cat burglar. You owe me big time."

Justin laughed. "Please don't tell me you've been caught doing something illegal."

"No, you got lucky there. Janet's secretary let me in, so we didn't break in. It was, let's just say, highly unethical."

Justin's tone turned more sober. "What were you able to find out?"

"I've made copies of the files on your list. Have you ever heard of New Federal Title?"

"Hmm, I don't think I have. Who are they?"

"I don't know." Stephanie underlined the name New Federal on her legal pad. "All Janet's loans have gone through First Pacific Title except for the loan files you listed. Those went through New Federal. There is no closing statement showing who the seller is in any of the files."

"That's strange. I can't imagine Janet not getting closing statements. I'll have one of my staff find out who New Federal is and who owns them."

"Justin, this part is really strange. Every one of the buyers in these files are Hispanic males, with declared income over a hundred and fifty thousand dollars annually, and they all lived at the same apartment building on Del Paso Boulevard before buying these houses. Something is weird about this."

"You're saying they all lived at an apartment building before buying five-hundred-thousand-dollar houses."

"Not only that, but I know the area the apartment is located in and it's not Beverly Hills. I plan to take a drive and pay the manager a visit this afternoon. He should remember his former tenants and can help track them down to shed light on who is behind this scheme. Janet's involved, but she's got help, probably from inside Whitney Homes."

"Good job, Steph. Be careful at the apartment complex. Any hint of trouble, call the police and get of there, fast. In the meantime, I'll try to find out something about New Federal Title Company. Take care."

"I will, thanks. One thing, though, Justin. If anyone knows anything at this apartment complex, they're not going to give up that information for free. How much can I give for what they know, and how will you get the funds to me?"

"I'll send a cashier's check for ten thousand to you tonight. Cash it and use it carefully. Make sure what you're paying for is useful information. Keep a tally of every dollar you dish out and be alert."

"Thanks, I will." She set the phone down on her desk. Googling MapQuest on her computer, she typed the address 222 Del Paso

Boulevard, Sacramento. She printed the directions and glanced at her watch. 12:30 p.m. Not enough time to eat. As she headed out the door, she snatched up her purse and shut off the lights. This was going to be an interesting afternoon.

Thirteen

Dilapidated buildings lined the street. Every other corner had a beat-up liquor store advertising "Lotto" in bold letters with the current amount available for the next drawing. Posters of peeling cigarette and beer ads lined the windows, along with dusty neon lights flashing Budweiser and Coors. Although it was early afternoon, numerous men stared at her from the front porches of their houses as she drove slowly down the street. Stephanie didn't feel threatened, but she didn't feel comfortable, either.

Driving a little further, she came upon 222 Del Paso Boulevard. She pulled into the complex and surveyed it through her windshield. It was a series of older buildings in what appeared to be clusters of eight. The parking lot was clean. The lawn, although slightly brown from lack of water, was neatly mowed. The project was aged, but it was kept up better than most on the street. A couple of young children played in a sandy area in the middle of the complex, their mothers close by on a bench under a large sycamore tree. They eyed her suspiciously.

Stephanie steered forward in her car, which was conspicuously newer than anything in the parking lot. Pulling into a space next to the rental office that read, "Reserved for future tenants," she shut off the engine and sat for a minute.

Okay, relax, she told herself. Take a deep breath. This is not Rodeo Drive, but it's not Baghdad, either. These people are just as nervous about me as I am about them.

She adjusted the rearview mirror, ran her hand through her hair, and got out. She was dressed in a white blouse and jeans. Nothing sexy, nothing flashy. Stepping into the rental office, she spotted an older Hispanic man in a small office to the left of the door. He was smoking a cigarette and reading a newspaper. A window air conditioner hummed from the wall across the room.

"Uh, excuse me, sir," she said, closing the door the behind her, "can I bother you for a minute?"

The man looked up, startled, and quickly put out his cigarette. "Of course." He gestured to the chair in front of his desk. "Have a seat. My name is José Cabrera. I'm the manager here."

Stephanie sat down and handed him a card. "I'm Stephanie Bernard, an appraiser for Burns and Finch. I've been working on a project nearby that's similar to your location, and I thought I'd check the comps here."

José studied the card, then put it on the desk. He leaned back in his chair. "Okay, Stephanie, what do you like to know?"

Stephanie took out a notepad and scanned it. "Is this a subsidized project, Mr. Cabrera?"

"Please, call me José. No, these units are market rate. The project needs some care, but the owners…" He shrugged. "All tenants are good tenants. They have jobs—all of them. They are all of them hard-working persons."

Stephanie hesitated before asking the next question. She glanced around the office for a second. On the wall were various cheaply framed pictures of José and what appeared to be his family or close friends. "Who is the owner of this place?"

José leaned forward. His smile disappeared and his face turned serious. "Why do you ask me this question? That has nothing to do with appraisal. If it is true you are appraising this project, you could find out this information you ask."

Stephanie chewed on her pen. She put her notepad on her lap. "José, you're right. I'm not here for an appraisal." She ripped a sheet out of her notepad and slid it across the desk. "This is a list of some of your former tenants. All of them, within the last two years, bought a Whitney Home here in town, ranging from three hundred fifty thousand dollars to five hundred thousand dollars in price." She looked out the window at the aging complex. "It doesn't fit that a group of your tenants would be able to afford houses that pricey." She looked back at José. "After each house closed, these people disappeared and we can't locate them. I was hoping that you could help me out."

José looked at the names and glanced nervously at his time-worn desk. He fumbled in his pocket for his pack of cigarettes. "Do you mind?"

"No, go ahead." Stephanie leaned back in her chair.

He lifted up a lighter from the desk and lit the cigarette, breathed a deep drag, and wiped his forehead with a handkerchief. His eyes scanned the parking lot, and when he spoke his voice was low. "I cannot talk about this here. I will meet at another time and place and tell some things. This information is not free. If I do something for you, my friend, you need to do something for José." He gestured at the pictures on the wall. "I have a family." The cigarette shook in his hands. "There are very bad people who would not like you to ask these questions, and you should be careful."

"Thank you for the advice. I can meet your needs, assuming they're reasonable and you give me true information. When and where can we meet, José, and how much do you need?"

"I will meet next week. I think two thousand, cash, to start, eh? I have your numbers on your card. I will call when the time is good." He stood up, putting out his cigarette and extending his hand. "I am pleased to meet you."

Stephanie thanked him and left the office. Driving down Del Paso toward the freeway, she pondered José. She could smell the stale cigarette smoke in her clothes.

I bet most of his tenants are illegals, and someone is using them to buy new houses. What I don't get is, what's in it for these people and where did they go after the sale closed?

Fourteen

Matt slammed down the phone and threw his pen on the desk. "Damn that Dick Samuels!" he shouted at the phone. "Just last week he told me I'd have the last shot at United Bank's next sale of securities."

Pete Ramsey appeared in the doorway, his arms crossed. "What's the problem, Matt? Lenders giving you grief?"

Matt looked up. "Yeah, I just lost a deal with United. My client tells me we have a deal to purchase two hundred million in mortgage-backed securities at a three-quarter-point premium. Before I formalize the deal in writing, the jerk gets an offer from someone else paying another eighth of a point in premium. He takes that deal and hangs me out to dry. I can't believe it!"

Pete looked down at his fingernails. "That's strange. I just finalized a deal with United Bank for the same amount. I wonder if it's the same deal." He looked right at Matt.

"Are you saying you stole a deal from one of my clients, Pete?" Matt's voice rose. "You know United Bank is my client. I've been working on that deal for months." He stood up and moved toward Pete. "I've wined and dined Dick Samuels for a long time to get those securities. You can't come along and undercut me. It's unethical."

Pete crossed his arms. "Sorry, Matt. You know the saying. The deal's not done 'til the check clears. In your case, the check didn't clear. You should have given United a better price originally." His eyes narrowed with his thin smile, making him look every inch the weasel he was.

"So now I'm in competition with you for my clients?" Matt walked up to him. "You have some gall."

"Don't take it so personally. You can do another deal with United next time."

"Yeah, next time." Matt glared at Pete.

"I'll see you around. Oh, uh, John wants to see you in his office in fifteen minutes." Pete turned and left.

Matt walked back to his desk, sat down, and ranted to the walls. That's the third deal I've lost this month, and the second time Dick Samuels has stiffed me. First, I lost that hundred-fifty-million-dollar package from Bank of the Northwest, and now this deal from United. How many other deals has that scumbag stolen from me?

He leaned back in his chair, clasping his hands behind his head, and stared at the ceiling. Out, he wanted out of here now. He rose, swiping up his cell phone, and dialed Drew as he headed for the dreaded meeting in John's office. "Hey, Drew, you ready for a drink?"

"Hey, Matt. Give me forty minutes and I'll meet you at Bubba Gump's. I feel like fried shrimp."

"Good deal. I'll see you there."

Matt rapped softly on the door. John had his back to him and spun around in his chair. "Matt, come on in, take a seat." He motioned to a chair across from his desk. "I want to chat with you about your numbers for the quarter. You've been with us for awhile now and you've done very well. New York is pleased with your effort." John lifted a report off his desk.

"Last quarter, you were one of the top ten traders in the company. It appears, though, your numbers have fallen off this quarter. I know it's not for lack of effort because my security spies tell me you're working late almost every night." He grimaced. "I don't want you to get discouraged, but this market has changed and it's getting tough."

"Thanks for the encouragement. You know I'm trying." Matt rubbed his hands together, feeling uncomfortable.

John looked up from his computer screen. "My nephew just closed a good-sized deal with United Bank." He squinted at Matt. "Weren't they one of your clients? How did that happen?"

Matt turned toward the window and caught sight of a large freighter crossing the bay. "I'm not sure, John. I just heard that myself."

"Did you do something to anger someone?"

Matt shook his head. "Not to my knowledge. I have a good relationship with them."

"That's strange." John turned off his computer. "Well, keep pushing. I need you to come through this quarter. Unfortunately, it looks like it'll be getting worse before it gets better."

"Okay, sir, I will. Thanks." Matt stood and left. He was steaming by the time he got to the elevator.

On his way down to the bar, Matt's cell phone registered a call from his mom. He took a deep breath before he answered. "Hi, Mom."

"How are you doing, Mattie?" she asked gaily.

Matt sighed. "It was a long day. How's Dad?"

"He's doing well. He's been really busy at work. The new tenants for the building he's working on want to move in early, so he's pushing his people to finish. The reason I called is to ask if you could come home this weekend and help your dad with a couple of projects around the house. He could use a little help. I hate to do this to you."

"Mom, it's no trouble. I'll drive up Friday afternoon and we'll get everything you need fixed up."

"Thank you so much, Mattie. I'll see you Friday and I'll have a nice meal, maybe the meatloaf you love so much with mashed potatoes."

"That will be great; I'm looking forward to that. I'll see you Friday."

Matt made it down to Bubba Gump's, pulled up a bar stool, and sat down. He waved to the bartender. "Hey, could I get a Coors Light?"

The bartender nodded and left. After a minute, he came over with a bottle and a cold glass.

Drew walked in. Matt pushed a bar stool out. "Hey, bud, have a seat. You can commiserate with me."

"Thanks." Drew turned to the bartender. "The usual for me. You look like someone stole your best girl. What's the matter?"

"Dick Samuels from United Bank sold me out on a big loan package. But get this. Samuels sold the package to Pete Ramsey. That weasel stole a deal from one of my clients!"

"You're kidding. Your boss's nephew? The slimy-looking one?"

"That's the one. He told me today he beat my price by an eighth of a percent and United took his deal over mine."

"That's unethical. You don't compete against your own colleagues. Are you going to tell Ramsey about this dude?"

Matt sighed. "I don't know what to do. John asked me why Pete closed a deal with my client and I didn't say anything. I don't want to come off as a crybaby, but it affects my numbers for the quarter." He placed a cocktail napkin under his beer. "I'm not sure John would do anything anyway. After all, Pete is his nephew."

Matt scooted his bar stool closer to Drew's as another couple of businessmen squeezed in next to them. The bar was crowded and unusually noisy for a weeknight. The bartender was scrambling around the bar, trying to fill orders.

"I don't know, Matt. If someone at my firm tried to steal one of my bank clients, I wouldn't let them get away with it without a price. I'd probably get fired, but at least I'd get the satisfaction of pummeling them." Drew caught a view of the bay. He stood up to check a large container ship floating about a half mile out, then sat back down.

"Yeah, that would be good, but I like my job and I want to keep it. I'll just have to be more careful and aggressive next time. I don't want to give that fool anymore opportunities to beat me out." A waiter walked past them with a steaming platter of shrimp, distracting Matt. "Those things smell great. I think I'll order up a plate."

"Yeah, I'll do a plate of shrimp, too. So what else is new?" Drew took a sip of his beer, his eyes wandering to a blonde on the other side of the bar. A middle-aged man in a black tuxedo sat stiffly at the piano across the room and started playing a robotic-like version of the Beatles' "Michelle."

"Well, I'm ahead of myself on my ten-year plan," Matt mused. "I've got a six-figure job and bought a new condo. I've got a big flat-screen. No Rolex yet, or second home, but they're coming. I wonder if Kathy Ann has heard about my success. I know Mom talks to her mother's friends." He smiled at the thought.

"Give yourself a pat on the back, Matt. You've done very well. I'm proud of you. So what's your weekend like?"

"I'm headed to Sacramento to help my dad with a couple projects."

"That should be fun. Nothing like a little urban renewal to spruce up the neighborhood." Drew grinned. "I, on the other hand, will be dating that luscious lady over there." He nodded his head in the direction of the blonde across the bar.

Matt glanced down the bar and laughed. "She's your type, all right." He turned serious again.

"Yeah, John Ramsey will really appreciate me leaving here Friday afternoon. First, I lose two big transactions and then I leave early for the weekend." He put his head in his hands. "This place can wear on you."

"Quit beating yourself up, man. You've been working like a dog. It's just a sign of the times. Deals are getting tougher to put together these days. The mortgage delinquencies jumped again last month, and expectations are that next quarter's foreclosure and delinquency reports will to be eye-popping. Last year we never even heard the word foreclosure. Now it's on everybody's lips."

"Last year, putting loan packages together and purchasing them was a snap. Now every deal has issues, and they take forever to work through. The pricing on these packages is over the top. What do you think is driving the change from last year?" Matt asked. "Man, I'm longing for the good old days."

Drew looked through the mirror behind the bar at Matt. "You know what I think? The old days are a thing of the past, Matt. My sources tell me the housing market hasn't only started to cool, but it's starting to slide backward."

Matt pushed his empty beer bottle out to the end of the bar and signaled to the bartender for another round.

"Sales of existing homes have been flat since Thanksgiving, and the latest New Home Sales Report shows sales are down three percent from this time last year," Drew continued. "This is not good news. A lot of people have been banking on their house's value increasing. They've been playing with the house's money."

"What do you mean, the house's money?"

"You know, like in gambling. You win a couple hundred bucks at the blackjack table and you're playing with the house's money, not your own. The difference is you don't have to repay the house's money if you lose at blackjack, but homeowners do. Unfortunately, many of them have spent all their equity and are literally over their heads in debt."

"Everything will be fine as long as their house values stay high, right?" asked Matt.

"Yes, it would be fine as long as values continue to go up. All these borrowers need higher values so they can refinance loans before they readjust to a higher rate—one they can't afford. If they can't refinance their loans because the values stall out, look out. The managers of major hedge funds, like ours, and purchasers of huge loan pools are cutting back on purchases of mortgage-backed securities based on the fact that the housing market has cooled. Forty traders were let go this week at my firm due to the volume decrease."

"How many traders were in your company?"

"Two hundred fifty. That's almost twenty percent of the trading force. We can't get the quality mortgage-backed securities we're looking for."

"Once other hedge funds figure out what's in their portfolios, will they start buying securities that have subprime loans again?"

"I don't know, Matt. I think we are just seeing the tip of the proverbial iceberg. If some of these borrowers can't refinance, the delinquency rate will soar once they start missing their mortgage payments." Drew took a handful of pretzels from a bowl on the bar.

"All the loans that were made in 2003 and early 2004 will be starting to readjust to higher rates in a couple of months. As delinquencies rise, the hedge funds will cut back on their loan purchases. Financial institutions will get stuck with their own loans, credit will start to dry up. Loans to individual homebuyers are going to be harder to get. That will slow the housing market even further. What happens after that will be anybody's guess."

"Man, you're not making me feel any better."

"Then let's change the subject. How's the lovely Stephanie? Is she still seeing your low-rent mug?"

"She's doing fine. I'll see her this weekend when I'm in Sac. You know, Drew, I really like Stephanie a lot, but there's this nagging feeling that she's not who she says she is. I don't know if she is putting up a front, is afraid to let her hair down in front of me, or what. Something is amiss."

"What's wrong with you? I know you had a bad experience with Kathy Ann, but that was years ago. Let it go. Not every relationship ends with someone getting hurt."

Matt turned and looked back at the bustling area behind him. Every table was taken by either well-dressed businesspeople or under-dressed tourists.

"I know. Stephanie is the real deal." He had to raise his voice to be heard over the growing volume of clinking glasses and spirited conver-sation. "I do care about her. There is nothing I don't like about her, and that's what scares me. I don't want to go all in and get burned again."

"Matt, the only thing standing between you and true happiness is your ability to let go of a bad experience. I have to admit Stephanie does have an aura of mystery about her, although I can't put my finger on why, yet."

"Yeah, she does seem to have another side that she's not showing." Matt turned back and stared into his beer. "With her, I just need some time to figure out what to do. Besides, I've got some coin in my pocket and I'm not sure I want to be tied down to one woman."

"I think you're making a mistake, my man."

Matt returned home to his freshly painted condo a little after 7:30 p.m. He removed his shoes to keep from dirtying the plush carpet, placed his briefcase on the sand-colored granite kitchen counter, then walked over and switched on the 42-inch flat-screen TV. The condo and the TV were part of his ten-year plan that was moving along nicely.

A turkey sandwich from Quiznos, and the slim bag of chips that came with it, would serve as dinner tonight. Matt plopped down in his recliner and turned to the TV to find black-bearded Billy Mays screaming at him to buy Oxi-Clean. Man, that dude hawks just about everything, Matt thought. I wonder who's worse—him or Vince, that carnie-looking ShamWow guy? It's gotta be the ShamWow guy.

He thought about his conversation with Drew. It made him uncomfortable and raised questions in his mind.

Are there going to be layoffs at my firm? Last year I was a rising star and now the market is turning sour. I just bought this condominium and am making payments of four thousand dollars a month. I sank most of my bonus money into the down payment. I've set aside monies in my saving account, but if I lose this job, it would be tough to replace what I'm making at Franklin Smith.

Rio City Café had a beautiful view of the Sacramento River. A couple of ducks paddled quietly on the river under the deck where Matt and Stephanie sat at a table shaded by a large umbrella. The old gold-covered I Street Bridge, connecting Sacramento with West Sacramento, glistened as the setting sun disappeared behind it. Muffled sounds of low conversation, mixed with the occasional tinkling of glasses, could be heard in the half-full restaurant.

Stephanie's Dior sunglasses made her look like a model out of a glamour magazine. Matt was leaning back in his chair, a 49ers hat shielding his face from the sun, wearing a golf shirt and a pair of khaki shorts that showed his tanned legs.

"Are you coming to the city anytime soon again, Steph? I was glad you came by and saw me last time. I still don't get why you have to drop everything and see this guy, Justin, on such short notice."

"He just lost his wife and he's such a dear friend. I can't help but want to help him."

Really? Matt wondered how dear he was to her. There was something funny about their relationship. Matt tossed a couple of bread crumbs over the railing to the river and watched the ducks quickly scramble after them.

Stephanie touched his arm. "So how's your parents' new house? Has it been everything they thought it would be?"

Matt took off his sunglasses and wiped them with a napkin. "They love it. I haven't seen my parents this excited about anything for a long time. I guess Whitney Homes builds a decent house. My mom says their service warranty department leaves a lot to be desired, but overall, they're very happy."

Stephanie sighed audibly.

"Wow, you sound like a huge weight has been lifted from you. What was that about?"

She squeezed Matt's hand. "I'm just so happy you came to town this weekend. I've been missing you. I'm not sure I like this long-distance romance thing. There are too many gaps."

"I'm glad I came, too. Work has been keeping me buried. A few months ago, selling mortgage-backed securities was easy. Now they're the E. coli of financial instruments. All the hedge funds are worried that their portfolios might get infected with bad mortgages."

A waiter came up to their table, dropped off their drinks, and took their dinner order.

"How's that co-worker you dislike? What's his name ... you know, your boss's nephew?"

"Pete Ramsey? He's his same old slimy self. Other than stealing my clients' loans, he's the same. It's weird. We had a conference call from New York a couple weeks ago and our CEO said that we were not to buy any more mortgages from certain lending institutions, one of which was Worldwide Funding." Matt noticed Stephanie stiffen. "So last week I'm going over a couple of my trades with our trading desk and there is a deal for fifty million dollars with Worldwide Funding that Pete initiated. I go back to Pete's office and ask him about it." Matt slid his sunglasses down to the bridge of his nose. "You know what he says to me? He says, 'I don't have to listen to New York; I know people.' Now what the hell does that mean, I know people? Give me a break."

Stephanie interrupted. "That's not right. Pete has a contact at Worldwide who is on the take, or maybe Pete's on the take. Are there any particular builders who use Worldwide exclusively?"

Matt put up his hands defensively. "Whoa, whoa, Steph. You're firing way too many questions here. I have no idea who Pete knows at Worldwide or if he even knows anybody there. As for builders, I have no clue." Matt leaned forward on his elbows. "Why do you ask about Pete's relationship with Worldwide? Do you know someone there?"

Stephanie picked up her wine glass and raised an eyebrow at Matt as she took a sip. She brushed back a loose strand of hair from her forehead. "No, I was just trying to figure out what might be driving Pete to do this to you." She shrugged and looked down at the river. "That's all."

Matt rocked back in his chair, eyeing Stephanie. Could Drew be right? Stephanie had a mysterious side. Maybe she was not all that she presented herself to be. He hated thinking like that, particularly when she looked at him the way she was right now.

"Hey, Matt," Stephanie said, taking his hand. "There's a big bash each year at the Hyatt downtown on New Year's Eve. They offer a fabulous room and dinner package. I realize it's just the end of October, but reservations need to be made early to get the deal." She turned her head slightly. "If you're in, I'm buying."

Matt smiled wickedly. "If it's free, give me three. You're on." He squeezed her hand. A large yacht sailed slowly under the bridge and a soft Patsy Cline song could be heard drifting up from the boat.

Stephanie pointed toward it. "Hey, Matt, there goes your boat."

His eyes sparkled and all else was forgotten.

FIFTEEN

At the Wailea Country Club, located on the southern tip of Maui, Taylor waved off the hostess and seated himself next to Guy, who was adding up their score cards.

"So what did I shoot, 90?"

"Nice try, Taylor. How about 97—and that was with those two gifts I gave you for not charging for a lost ball. But look on the bright side. While you were searching for your lost ball, you found three other ones. You're ahead of the game by three bucks. Oh, but there's one other thing. You lost three hundred dollars to me. You can pay up anytime now."

A waitress in a Hawaiian shirt and khaki shorts approached. "Can I get you gentlemen anything to drink?"

Taylor looked up at her. "What took you so long? A man might die of thirst around here. Get me a rum and Coke, and get this guy the same."

The waitress recoiled. "Anything else?"

"Nope." Taylor turned back. "You know, Guy, this is the third time this week you've beat me. You'll need to give me more strokes next time."

"Quit whining." Guy picked up a pencil, signed their scorecard, and handed it to Taylor. "I was lucky. You've had a string of bad luck lately. You'll make it up tomorrow."

"Oh, I forgot to tell you. I can't play tomorrow. I've got company in town. I'm going to be real busy."

Guy gave him a look. "Really? You'll be spending a lot of time on your back, I assume? It's been awhile, hasn't it, since you brought that broad here last? Was it last June?"

"You have a good memory and you assume right, my friend. Janet flies in this afternoon. But the first thing I'm gonna do is show her the lot I told you about that I've put in escrow. It closes next week, and my architects are designing the home as we speak."

"What will it cost to build?"

"The lot was eight million and to trick it out, uh, about twenty-two million. It'll take another three million to furnish it."

Guy threw his hands in the air. "Good grief, Taylor, that'll be your fourth home. You just finished that monster in Granite Bay a couple years ago. How you gonna pay for all this?"

"Come on, Guy. How do you think? I'm going to sell more homes. Heck, this year isn't quite up, I've made sixty million so far, and I'll easily make eighty million next year in '05. And I'm raising my house prices."

"You should be careful. Remember what happened in the early '90s? The market was hot and all of a sudden, almost overnight, it seemed like someone hit a switch and buyers disappeared. If I recall correctly, you had to get your pal, Mark Bernstein, to bail you out and you damn near didn't make it."

Taylor leaned back in his chair and put his hands behind his head. He looked out the balcony and watched a group of golfers practicing on the putting green.

"That was different circumstances. First of all, you had over two hundred and fifty savings and loans go bust, and the feds came in and bailed them out. Then, they unloaded the savings and loans' problem real estate by giving it away. As builders, we couldn't compete with the cheap lots and houses that flooded the market. It took awhile for the inventory to be absorbed."

Taylor examined the scorecard. "On top of that, we were in a recession, and four large military bases were shut down in Sacramento. The area lost eighty thousand jobs. This time we're dealing with traditional banks that are more regulated and won't make construction loans to every Tom, Dick, or Harry who can swing a hammer." He pointed to the card. "Hey, I got a five on number seven, not a six."

Guy snatched the scorecard, changed the number, and handed it back. "Okay, you shot a ninety-six. You still lost."

Taylor took a swig of his rum and Coke. "Anyway, there's a lot of money available out there for homebuyers. Lenders are coming up with new programs all the time to help people get into homes. And as long as there's money for buyers, I'm going to keep building houses. I'm going to double the number of houses I build this next year, and I'm going to double *that* number in 2006."

"How many lots did you purchase during last year's buying spree?"

"Right now I've got over four thousand lots in the Central and Sacramento valleys in inventory, as far south as Bakersfield and as far north as Yuba City."

"That's a big area to service. Didn't you leverage most of the lots with bank loans?"

"Yes, three different banks financed the three-hundred-fifty-million-dollar debt on them."

"Holy lord! That's a lot of monthly interest! I hope you're right about the market. If it cools, you better think of a good exit plan."

"I'm not worried. Like I told you, this market is good for another five years. By then, I'll be worth a billion dollars."

The waitress came back to their table. "Can I get you another round?"

Taylor tossed his drink down and handed her his glass. "That would be a good idea. Get us both another round."

"Speaking of dollars, how did your bet on the Southern Cal/Notre Dame game go?" Guy asked.

Taylor looked down at the table. "I put five hundred thousand on those overrated Fighting Irish, and they lost. SC squeaked by." He turned his head to the TV. "I'm not worried. I'll make it up on the Super Bowl. I like the Philadelphia Eagles this year."

Guy pointed to the TV promoting an upcoming Oprah Winfrey show with guest Dr. Phil. "Look, Taylor, it's your twin brother coming on Oprah. You're just fatter than him." He laughed.

Taylor grinned. "I don't need to look like Pierce Brosnan with all I have. You remember all those girls in high school who made fun of me and called me a geek? They'd be lining up around this golf course right now for a piece of my fat wallet."

Guy shook his head. "I can't believe you lost five hundred thousand dollars on a football game, Taylor. You're an idiot."

Taylor's cell phone rang and he answered it. "Hi, Janet. You made it okay?"

"I sure did, baby, thank you," she answered.

"Great. How was the flight?"

"Smooth. I slept most of the way. I just love your beautiful jet."

"You like your suite too, huh? It's the best they have."

"I believe it. It's got great views. I love coming to the Four Seasons," she purred. "I'll show my thanks later."

"Well, all right then. I'll come by your room around seven."

Taylor hung up the phone and set it on the table. "Well, Guy, sorry to have to leave this stimulating conversation, but there's a woman waiting anxiously for me. So I'll see you in a few days."

"Call me when you get free, and we'll play more golf. I need the money."

Taylor flipped him off as he left.

Taylor had just gotten out of the shower when he heard the house phone ring. Toweling off, he answered the bedside phone.

"Hello?"

"So what are you doing?" He instantly recognized Monica's voice.

"Nothing at the moment. I played golf with Guy this afternoon. I just got home, took a shower, and now I'm talking to you. I'm heading over to meet him and Bill Benson for dinner in a couple of hours."

"Are any of the wives invited or is this another 'stag night'? Why don't you just stay at home and watch TV like most people do?"

"I don't know—it's up to Bill and Guy if they want to bring their wives. And I don't feel like sitting at home watching TV. What the hell difference does it make to you? You're in Palm Springs and I'm here. I'm not checking up on you all the time."

"You have no reason to check on me. But you, on the other hand … that's a different story. I'm not feeling real warm and fuzzy about our relationship right now. Ever since the sheriff's party you've been acting strange. You promised if I spent more time with you, you'd try to work on things."

Taylor yawned, walked back to the bathroom, and threw the towel over the shower.

"That was a month ago and your attitude hasn't changed." Monica's voice rose. "You don't care. You haven't even called in three days."

Taylor picked a pair of slacks out of his closet. "You're being paranoid. Look, I'm running late. I'll call you tomorrow."

Monica's voice quivered. "Taylor, you better figure out what it is you want. Don't let me find out you're cheating on me or I will make your life miserable. Get yourself together." Click.

Taylor walked into the bedroom to set the phone on the nightstand and stared at it. "What a pain in the ass." Then he smiled. "If you only knew I have a date with the lovely Janet Waller, and I'm not gonna keep her waiting."

Taylor quickly made the four-minute walk from his house to the Four Seasons, entered the lobby, and headed toward the elevators. A couple in colorful Hawaiian print bathing suits entered the elevator with him. Stepping onto the twenty-fifth floor, he headed to the end of the corridor, stopped at room 2560, and knocked firmly. The door opened and there stood Janet in a white lace see-through nightie. She held two rum and Cokes in her hands.

"I thought after your golf game you might like to relieve a little stress before we go out. What do you think?"

Taylor looked her up and down, smiled, and said, "That's a wonderful idea. You look mighty sexy."

Janet looked into his eyes, smiled back, and said, "Come on in." She set the drinks down, pulled his face with her hands, and kissed him on the lips. He stumbled through the door and into the room. Janet held him closer and yanked at the buttons on his shirt. Taylor clumsily pawed at her breasts and kissed her neck. Taylor attempted to lift the nightie over her head as they tumbled onto the bed.

An hour after leaving Janet's room, the couple sat for dinner in the Sterling Room of the Four Seasons. They conversed over a mouth-watering leg of lamb with a rosemary port reduction sauce. Janet remarked, "What a wonderful afternoon."

Food still in his mouth, Taylor asked, "How is business?"

"We're about to get into the holiday season and things will slow down. August and September were a little slow, but things will kick in after New Year's. It's tough that lenders are being more careful and starting to crack down on verifications and such. But you know, I've been in the business for so long, stuff like that doesn't faze me." Her eyes twinkled over her glass of wine. "Our little operation is clicking along smoothly."

A breeze came up and blew through the open-air restaurant. Janet looked out at the waves crashing on the beach. She took in a deep breath of the ocean air. "I love this place. The sunsets are magnificent. Look how pretty those colors are on the horizon."

Taylor turned and scanned the sky.

"There was a problem with lot 34 in the Cambridge subdivision," Janet said. "The appraiser wouldn't hit the sales price you wrote it up for. I managed to get around that obstacle by making a few changes. I sent the file to Worldwide Funding and it should close the day I get back to the mainland."

"I knew you could handle those types of problems." Taylor emptied his wine glass with a long sip. "I love these double escrows. I never take title and no one ever knows I made any money on the deal, including the IRS."

"It only works if there's an appraiser, a buyer, and a loan officer in on the scam," Janet said. "We've got two of the three, and with a little doctoring, I can get by the appraisal problem. This market is starting to worry me."

The waiter came up and refilled their wine glasses. "The way I see the market, Janet, is that this is the lull before the storm. Next February or March, the market is going to come alive and it'll be a feeding frenzy again. That's only a couple of months off. I'm going to ramp up my operations and start on at least twenty new homes at each of my subdivisions." He took a bite of the lamb and wiped his mouth with his napkin. "I'll be ready to fill the buyers' needs way before the corporate builders wake up from their winter slumber. I want to be the largest builder north of Bakersfield by the end of 2006, and the largest builder in California by 2007."

"Wow, Taylor. That's a daunting task. You'll have to build a boat load of houses to beat out CB Homes."

Taylor refilled her half-empty wine glass. "I know, but my people have talked to some of their people, and I understand that they plan to be very cautious this year. So are Broadstone Homes and Pacific Rim Homes. What a bunch of gutless wussies. They all sit around in their boardrooms and look at charts and statistics. They wouldn't know a good deal if it hit them in the head." He took a sip of wine.

"I don't have to read the *Wall Street Journal* to know what's going on in my industry. I'll look like a genius—a very rich one, I might add—by year's end. The corporate boys will be sitting with their thumbs in their ears whistling Dixie." He raised his glass as if in a toast. "And you and I will continue to do our little side deal to the tune of sixty homes this year. That'll be big-time dough we'll be makin'."

She raised her glass, and clinked his. "I like it. If anyone can pull this off, Taylor, my money's on you. I've seen what you've done in the past and you have an impressive track record. I meant to ask you regarding our venture. I know you give me a portion of the proceeds, but don't you have other partners in this?"

Taylor flipped his hand dismissively. "I do, but they're inconsequential. They have no say in what I do, and I pay them whatever I want."

"Don't they want an accounting of what closes, how much money is made?"

Taylor laughed. "They're on a need-to-know basis. They're very happy with our arrangement."

Janet dabbed her lips. "I don't want to be nosey, but who are these people?"

Taylor leaned back in his seat. "You don't want to know."

Janet watched a sparrow hop over to the table next to theirs, pick up a bread crumb, and fly off. "When will you be headed back to Sacramento?"

"I'm hanging around for a big poker tournament next week. Big money, major players. I'll probably go back in three weeks. That reminds me, I need to call Artie Tennelli and place my bet on the Rose Bowl. I'm putting five hundred thousand dollars on Michigan. I hate the Texas Longhorns. Besides, I've got six points."

"You're betting five hundred thousand dollars on a game?" she gasped, clutching her heart. "I'd never be able to watch. I'd be a nervous wreck."

"I place bets like that all the time. Anyway, when I get back to Sacramento, I'll be ready to turn loose the dogs and start major building."

Janet cuddled in close. "Is your wife coming back anytime soon?"

"I doubt it. I sent her packing a couple of weekends ago. I don't think our marriage will last much longer."

Janet ran her fingers through her hair and couldn't help smiling. "Three weeks without you is going to be a long time. I'll miss you."

"Well, I'll miss you, too, but in the meantime we've got four days together."

Taylor sat at his breakfast table drinking a cup of coffee. The TV was tuned to a local Hawaiian station, but he wasn't paying attention to it.

He picked up the phone and dialed his office. A young woman answered. "Whitney Homes, this is Brittany, how can I help you?"

"Yes, can you get Paul Bayless for me?"

"Can I tell Mr. Bayless who is calling?"

"You can tell him your boss, and his boss, is calling."

"Oh, excuse me, Mr. Whitney. I didn't recognize your voice. Hold on while I get him for you."

Paul Bayless was the chief financial officer for Whitney Homes and ran the day-to-day operations. Although Taylor owned the company, he had effectively turned it over to Paul years ago. Except for the enormous amounts of money Taylor was withdrawing from Whitney Homes for his personal use, Paul had the company running smoothly.

"Hello, Taylor. Long time no hear. How's Hawaii?"

"Hi, Paul, it's wonderful. Too bad you have to run a company. You'd love it."

"I'm sure I would. What can I do for you?"

"Nothing, I just thought I'd check on things." Taylor walked out of the house onto his deck and leaned over the railing. "How are sales?"

"Sales have been slow since before Labor Day. All our subdivisions throughout California are experiencing the same thing. Traffic is strong, but buyers are holding out. It's probably the summer hangover."

"That happens every year; it's nothing new." Taylor looked down at the beach below him. A couple crabs were inching their way toward the shade of the deck. "Things don't get going until after the new year. How are closings?"

"They're holding up well, except the buyers are stringing things out. Our lenders are tightening lending policies and forcing buyers go through more hoops."

"Which ones are giving you trouble? Do they know who they're doing business with?" Looking down at the two crabs, Taylor turned over his coffee cup and spilled coffee on the rail. The steaming liquid hit both crabs on the back and they scurried back to the water. His lips curled. "You tell them if they don't step up and start making these homes close, Whitney Homes will go elsewhere. Northern States Mortgage and Advantage Mortgage would trip all over themselves to get our loans."

"Of course I spoke with them. It's a sign of the times. Wall Street investors are demanding more documentation from buyers and taking a closer look at loan applications. It has only affected a few deals. Another thing is lot 34 at Chesapeake Village didn't appraise out. The appraisal is seventy thousand dollars short of the sales price. That's one you're buying, right?"

"Yeah, I'm buying it personally. How did that low appraisal happen?"

"The appraiser can find no comparable sales to justify the sales price."

"What's the name of the appraisal firm?"

"Burns and Finch. They're one of the best firms in town."

"Those people have done this to me before, coming up short on the appraisal. I'll take care of it. I want you to increase prices twenty-five thousand dollars per house on every subdivision we're building."

"I don't know, Taylor. Don't you think that's a little extreme? I mean, sales are slow. I spoke with people at both Pacific Rim Homes and Broadstone Homes. They're saying the same thing. In fact, Broadstone's Quail Crossing is giving away twenty thousand dollars in upgrades in an attempt to move inventory."

"You know what, Paul? Those big corporate builders don't know anything." Taylor refilled his coffee and walked out onto the deck. "Those chumps spent a lot of time in Ivy League classrooms chasing theories and reading books. I've been in this business for over thirty years. I pay no attention to what they're doing and never have."

"Well, I'll go ahead and raise the prices, but I think it's a mistake."

"Just watch what happens—we'll sell more houses. Also, I need you to wire ten million to my personal account." He leaned back over the railing, looking down at the beach below. A couple more crabs were ambling toward his house. "I saw a nice Ferrari in Kaanapali I want to buy."

"Ten million! What are you going to do with ten million? Don't you already have a Ferrari here in Sacramento?"

"Yeah, I have one, but it's not here. And I'm closing on my new lot next week."

"Well, we're getting a draw in from the Bank of Lexington for approximately seventeen million on Friday."

"That's perfect. Wire me the ten million on Friday."

"What about our subcontractors, Taylor? We owe them a lot of money. We've been putting off paying them for a long time and they're antsy, especially our engineers. We owe them about one-point-five million for the work on the Bickford Project."

Taylor sat down in a deck chair and put his feet up on the railing. "Screw 'em. Tell them we'll pay them next month."

"That's what you told me to tell them last month and we still haven't paid them. Also, Jake Burgess, our framing contractor on the Waterford project, was here at the office looking for a check. He was hot when we didn't have it and threatened to kick your ass off a roof if he sees you. I think he's not playing—you better be careful."

"Screw him, too. What about our month-end closings? Shouldn't we close about forty homes this month?"

"No, we'll be lucky if we close twenty and that money has already been spent."

"Well, you'll figure it out. That's why I pay you the big bucks."

"Thanks a lot."

"Next Tuesday, send the jet here for Janet Waller and take her to the mainland."

"Again? You realize it costs forty grand to take that jet back and forth from Hawaii?"

"I'm aware of the cost, but it's my plane and my money. Besides, every woman is expensive. Some just cost more than others."

"If your wife catches you, it could get very expensive," Paul said.

"No worries, my friend. The wife is too busy shopping at Nordstrom's or the Diamond and Gold Vault to worry about my comings and goings." He stood up and walked back into the kitchen and poured more coffee. "How things have changed. When she met me, she used to shop at Ross. Now she gets nauseous if she even drives by one of those stores. It's nothing but the best for Monica these days."

"Well, you created that monster. I'll wire the money to you on Friday. Is there anything else?"

"Nope, that will do it."

"Hit 'em straight."

"I always do."

He leaned over the deck again and poured more coffee on the crabs below. Smiling at their distress, he looked up and peered over the horizon. He muttered, "This view was getting old. It's time for a change of scenery."

Sixteen

Barbara knelt in the flowerbed near the sidewalk in front of her new house, planting annuals. A straw hat guarded her face from the sun and leather gloves provided protection for her hands. Markus was lying on his stomach on the lawn next to her, his front paws clinging tightly to a rib bone as he gnawed on it intensely. She arranged a combination of pansies, snapdragons, and mums in a variety of colors. Admiring her flowerbed, she said, "My, it's so festive." On this beautiful spring-like day at the end of November, she basked in the warm sunshine, a pleasant change after the last two months of constant dreary weather. "What do you think, Mattie?"

Matt was digging with a shovel, working the soil next to her. He checked out her handiwork. "It looks very cheerful, Mom. You've done a nice job."

An older Ford pickup pulled up to the house directly across the street and a Hispanic man who appeared to be in his mid-thirties got out of the car. He wore jeans and a dirty white T-shirt under a loose-fitting brown shirt that almost hid the tattoos on his chest that crept up to his neck. He stared at the roofline of the house from the driveway.

"Look, I wonder if that guy knows the owner of the house," Barbara said. "It's the exact floor plan as ours and has been finished for awhile, but no one has moved in yet. I'm gonna find out."

Barbara stood up from the flowerbed, dusted the dirt off her jeans, and walked across the street. She peeled the glove off her right hand and extended it to the stranger. "Hi, I'm Barbara Whiteside. My husband and I live across the street. Do you know the owner of the house?"

He shook her hand, his dark eyes darting around the neighborhood. "Yes, I am Manuel Garcia." His accent was heavy. "Uh, I own this house." He looked over at the house uncomfortably.

"You're kidding me," Barbara exclaimed, then caught herself. "I mean, congratulations, and, ah, welcome to the neighborhood."

After instructing Markus to stay, Matt wandered across the street and joined them.

"I was visiting relatives in Mexico and just came back to check the house." Manuel surveyed the house. "It looks very good to me."

"Are you planning to move in soon? It really turned out nice." Barbara stared at his house, shielding her eyes from the sun with her hand. "Your color scheme was my second choice for our house, but I love how it looks on yours. Oh, this is my son, Matt."

Manuel looked at Matt and nodded. "No, I don't plan to move in. When Whitney Homes puts out the price list for phase four on Saturday, I will put a price on this house just below their prices. Guess you could say I'm—what do they call it— a 'flipper.'" He smiled broadly, showing off a mouth that was in major need of dental work.

"What's a flipper?" Barbara asked.

"A person that buys a house, but they never move in. They flip it. They sell it right after it's finished. I will try to sell my house for a little cheaper than the builder. I will make a good profit."

"Do you have any idea what price you're going to try to sell this house for?" Matt asked.

The man looked over his shoulder at the house. "I bought this place for four hundred sixty thousand. I'll try to get four hundred eighty-five thousand."

"Wow! Will you list it with a real estate agent?" asked Barbara.

"No!" He glared at her with disgust. "I will not pay thirty thousand dollars to a lazy agent to do an hour or two of work. Manuel can do that himself. This house should sell fast."

Matt shielded his eyes and looked down the street. "I guess you might get that price. The market is still hot."

"That's really interesting," Barbara said. "I wonder if that's why there are so many homes in our phase that were sold but remain unoccupied. In our phase of twenty homes, five sat vacant for over six weeks before someone finally moved in."

"I don't know," Manuel said. "This is the first time I am buying a house."

"Did you buy this house from Taylor Whitney? Somebody told me he bought it."

Manuel snapped his head around. "Who said this to you? That is not true. I bought this house."

"Sorry, I didn't mean to offend." Barbara put her hands up defensively. "Flippers, that's funny. Well, it was nice to meet you, Manuel, and good luck with the sale of your house. Let's go see what your dad's up to, Mattie."

"Nice to meet you too, Barbara, Matt. If you know someone who wants to buy, let me know."

"Sure, I'll keep it in mind," Barbara said.

They walked across the street and watched him drive off out of the subdivision.

"Flippers. Now I've heard everything," Barbara said. "He'll probably pull it off."

"That guy is weird, Mom. He looks like a wannabe gangster. I'd be careful around him. I hate to be negative, but he doesn't look like he could afford to fix his truck, let alone own a house."

"I was thinking the same thing, but I didn't want to be nosy. Maybe he won the lotto or something." She and Matt walked through the side gate into the back yard. Markus, bone in tow, tail wagging furiously, followed them.

"Hey, Stan, where are you?" Barbara called out.

He shouted back, "Over here on the other side of the garage."

She walked around and found him on his hands and knees fiddling with a plastic PVC pipe.

"What are you doing?"

He stopped and looked up at her. "I was thinking of getting one of those small storage sheds so I can take all my tools and stuff out of the garage. I want to run an electrical line to the inside. In order to do that, I need to dig a trench and run this pipe under the shed so I can run the electrical through the pipe."

"Hey, we just met the owner of the house across the street."

"Which house?"

"The one that's the same plan as ours, directly across the street. You know—the vacant one."

"Oh, yeah, when's he planning to move in?"

"He's isn't moving in. Get this: He's a flipper."

Stan looked up at her. "A flipper? It sounds like some kind of dolphin."

Barbara laughed and explained.

Matt added, "He seemed out of place, Dad, and uncomfortable."

Stan sat back on his haunches. "Interesting."

"Yes, he seemed intense," Barbara said. "When I told him I thought Taylor Whitney bought the house, he almost bit my head off. I'm not sure why he was so sensitive about that. I was going to visit Maggie at the sales office tomorrow to see how the balances of the houses are selling in this subdivision, so I'll ask her about that guy's house. I haven't checked with her since last month, so I wonder what the prices of new houses are. I also want to talk to her about our service warranty issues. Not a single thing has been done on our walk-through list."

"Why not?" Matt asked. "Have you called their office?"

"I've called their office many times and they tell me they'll get someone to come out and take care of our list, but nothing happens."

"You would think their customer service would be better than that." Matt shoveled dirt out of the trench Stan was working on. Markus moved in, giving the trench a curious sniff. Finding nothing of interest, he backed away.

Stan said, "I'll go with you to the sales office tomorrow. We could walk there and get a little exercise."

He stood up and Barbara wrapped her arms around his neck and kissed him on the lips. She jerked back and wrinkled her nose. "Gosh Stan, you stink."

He laughed. "What did you expect, Chanel Number Five? I've been out here for two and a half hours working like a dog. It's hot today."

Stan turned to Matt and they surveyed the yard. "You know, we took all the money we made on the sale of our first home and poured it into this back yard. It turned out nice, but it sure was expensive."

"Will we have any savings when we're finished with the yard?" Barbara asked.

"We haven't spent every cent. But look at it this way: Depending on the price release of the next phase, we may have gained about seventy thousand dollars in equity on this house."

"Well, we can find out what Whitney intends to do in their next phase tomorrow after church," Barbara said. "How are you feeling, Stan? Are you feeling any better today?"

Stan wiped his forehead. "I'm okay. The new inhaler seems to help. My breathing has been better the last few days."

Barbara turned to Matt. "Your dad has been feeling sluggish for the last month and he's really had to force himself to go to work. After about the third trip to the doctor, he's finally been feeling better."

"Has it gotten worse than before, Dad?"

"Yeah, about a couple months after we moved here, I started having days when I can't catch my breath. Then it goes away and I'm fine. This new medicine seems to be working. I hate being sick and we have bills to pay, so I can't afford to miss work."

"Your health is more important than work, Stan."

SEVENTEEN

Stephanie parked her car in the lot behind the building and walked around to the front. Dressed casually in a sweatshirt, loose-fitting jeans, and a beat-up baseball cap, she came to the entrance of El Toro También. As she pushed open the door, the bell rang.

The smell of cumin, chilies, enchilada sauce, and corn tortillas filled the busy restaurant. Mexican music played softly from a corner juke-box, while the chefs scrambled to prepare orders set on the counter by the waitresses. The walls held various portraits of famous bullfighters in different stages of battle, and the tables and chairs reflected many years of service, with too little time spent on maintenance. Pausing for a moment, Stephanie scanned the room until she spotted José in a booth toward the back of the restaurant. Although it was barely dusk outside, the place was dark.

She moved quickly to the booth and slid in. "José, it's good to see you. How have you been?"

José held out his hand to shake. "Very well, thank you." He motioned for one of the waitresses. "Would you like some food or drink? The chile verde is very good."

"Thanks, I'm not hungry." A waitress came to their table. "I would like an iced tea."

José spoke to the waitress in Spanish and she nodded and turned to the kitchen.

Stephanie set her purse beside her. "I was worried that you had changed your mind and wouldn't be calling me."

"I'm sorry I didn't get back to you as I said I would. Many things have kept me from calling you. You brought the money, yes?"

Stephanie felt inside her sweatshirt and half-exposed an envelope. "I did, but I must have an idea about what information I'm paying you for. Give me an idea of what's involved here."

He surveyed the restaurant. "I don't want to scare you, but you are looking in dangerous areas." He wiped his forehead with a napkin, his tobacco-stained fingers standing out. He looked at the front door nervously. "You know who owns the building, *sí*?"

"Maui Partners, LLC is the owner, and an attorney out of LA is the agent for service, but I don't know who owns Maui Partners, or who is in charge." She paused while the waitress set a glass of iced tea in front of her. "Thank you." She tugged the wrapping off a straw and put it in the drink. "But what does the ownership of this property have to do with your former tenants buying these houses and disappearing?"

"I don't know everything, Miss Stephanie." José looked over his shoulder. "But I know a man named Mr. Whitney owns the complex with a man named Carlos Diego. Carlos is part of the drug cartel in Tijuana. He is a ruthless man." He shook his head from side to side. "When he tells someone to buy a house, they buy a house."

Stephanie sat shocked. Taylor Whitney! What was going on here? "So are you saying that your former tenants were forced to buy houses from Whitney Homes? Why?"

"It is what I say. Why? I do not know these things. There are stories that the men who buy these houses are paid five thousand dollars in cash and told to go back to Mexico and never come back, or else. Five of those men, they spend all the money in Mexico. Then they come back to Sacramento to look for work. They are seen one week only, then no one sees them since."

This fraud is deeper than it seems on the surface, Stephanie thought. I bet the reason Carlos and Taylor don't want these guys back in the U.S. is to keep them from talking to the authorities. Or someone like me will find them and find out what's really going on.

"José, I need to get to the bottom of this before anyone else gets hurt. I appreciate what you've done so far, but I'm going to need more help from you."

José put his hands in the air defensively. "Please, Miss Stephanie. I have told you too much already. I am scared—these people are bad. I wish you luck. Give me the money and I go."

She pulled the envelope out of her sweatshirt and slid it over. He picked it up, slid out of the booth, and left the restaurant, leaving Stephanie with her thoughts and the bill. She fumbled nervously in her purse for some money for the check. I need to call Justin, she thought. This is out of my league.

As she drove from the restaurant, it began to rain hard. Stephanie's windshield wipers were working overtime, and the encroaching darkness made it difficult to see. She dialed the phone and connected to voicemail. "Justin, this is Stephanie. I need to talk to you ASAP. I've learned a few things about the Whitney files and would appreciate it if you'd call me back."

A black Mercedes with tinted windows drove up next to her car as she drove along the freeway. Stephanie's heart started racing as she stole sideways glances at it. She sped up but the Mercedes kept pace. She slowed down to let the car pass, but the car slowed to her pace and she started to panic. She jumped at the sound of her cell phone. The Mercedes pulled up half a car length and then steered toward Stephanie's car, pulling away to avoid a collision at the last second.

"Justin, thankfully you called," she said almost hysterically. "You've thrown me into a bigger mess than either of us imagined. Someone is forcing illegal immigrants to buy Whitney Homes and then sending them back to Mexico permanently. I'm driving down Highway 50 and

I've got a black Mercedes next to me. It won't stop tailing me. It keeps pulling up alongside me, then dropping back behind me. I don't know what to do."

"Slow down, Steph, you're talking so fast I can barely understand you. Are you okay? Can you see who's in the Mercedes?"

"No, I can't, but wait—it looks like there's a wreck up ahead. I can see police lights. I'm pulling over there." Just then, the Mercedes gunned its engines and sped away. Stephanie relaxed her grip on the steering wheel.

"Steph, are you there? Is everything all right?"

Stephanie breathed a big sigh. "Yeah, Justin, I'm fine. Just a bit rattled." She checked the mirror as she drove. "The Mercedes took off. I'm heading home."

"Can you come to the city tomorrow and go over what you have? I need to see what you've uncovered. Whatever you do, don't go to the police. I'll explain when you get here."

"Okay, Justin, I'll be there by nine. Just one more thing: I have to tell Matt what's going on here. He isn't involved and I can't stand deceiving him any longer."

"Let me think about that before you do anything."

"It wasn't a request. I'm telling Matt everything."

"Just come see me first."

"All right, Justin. I'll see you in the morning, but I'm not waiting another day after that." She sped into her driveway and hit the garage door opener. After pulling in, she closed the garage and ran for the house. Closing the door behind her, she locked it. She leaned against the door and caught her breath, and then glanced up at the clock in the kitchen. It read 8:10.

Oh no, I've got to hurry—Matt will be here in a half hour. I can't play this charade any longer. After tomorrow, I'm telling him everything.

Mimi's Cafe was less than half full, not unusual for a Sunday evening. Matt perused the menu while Stephanie set hers in front of her and stared down at it. Matt put his down as well. "What do you feel like, Steph? A burger or a salad?"

Stephanie snapped to attention and glanced at the menu. "Ah, I, uh, I'll just get a salad. I'm not that hungry."

"Stephanie, is something wrong? You barely said two words tonight."

Stephanie reached across the table and touched Matt's hands. "I'm sorry, Matt. I've been thinking about issues at work and my mind has been out there all afternoon."

"Do you want to tell me about it?"

Stephanie adjusted her red turtleneck sweater. "It's Janet Waller. It's a lot of things. I really don't want to get into it right now. I'll deal with it tomorrow."

The waitress brought their orders and set them on the table in front of them. "Can I get you anything else?"

Matt shook his head. "No, thanks." He picked up the cheeseburger he had ordered and paused before taking a bite. "I don't know, you've been acting different. I hope whatever is bothering you gets resolved."

Stephanie pushed around at her salad and looked into Matt's eyes. "Don't worry. It will be resolved—soon."

Eighteen

The headlines on the front page of the *Wall Street Journal* screamed, "Pacific Financial Collapses, Subprime Mortgages Sink It." Matt placed the paper on his desk and took a sip of his coffee. He furrowed his eyebrows, thinking, Wow, they were a bigger hedge fund than Franklin Smith. There've been rumors on the street that Pacific was having liquidity issues, but not this. I wonder if Drew saw this.

He dialed Drew's number.

"Hey, Matt, did you see what I just saw?"

"Jeez, Drew, those guys were the big boys, the A-players. What happened?"

"What's happened is all those risky loans that these hedge fund firms have been falling all over each other to buy for the last few years are starting go bad. Borrowers are defaulting at alarming rates and nobody wants to trade the subprime-mortgage-backed securities."

Matt heard a beep in his earpiece indicating an incoming call. The ID showed it was Stephanie. "Drew, I'm getting another call."

"No problem, bro. Just watch; Pacific is just the first of many. Talk to you later."

He hit the answer button on his phone. "Hello?"

"Hi, Matt, how are you?"

"I'm great, thanks."

"I have something important to talk to you about," she continued. "I'm about halfway to the city to meet with Justin and I hoped we could meet for lunch."

Matt sat up in his chair. "Another emergency meeting, huh? Why didn't you tell me last night when we had dinner?"

There was a ten-second pause. "I will explain."

He spun around in his office chair and looked out at the morning fog covering most of the bay. He watched the headlights of cars coming across the Bay Bridge from Oakland. He would like an explanation. Stephanie had been very preoccupied and quiet lately, very unlike her. Something was bothering her. "Sure. What time were you thinking?"

"I'm thinking close to twelve-thirty. I'll call you when I'm finished and we could walk down and grab something at Pier 39."

"Okay, Steph. I'll wait for your call." He hung up and stared at his phone. And here it comes—Kathy Ann all over again. She's gonna tell me she and Justin have been seeing each. Damn it, why did I let myself get involved? I keep losing focus on the plan. This will be the last time.

Hundreds of seals lounging on floating rafts attached to large posts bayed lazily at the tourists, who were eagerly snapping pictures from the back end of Pier 39. Seagulls squawked as they fought over food morsels thrown in their direction. An occasional tern, flying above the fray, would fold its wings and fall like a dart into the water, only to emerge a few seconds later with a traumatized anchovy in its beak. Matt could relate to the small bird, as it had to fly through a gauntlet of hungry seagulls to finally enjoy its catch. He thought, If that doesn't typify Wall Street, nothing does.

Matt and Stephanie walked by this spectacle as Stephanie filled the air with idle talk about the birds and passersby. When they approached Sea Lion Restaurant, overlooking the floating mountain of noisy blubber, Matt opened the door and held it as Stephanie entered. In his haste, he'd left his coat at the office, but the establishment looked casual enough. Stephanie looked remarkable as ever in a beige business suit with black pumps.

The lunch crowd had thinned out, so a booth by the window was easy to find. The waitress, looking weary in a stained apron and dark slacks, took their order, then left for the kitchen.

Matt glanced out at the sea lions, which hadn't moved much and didn't look like they would anytime soon. "Well, I'm glad we covered all the small talk on our way here. You said you have something to tell me." He gave Stephanie a penetrating look. "Well, let's hear it."

Stephanie took a deep breath. "Where do I begin? You may have guessed I haven't been straightforward with you."

Matt swallowed hard. He listened intently as she spilled out her confession that she was working undercover and that Justin was her boss. At least he wasn't her lover—that part was good.

She stopped talking and looked at Matt. When he said nothing, she continued.

"We've been investigating Janet Waller, Taylor Whitney, and the bank fraud they are allegedly committing. I wanted to tell you, Matt, but I had to be sure you were not involved. My feelings for you have always been completely honest. I hope you know that."

Matt rose from the table. "I hope you don't mind, but I need a little air for a moment." He could feel her eyes watching him as he slipped outside to the pier and took some deep breaths. She was a spy, and he had been a suspect. Her feelings were real. Were they? What was he supposed to believe?

He re-entered the restaurant partly out of curiosity and partly because his heart still wanted her—wanted her to be real.

Stephanie talked nonstop for several minutes, revealing detail after detail. No wonder things didn't seem right at Franklin Smith. There *was* someone there who was in on this illegal deal. Was it Pete? Then, something else came to Matt—his parents…their new home.

Their food had arrived, but eating was the last thing either of them was interested in doing. Stephanie moved the food around on her plate. "There's one more thing." She felt down to her leather briefcase and pulled out a file. She looked at it briefly and handed it to Matt. "It's your parents' file. I copied it from Janet Waller's office. She wrote them a bad loan, Matt. It could come back to haunt them."

Matt looked at the file, his face burning red.

"So, now you know everything I know, Matt. I'm sorry to have deceived you, but I had no idea when we met our paths would cross this way. I wanted to warn you, warn your parents."

Matt watched her face. She seemed to be telling the truth, and certainly she could not have planned him walking out of the elevator the minute she was dropping off her packages that first day.

"Did you know anything about this fraud before my parents bought their home?"

She reached over and touched his hand. "I only knew a little when I met your parents. I lacked proof, so how could I tell you? There was nothing I could do without compromising my job. When I took the assignment, I agreed to keep my role secret. I did it as long as I could stand it. Yesterday, I finally put my foot down and told Justin that I was telling you everything."

"And Justin just said 'That's cool,' and he was okay with that?"

"Not exactly. He knows I'm telling you everything, but he wants me to take a break from the case and let him do more research. He told me to take a couple weeks off until after the first of January."

Matt looked down at his watch; it still wasn't a Rolex. His boss back at the office would be wondering where he was, and his food wasn't looking that appetizing. "I have to get back. The financial markets are in a tizzy."

"Are you okay?"

"So you were investigating Franklin Smith and me? You've got all my parents' personal information in a file, and you do nothing while they take on an outrageous loan that they won't be able to afford? No, I'm not okay. I'm dumbfounded. How could you do that?" Matt's voice was rising. He threw his napkin onto the table. "I feel like I've been betrayed, Stephanie. You knew a huge secret and kept it from me."

She took his hands. "Matt, please forgive me, but it was not intentional. Never in my dreams could I have known we would be dating. I've agonized many times over the situation. I'm sorry, Matt, I truly am."

Matt stared into her eyes, his face blank. Another woman, another deceit. He signaled to the waitress to bring him the check. "I need to think about things, Steph. A lot of information has been dumped on me and I need to decompress. Let's go."

Outside, Stephanie attempted to give him a hug. "Matt, I'm not canceling our New Year's Eve date."

Matt looked at her blankly.

NINETEEN

Christmas lights from the tree threw soft lighting around the room. The TV flickered with the action of a football game. Matt sat on the couch opposite his dad, who was relaxing in a recliner—both fixated on the game. Stan pushed the sound down on the remote.

"Are you going to see Stephanie tonight?"

"No, we met earlier and she was heading to her grandmother's. We'll be spending New Year's at the Hyatt tomorrow night. You know, Dad, one minute I think she's God's greatest gift and then the next, I find out I don't really know her."

"Why do you say that? I thought you two were getting along well."

"We were—I mean we are, but things have come up that have caused me to re-evaluate. I'm just being cautious."

"What has she done to make you question the relationship?"

"She had been keeping secrets about her employment from me and other things I can't get into. She's come clean on everything, or so she says, but I just don't know."

"Look, Matt, there are bound to be things she hasn't told you, just as there are probably parts of your past you haven't disclosed to her. Give her the benefit of the doubt. I know you care for her deeply—loosen up. Don't be afraid to follow your heart."

Matt tossed the remote up and down in the air. "I don't know, Dad. You're probably right, but I can't shake these doubts."

Their room for New Year's at the Hyatt overlooked César Chavez Park, right in the middle of downtown Sacramento. From the nineteenth floor, Matt looked out the window at the twinkling red and green lights strung through the leafless trees. Directly below, crowds of people wandered down the sidewalk, dodging into taverns and nightclubs. He turned around, sat on the bed, and stared blankly at the Holiday Bowl game on TV.

Matt's stomach growled. His watch said 6:30—was she ever coming out? He stared at the closed bathroom door, pushing away his doubts again. "I hope I'm making the right decision coming here," he murmured to himself.

Thirty seconds later Stephanie emerged, wearing a flowing red cocktail dress with a black shawl, red pumps, and a small sequined purse. Curly brown hair cascaded down to her shoulders. She wore a small diamond necklace around her neck.

Matt stood up. "Wow, you look gorgeous. I'll never complain about the time you take to get ready."

"Thank you, Matt. You look handsome yourself. That's a sharp suit. I like your red tie."

Matt blushed. "Thanks. Well, shall we? I'm ready."

"Let's go."

Matt held the door for her and followed her to the elevators. He reached for her hand and held it, and she glowed.

Two minutes later, they were inside the huge ballroom handing their tickets to the maitre d', a small man dressed in a black tuxedo and a black bow tie. He scanned the list of names on his podium, smiled, and said, "Follow me, please."

He stopped at a table near the orchestra and pulled out a chair. "Here you are. You may sit anywhere at this table you like." With smooth indifference he added, "You may start to eat whenever you wish." He pointed to a group of tables brimming with steaming food. "The plates are at the buffet tables and, as you can see, the line starts on the left. The band will begin at nine o'clock. Enjoy your evening." Before they could thank him, he had turned away and was hustling back to his station at the entry.

Matt held Stephanie's chair as she sat down. She looked up at him. The lights made her red dress shimmer and the black shawl around her shoulders added to her sensuousness. "These centerpieces are gorgeous. Such pretty lilies."

As they watched, a harpist softly plucked out a tune a few feet away. She was a young woman, no older than twenty, dressed in a white formal dress with spaghetti straps. Her long blonde hair almost matched her honey-colored harp. The room was quickly filling up and the noise level was rising.

As Matt waited for the waitress to bring the drinks they ordered, he surveyed the room. This reminds me of the Christmas Ball at Santa Clara after my freshman season, he thought. Kathy Ann had looked so stunning. He pushed that memory away. He knew what he was doing this time...at least, he thought he did.

Matt nodded at the harpist. "This is great—we have our own private musician."

"I noticed. She's really good." Stephanie glanced around the ballroom. "The women here tonight are stunning. See that woman in the long aquamarine dress with the silver sequin trim? That is a beautiful dress."

Matt looked. "That is a pretty dress. Yours looks better."

"You're so sweet, Matt, thank you." She leaned over and kissed him on the cheek.

"Are you ready to eat?" he asked.

"Absolutely! Let's go."

When they returned, plates full, the table for eight had filled up. They resumed their seats and nodded hello. Introductions began. There was a banker, a title officer, a real estate broker, and a teacher. The couple seated next to them was the last to introduce themselves.

The man was tall, slender, around fifty, and wore a dark suit. His wife was pretty, petite, and a few years younger.

"Hi, I'm Preston Carson and this is my wife, Karen."

"Nice to meet both of you. I'm Matt Whiteside and this is my girl-friend, Stephanie Bernard."

"It's nice to meet you. You two make such a nice couple."

"Thank you, Karen," Matt said. He looked around the room. "How many people do you guess are here, Preston? Four hundred?"

"Probably close to that. It's a big room."

Stephanie put a cardboard tiara on her head with the year 2005 outlined in silver on it. "They did a nice job with the decorations. Aren't the centerpieces beautiful?"

Karen nodded. "It looks like they threw a bucket of confetti on each table." She looked up at the 12-foot-high ceiling and pointed. "Look how many balloons are in those nets. We're going to be knee-deep in them when they're released."

Preston eyed Matt and Stephanie. "Are you two from Sacramento?"

"Steph is from here," Matt said. "I was raised in Sacramento, but now I live in San Francisco."

Preston took a bite from his plate. "Have you tried the veal marsala? It's delicious. What do you do in San Francisco, Matt?" he asked.

"I work for Franklin Smith, the hedge fund," Matt said. "I trade mortgage-backed securities."

"Really? That's an interesting position. Given this market I'll bet it's exciting."

"It's definitely an interesting field. Before I was involved, I had no idea how real estate mortgages permeate our economy." Matt picked a roll out of the basket. "But now I know how mortgages are packaged together, and sold as one mortgage-backed security, like a stock cer-tificate. A firm like mine buys, owns, and sells that security."

"That's pretty cool. Me, I'm just a homebuilder here in town. The people who buy my homes take out mortgages that your company even-tually buys. Is your firm showing any concern over the housing market?"

"My firm is based in New York, so we deal with Wall Street types all the time, and they're getting concerned with the skyrocketing home prices. Nobody is screaming that the end is near, but they're definitely watching the main markets, like California, Florida, and Arizona, for any sign of stumbling. I hope the market stays strong—my parents recently bought a new home and I have a new condo."

Preston nodded. "What do you do, Stephanie?"

"I work for an appraisal firm here, and we've seen no signs of a slowdown," she answered. "We're buried with requests for both refinances and purchases."

"What firm do you work for, Stephanie?" Preston asked.

"Burns and Finch."

Matt rolled his eyes, but no one noticed. Still playing the role, Stephanie, he thought. When will this act end?

"I know your firm well. Your boss, Bob Burns, is a great guy. We go back a long way. His wife, Megan, is one of Karen's close friends."

Karen took a sip of wine. "She and I get together every other week for lunch at Slocum House in Fair Oaks."

"I enjoy working for them," Stephanie said.

"You said your parents bought a new house recently, Matt." Preston carved into a thick piece of prime rib. "Do you know who the builder was?"

"Whitney Homes. My parents are very happy with their house so far."

"Whitney builds a nice home. He's the largest builder in town."

"Whitney may be the largest," Karen smiled, "but Preston builds the best."

Preston squeezed Karen's hand. "My wife is such a comedian. She loves to brag on me to embarrass me. Well, enough about that. Where'd you go to college?"

"I started at Santa Clara and finished my degree at San Jose State."

"Did you play ball at Santa Clara, Matt?"

"Yes, I played three years before tearing up my knee. I concentrated on school after that. How about you? You look athletic enough to have played."

"I went to USC and played football as a backup quarterback. I love college football. Karen and I try to catch either the Stanford-SC game or the Cal-SC game, depending on who's in town. We love tailgate parties."

"You played at USC? That's impressive."

"Are you still a college football fan?"

Matt's eyes lit up. "Absolutely, I love it. I can't get enough of it. What do you think about SC's chances in the Rose Bowl tomorrow?"

"They're gonna kill Ohio State. The Big Twelve can't compete with the Pac Ten. SC's way too fast. What are you doing tomorrow? We're taking off right after we have brunch and heading home. We live about twenty minutes away in Granite Bay. There'll be a big pot of chili simmering on the stove. A couple of friends are coming over to watch that game, followed by the Orange Bowl later. Why don't you come by?"

Matt looked at Stephanie. "What do you think, sweetie? I don't have to be in the Bay Area until Sunday."

Karen jumped in. "Come over, Stephanie. You and I can find something to do while these fools relive their past. There's a great little shopping center right around the corner from our house and they're planning a football widow's sale all day tomorrow. We'll have a great time while they enjoy their football and chili."

"Karen, you said the magic words," Stephanie responded. "Shopping and sales. I'm in. I only need to run by my house to feed my cat. What time should we come over and what can we bring?"

"Yeah, Preston, do you need any snacks or beer? I hate coming over empty-handed."

"You don't need to bring a thing. Karen and I both love to cook, so we've had this dialed in for a few days. I've got plenty of beer, wine, or whatever you need, so don't worry about a thing. Just come on by and enjoy the game."

"That sounds like fun. Steph and I will be there."

The band struck up with Cool and the Gang's hit "Celebration." Stephanie tugged at Matt's hand, pulling him out of his chair and onto the dance floor. "Come on, big fella. It's time to shake it up a little."

"You don't have to beg me. Let's get after it."

When they came back to the table, Matt had loosened his tie and rolled his sleeves up. "You two make a beautiful couple," Karen said. "You could have just walked off the cover of *People* magazine."

Matt nodded at Stephanie. "Steph is the beautiful part of us. I'm just a prop. But thanks for the compliment."

The band started to play "Auld Lang Syne," and Matt looked at his watch. "Wow, it's midnight." He reached for Stephanie's hand and pulled her up.

With her arms around his neck and her head on his shoulder, they swayed to the beat. Silver, red, white, and blue balloons, with matching confetti, drifted slowly from the ceiling. The disco ball hanging over the dance floor bounced lights all around the room. Stephanie lifted her head and looked into Matt's eyes. She leaned forward and kissed him on the lips, hugging him tightly. She whispered in his ear, "I wish this night would never end."

TWENTY

S itting in his Bentley outside his house, Taylor fumbled with the remote, hitting one button after another until he finally pressed the correct one. The six-car garage remote confused him.

He drove the Bentley through the opening, parked, and shut off the engine. He got out and stood for a second, admiring his collection of cars. Monica's white Mercedes was to his left, the Ferrari on the other side, and next to that a yellow Porsche. They were all washed and parked neatly.

As he shut the car's door, he looked down at his diamond-encrusted Rolex watch. He mused, This watch is more expensive than most people's homes. It was slightly after midnight and he had arrived home from another night with Janet.

He lumbered through the laundry room, which was as big as many of the homes he built, and strolled into the kitchen. The dozen red roses he had sent his wife for Valentine's Day sat drooping in a crystal vase on the counter. There at the breakfast bar sat Monica, thumbing through an *Architectural Digest* magazine.

Oh boy, he thought. Here we go again.

She looked up from the magazine. "Did you have a nice evening?"

He shrugged. "Yeah, it was fine. The hearing in Elk Grove for the Belmont project went on longer than I expected."

"Is that so? So you were at a planning commission meeting all night? That's odd. You've never attended one of those in the ten years I've known you. All of a sudden, you want me to believe that you're attending planning commission meetings when you've got fifty employees whose only job it is to attend those meetings? I don't think so. What were you doing at the Bistro Capri at nine o'clock, and why did you follow Janet Waller after you left?"

"What are you talking about?"

"Don't play stupid!" she screamed. She grabbed a bowl that was sitting on the counter and flung it at him. He ducked; it crashed into the refrigerator and burst into a thousand pieces. "I saw your damned car at the Capri and I saw you walk out of there with that tramp Waller. Did you two have a fun romp in the sack, you piece of trash?"

"Quit being an ass," he shouted back. "I had a legitimate reason for meeting Janet Waller. We needed to meet and go over a few files."

Monica stood up and threw a glass at his head, missing by an inch. It shattered off the counter's backsplash. "Review files my butt," she screamed. "When you were screwing her, did it ever cross your mind, 'Hey, this could be dangerous if I get caught— my wife might not appreciate me screwing around'? Well, guess what, you got caught!"

"Quit screaming at me! I'm tired of you accusing me of screwing around. If I'm gonna get in trouble for it, then I'm gonna start doing it."

Monica kept screaming. "Listen up you jerk. I'm headed to Palm Springs tomorrow and I'll be there indefinitely. I would suggest you keep a low profile with your screw buddy while I sort out what I am going to do. I'm calling my new attorney in the morning. You remember Mary McDougal, don't you? I'm sure she will relish another shot at you."

She pucked the first plate she could get her hands on and threw it at him, missing again, but shattering it all over the floor. She hissed, "That is going to be one expensive affair you've had! I'll make you regret this little indiscretion for a long time. I hate you! I hope you die a painful death." She turned and stomped out, slamming the door so hard the whole house shuddered.

Taylor sat down in one of the seats at the breakfast bar, surveying the damage. Well, good. I won't have to listen to her nag at me for a couple of weeks. It will give her a little time to cool off. If she tries to divorce me, I'll bring her forty-thousand-dollar monthly shopping sprees to a screeching halt.

Monica's calico cat, Tuffy, came around the corner cautiously. He wandered into the kitchen, saw Taylor, and immediately arched his back and hissed. After a long pause, Tuffy turned and sprinted out of the kitchen and down the hall.

Taylor watched him go. "It's a good thing you're headed to Palm Springs with your mistress there, 'cause I'm about to take you for a long drive. You've just used up one of your nine lives."

Twenty-one

Taylor strolled into the office and set his briefcase on a chair in front of his desk. He glanced at the office walls, which were decorated from top to bottom with awards from a variety of home-building trade groups. Paul Bayless leaned his head in. "What time can you be ready, Taylor?"

Taylor replied without looking up, "How about in fifteen minutes? I want to hurry this up. I've got a tee time at one o'clock at Twelve Bridges."

"You'll probably want to cancel that. We've major problems to deal with today, and I'm not sure we can address them in that short time."

"What are all the big issues? Isn't that why I pay you so much? Aren't you here to solve problems?"

When Taylor walked into the conference room, Bayless, John Wilson the controller, and all the senior project managers of Whitney were already seated. They nodded to Taylor, who took his position at the head of the conference table. He nodded at Paul. "You called the meeting, let's go."

Bayless went to the blackboard. "First off, sales were dismal last year. We closed one hundred thirty homes, down from two hundred thirty the previous year. Taylor, last March you wanted to be aggressive and get a jump on the competition and for Whitney to be in a position to deliver homes to the market. You felt this home-buying slowdown would be over by the second quarter. With that in mind, almost five hundred homes were started, and currently almost half of those are standing inventory. Weekly payroll is a half million. We are not getting enough in monthly draws from our banks to cover overhead, subcontractor bills, payroll, and all *your* personal expenses. We anticipate closing twenty-five houses this month to generate about a million dollars. That's the good news. The bad news is we owe roughly four million. That number will climb monthly until we sell off our inventory."

Taylor put his hand to his mouth and yawned. "That's easy. Get rid of the standing inventory. Sell off all the finished houses. You say we've got a hundred and fifty homes that are finished—let's sell them. Why haven't they sold?"

"Taylor, we've been trying to sell them. Haven't you been paying attention to reports? The new home market is in the dumps. We've tried every marketing gimmick known to man, but houses just aren't sell-ing. We've used the papers, the TV ads, radio, on-site remotes, circus animals, free concert tickets...you name it; we've tried it."

"Who's our ad agency?"

"Morrison and Associates."

"Get them on the phone and kick them into gear. We need more buyers."

"With all due respect, we can't just call them and as you say, 'kick them into gear.' Number one, they're doing a great job of getting people to our subdivisions. We've had more traffic going through our model complexes than any other builder in town. Number two, we owe them money and they've been very patient with us. It would be unwise to kick that hornet's nest." Paul handed a sheet of paper he had been reading to John Wilson, who was sitting next to Taylor.

Everyone in the room sat ramrod-straight. Paul continued, "I know what you're going to say next is, 'If we're getting all the traffic but no sales, there's something wrong with our salespeople.' It's not just Whitney Homes. Every builder across the state is struggling with sales. Buyers aren't buying." Everyone, except Taylor, silently nodded their heads.

"We've lowered prices to the point where, in a couple of cases, we have to bring a check to escrow to pay off the bank. We owe more than the house sells for. There's no relief in sight. We need a major influx of cash or we could go down."

Taylor's face turned red as he gripped the armrests of his chair firmly. "What do you mean, go down? We're the largest builder in Sacramento. We always raise cash. Are you out of your mind?"

"No offense, sir, but raising cash isn't that easy right now," said Steve Bayless. "The credit markets are tight and our other investor sources are sitting on the sidelines. They're aware of housing market conditions. We've called out to many of our usual sources, but they have passed on our offers."

"You aren't trying hard enough. Do you know how many times people come up to me and ask, 'Can I invest in a Whitney Homes project?' It happens almost every day, that's how often. You should be able to raise ten million in an afternoon. This company makes money and everyone knows that. They all want a piece of the action."

Paul put his hands on the conference table, leaned forward, and looked Taylor in the eye. "Could you in good conscience put an investor in the River Knolls project in Merced? How about the Pheasant Run project in Bakersfield? We all know those projects won't make a dime. We know they will lose money. Do you think we should bring in new people with additional money to invest in projects we know will lose money? Our investors are well-informed."

Taylor looked at him, his lips quivering, eyes narrowing. "Now is not the time to get a case of the moralities. We need money, so go out and sell our company's name. New investors don't have to know the individual project situation. All they need to know is they are investing with Whitney Homes and that should be enough."

Paul sighed. "We have to be careful with the disclosure laws on these investments. We can't hide problems we're aware of, and then later throw our hands up and say, 'Oh, didn't we tell you? That project was a loser, so sorry.' That's how people end up in jail."

Taylor rose from his chair. He pointed his finger and waved it at Paul. "Don't be such a sorry wimp. Get your marketing team out there and come back with new investors." He looked around the room. "All of you need to stop loafing around and start raising money."

Paul straightened up and loosened his tie. "Jennifer, get your marketing team rolling and see what you can scare up. The only viable projects we might be able to raise money on are the North Natomas subdivision or the Fairfield one. Try and find investor money, quickly. But make sure you explain and document the risks of investing with us. I don't want any surprises down the road if these projects don't pan out."

Jennifer got up and gathered her notes. "I'll get right on it, sir."

Paul turned back to Taylor. "How about selling off pieces of land? We've a few vacant parcels that are at least three years away from building. Why don't we take a few of those to market? We might be able to get two or three parcels sold before the market deteriorates any further."

Taylor sat down, slamming his hands on the table. "Paul, why in the world would I do that? I've got land that will keep this company in business for the next ten years. I don't want to have to buy that same land back two years from now at a higher price. You'd better snap the whip on your salespeople, your superintendents, and the marketing company to generate more sales."

"Taylor, we do need to take immediate steps. It's imperative that we cut our payroll drastically. I'm suggesting we cut two hundred jobs by this Friday. We also need to decide which subs to pay immediately. Our framer and foundation subcontractors have filed bonded stop notices at the Portraits subdivision. We need to pay them a quarter million to get those notices lifted. The construction lender cannot fund anything further until those notices are removed."

"Will the press get wind of our layoffs?"

"I don't see how that can be avoided. Is there anyone who you want me to spare with these layoffs?"

"I don't care who you get rid of. You can start with my cousin."

"Andrew? You know his wife had their first child last week."

"She did? Great, tell him congratulations for me. Let him go, and get rid of any other deadwood we have hanging around here. How did you allow these stop notices to be filed at the Portraits? Is that why there haven't been any closings from that subdivision in weeks?"

"That's one reason. Do you remember the five million you took out of the company earlier this year, and ten million dollars you took out last October? Those funds were earmarked to pay subcontractors. We owe the engineering firm at least two million. If we don't make a substantial payment to them by Friday, they'll sue us."

Taylor banged his fist again. "Damn it! I've given them enough business over the years. They can wait for their payment. They always threaten to sue, those leeches, but they won't follow through because they want my business."

"The engineers aren't fooling around this time. Their attorney isn't playing games. We may need to liquidate unnecessary assets. They cost a fortune to maintain, and we're getting no mileage from them as far as improving our business."

Taylor's eyes bugged out. "Forget it, Paul!" he screamed. "I know where you're going. Why don't you do a better job of getting these houses built and sold? If you would concentrate on that, we wouldn't be having this discussion." He took a deep breath and looked around the room. It was eerily quiet and nobody moved. "Is there anything else?" Taylor looked down at his Rolex, then around the room. "You slobs better start doing what I'm paying you to do. Raise money and sell houses. If you can't do that, there are plenty of people out there who would kill to work for Whitney Homes." He got up, walked to his office, picked up a stack of papers, and left the building.

He could see his staff watching him in stunned silence through the conference room windows as he walked to his car. He jumped into his freshly waxed red Ferrari, gunned the engine, and raced out of the parking lot.

Just before he arrived at the Winchester Country Club, his cell phone rang. He hit the "on" button to his Bluetooth ear set and answered, "Hello?"

"Taylor, this is Artie Tennelli. We talked two weeks ago and you told me you would clear up your debt from the Super Bowl. I haven't seen it yet and my people aren't happy. They're not a bank. They don't make loans."

"Sorry, Artie. I was traveling the last two weeks and forgot. What is the amount you need?"

"You might have forgotten, but my people didn't. They don't like slow payers. You owe six hundred thousand dollars, and if I don't receive a cashier's check from you by Friday, it will go up to seven. Don't try to play games, because these people don't."

"I'll get it to you Artie, I promise."

"I'll be looking for it."

Taylor hung up his cell phone and stared at it. "I'll get the money to you when I'm good and ready, Tennelli." He stopped the car with the engine running and stepped out.

A young attendant helped him with the door. "Good afternoon, Mr. Whitney, are you playing golf today?"

"What do you think, I just came up here to admire the view?"

"I'm sorry, sir, I was just asking."

"Be careful with my car. Don't jack around with it if you know what's good for you." He turned and headed for the clubhouse as the attendant stood there, juggling the keys in his hand.

Taylor's cell rang again. He looked at the phone, but didn't recognize the number. "Hello?"

"Taylor? Taylor Whitney?"

"Yeah, this is he—who are you?"

"My name is Mike Sherman—you know, Sherman Construction, the contractors who framed your Portraits project, the ones you owe about three hundred thousand dollars to? Now do you remember?"

"Yeah, I remember. Who gave you this number? Lose it. If you want money, call my office." He snapped the phone shut and shouted at it. "Stinkin' subs!"

TWENTY-TWO

The conference room on the twenty-second floor of Embarcadero Number Four was richly decorated, with heavy, dark oak paneling lining the walls. The ceiling was covered with stamped copper, and a large, circular oak table sat dead center surrounded by sixteen leather-bound captain's chairs. Matt and Stephanie sat next to each other. Justin and a bald, burly man sat to their left. Worldwide Funding's huge logo hung on the wall behind them.

Justin handed them a sheet of paper. "I really appreciate you both coming in on a Saturday to discuss this situation." He gestured to his left. "This is Greg Cranston. Greg has been with us for twelve years investigating loan fraud and other questionable dealings with World-wide. I don't think we've ever seen anything as large or as sophisticated as this fraud ring."

"However, when you say sophisticated, I think you are giving these crooks too much credit," Greg Cranston said. "It's sophisticated in the number of players involved, and its uniqueness. Who would have thought of using illegal immigrants to defraud a bank—or quite possibly banks?"

Matt looked up from the sheet in front of him. "Mr. Cranston—"

Cranston held up his hand. "Please call me Greg."

"Okay, Greg, what can we do for you? Why don't you just call the police or the FBI and have the principals arrested? It seems to me you've got enough evidence to at least start a formal investigation."

"That's a legitimate question, Matt." Justin adjusted the sleeve of his denim shirt, which was rolled halfway up his arm. "Since you are in the mortgage securities business, you know just how bad the real estate and mortgage business is getting. Worldwide has made a boatload of loans over the last three years and just about half of them were in the subprime category. Needless to say, we've been pounded by the declining market and rising delinquencies. We are a public company, and as such are sensitive to bad public relations. If we were to go to the police or FBI, it would be all over the press within hours. It could cause a run on our stock price and wipe out our company. You probably read about Pacific Financial's collapse last month. They were put out of business in a day and we don't want that."

"I understand that," Stephanie said, "but how are Matt and I going to help? I told you I was scared to death the last time I was investigating. These people mean business." She pointed at Matt. "We're a couple of amateurs."

Greg laughed. "Stephanie, you give yourself no credit. You quickly discovered things I had overlooked. Here's how you two can help. We won't put you into any dangerous situations. But I know you can get closer to Taylor Whitney's and Janet Waller's operations." He looked at Stephanie. "You've done a tremendous job so far with Janet, but we need more. Someone has to be steering these buyers to either Janet or Taylor. Who is that person? How are the proceeds of these fake loans being split? Follow the money." Pointing at the sheet in front of him, he continued, "These buyers have to be somewhere. You need to find them and figure out what they're getting out of this."

"All right," Matt said. "Say we solve this and figure out who's who. What is the bank going to do next and who will be watching out for us? What's in it for us?" He thought for a moment. "Also, you've indicated someone at Franklin Smith has been actively buying these loans that were originated by Sunset Mortgage for Whitney Homes. That means there must be someone on the inside at Worldwide, too."

Justin took a sip of coffee from a Starbucks cup. "If we get to the bottom of this scam, we will quietly meet with those involved and give them an ultimatum. Pay us back or go to jail. It's very simple. We will still lose money, and I'm sure we'll never recover everything. As for you, Matt, Stephanie's already being compensated, but I will pay you five thousand a month and a bonus of twenty-five thousand if we solve this." He handed Matt a check. "Here's your first month in advance. As to your next question, yes, somebody is on the inside here at Worldwide. We think we know who that is, just as you have an idea who is on the inside at Franklin. We don't want to move on them until we get everyone involved lined up. Just out of curiosity Matt, why are you getting involved?"

Matt shifted in his chair. "It's simple. This market has changed, and I need the money. I'm also tired of getting ripped off in my own office by people who are trading illegally."

Greg motioned to Matt. "We will protect you at all times and if there's a conflict with your job, I will personally visit John Ramsey and make him understand your importance here. He'll understand. Just don't get caught doing anything illegal, because then my hands are tied."

Greg slid a card across the desk to Matt and Stephanie. "I'm available anytime, day or night. If you need anything, call me. You also can call Justin as you have before. We're both available."

Matt stood up and shook hands. "I guess we have our marching orders." He sighed as he folded up the check and put it in his breast pocket. "I hope we can help you out."

Driving across the Bay Bridge toward Sacramento, Matt scanned the bay as a tanker and a fleet of sailboats negotiated across the large expanse of water. Traffic was light for a Saturday, and he was making good time. Stephanie put her hand over his and he squeezed it back.

"Matt, you haven't said two words since we left Justin's office. What do you think?"

"I'm wondering if we have bitten off more than we can chew. I'm still spinning from all the information."

"I'm wondering the same thing. We are either adventurous or just plain crazy." Stephanie rubbed his arm. "Only time will tell."

"I think you're right on both counts. I was just thinking, my parents have been having a hard time getting any warranty work done by Whitney Homes. I could step in for them and see if I can't get closer to Taylor Whitney. They asked Preston Carson to help them, and he's set up a meeting with Taylor. I should go instead of my parents."

"Matt, that's a great idea. I'll bet Preston could help you get with Taylor. As for myself, I know I can get more out of Janet's assistant, Carol. We could do another late-night visit to Janet's office if we have to. I also need to talk to José Cabrera again, but I'd like you to come. There's got to be a way to find some of these fake buyers."

"We need to be careful, Steph."

TWENTY-THREE

Taylor sat at the head of the conference table and scanned the room. With him were Paul Bayless, his chief financial officer, and Blake Wilson, his corporate counsel. Across a heavy table sat two senior vice presidents from Bank of the Northwest and their two attorneys, William Moore and David Johnson.

It was the fourth week of January and Taylor was more than a little miffed that the meeting had been called by the bank. 2006 had not gotten off to a good start. A pitcher of water and crystal glasses sat unused at the center of the conference table.

I hate these stupid meetings, Taylor thought. These mindless attorneys and corporate MBA's think they know more than I do about home building. How dare they force me to come back from Hawaii early.

It was quite a contrast in clothing, with Taylor dressed in a golf shirt and slacks and the balance of the crowd in suits and ties. The bankers were stiff and sat ramrod-straight while they talked. Taylor slouched in his chair, one foot dangling over the arm. Wilson and Bayless fiddled nervously with their pens.

After a round of pleasantries and small talk, William Moore got to the heart of the matter. He spoke in a low monotone. "Mr. Whitney, we're trying to determine the status of the four projects to which there is a current one hundred twenty-five million dollars' outstanding loan debt. We've received over thirty-five mechanic's lien notices on these projects for roughly three-point-five million dollars. According to our records, between all these subdivisions about seventy-five homes have been started. What seems to be the problem with all these liens?"

Taylor cleared his throat and looked over at Moore. "We've had a lot of cancellations over the last two months. There are people who signed up to buy homes and then changed their minds and canceled the contracts. As far as the liens go, we've had quality control issues with subcontractors who have not been performing to our standards. When that happens, we withhold funds until their work improves."

William straightened out his tie and said, "Excuse me for a second, Mr. Whitney. I can understand that type of business philosophy regarding standards for your subs, but three-point-five million dollars in liens is excessive, don't you think?" He picked a legal notice from a stack of files and held it up. "There are also bonded stop notices on more than one of these houses that must be remedied, or we can't fund anything further. Are you going to address these notices? These mechanic's liens are from subcontractors whose work has already been funded. Where is that money?" He stared intently at Taylor. The whole room was deathly quiet.

Taylor cleared his throat. "Well, that money is used to pay our bills. We need money to run such a big company, and as the funds are available we use them." As he spoke, he swept his arms around the room as if to point out to everyone that all the pictures and trophies there didn't just fall out of the sky.

Taylor's attorney, Blake Wilson, held his hand up to Taylor and jumped in. "What Mr. Whitney is trying to say is funds that are disbursed to Whitney Homes by your bank are used to move projects along. Whitney pays the bills that are directly related to the subdivisions that we borrowed against."

Taylor interjected, "That's not what I'm saying. When we get your funds, we use them as we see fit. You people don't know how to run a home-building firm. We use those funds to pay our bills and keep the houses moving toward completion." He again pointed at the pictures on the walls. "We've been doing this for fifty years and we've never had anyone question our business practices until you came along." Taylor made a sweeping gesture with his hand to include all the people in the room.

Blake tossed his pen on the legal pad in front of him and asked, "Can we take a ten-minute break?"

Everyone around the table nodded. Blake rose from the table and headed for the door. He looked directly at Taylor and indicated with his head for Taylor to come with him. Once outside the conference room, he pulled at Taylor and ushered him into a nearby office. Paul Bayless followed them in and shut the door.

Blake spoke in a hushed tone. "Taylor, do you know what you're doing? You can't tell a bank that the money they've disbursed to you for subcontractors has been used for other purposes. That's called diversion of funds and it's illegal. You can say that you've had cost overruns or that you've had theft on the job, but you can't say that you are using their money for anything but the construction of homes. You can't say money the bank has earmarked for the construction of houses is being used to cover the overhead of your company. They will come after you hard."

Taylor looked at him. "I don't care, Blake. They've never run a toy train set, let alone a multi-million-dollar business. I know what I'm doing and they aren't going to bully me around. If I need ten million dollars for whatever reason and it's in our account, I'm taking it and I don't care where it came from or what it's supposed to cover."

Paul Bayless joined in. "Taylor, we need the bank's cooperation in order to keep receiving our funding. The last thing you want to do is anger them or make them nervous. They'll start looking through our records. At your request, there have been many questionable bookkeeping practices over the last two years that could lead to real problems if they request an audit of our books."

Taylor was indignant. "These bankers' jobs are to fund Whitney Homes's money, and we can take it from there. I don't need a Stanford

MBA bean counter telling me how to do things. I will do it the way I always have, whether they like it or not."

Blake stared at Taylor. "Don't ever tell me you weren't warned." He looked at Paul. "Let's go."

Back into the conference room, William Moore asked, "Are we hearing correctly, Mr. Whitney, that when the bank funds you money, it may or may not go to pay for the work that it was intended to pay? Are we also hearing that you have used money intended to pay for permits for other purposes?"

Taylor looked at him condescendingly. "We could have done that. I don't keep account of every dollar you've given us from the last three years, but we've probably used your funds for any purposes that were necessary at the time."

One of the senior vice presidents for the bank spoke for the first time. "Mr. Whitney, your firm provided us with a financial statement signed by you in August of last year that shows Whitney Homes to have ten million dollars in the bank. That same statement shows accounts receivable of six-point-five million. Are these funds available to you currently? Because, if so, we want you to pay down a portion of the principal on your loans and bring the loans back into compliance, as is stated on your loan documents."

Taylor leaned forward with his hands under his chin. "First of all, I don't know where that money is, how much is there, or if it's still available. But the last thing I'm going to do with my cash is to pay your loans down. You can get your funds same as you've always gotten them—when we close a home, you get paid. It's a simple formula that has been working for decades, and I'm not changing it for you, or anyone else."

David Johnson, the attorney from Bank of the Northwest, spoke calmly to Taylor. "You realize, Mr. Whitney, you are out of compliance with loan documents you signed, and that we can suspend funding at any time until you bring the loans back into compliance? I want to make this crystal clear. We don't want to stop any of your projects, as we would rather see you successfully complete them. That's in the best interest of everybody here, including the bank. We want to work with you, but we need your cooperation."

Taylor leaned back in his chair and pointed a finger at the attorney. "You need me more than I need you. I owe too much money for you to dictate your terms to me. Your bank cannot afford to let me fail. Like you've said, Whitney Homes owes over a hundred and thirty million to your bank. I know what I'm doing, and if you want to see that money, you'll continue to fund us and get out of the way. We've been through a market like this before and survived. We'll get through this one. You put out the money, and we'll build the houses. It doesn't get easier than that."

There was an awkward silence as Taylor's words hung in the air. All four bank representatives stared blankly at Taylor. After an uncomfortable period of silence, Dave Johnson turned to William Moore and shrugged. "Well, I guess we're finished here. Taylor, I do want you to remember one thing. You personally guaranteed every one of these loans, which allows us to go after everything you own. Gentlemen, we thank you for your time and we'll be in touch." He stood up and shook hands with everyone and left the room. He headed to the front door and walked out, Moore close behind him.

Paul followed Taylor into his office. "Taylor, listen to me. You can't treat these people as if they were ignorant. We need them and we need them desperately. We have been unable to raise a significant amount of outside capital, even by offering our best properties as an investment. Trying to get money out of a Wall-Street-type firm is out of the question. They have put a lending stop on anything that smells of real estate. Our only hope is that we can work with our existing banks to keep money flowing. You cannot insult them and expect them to do you any favors. It just won't work."

Taylor was admiring a trinket on his desk. "I don't want to hear about what you think. I know what I'm talking about. They need me and they can't allow me to fail. Do you think they will say to their board of directors, 'Oh, we lost a hundred thirty million dollars because

Whitney Homes wouldn't do things our way'? They are running scared. Just continue doing what we've been doing and it will all work out."

"You've got your head in the sand," Paul scolded. "I'm calling the bank tomorrow to see if I can mend some fences. It's time to get rid of the jet and yacht, pronto! Cutting payroll has helped, but we're still losing money at a deadly rate every month. We would use any funds from the sale of the jet and the yacht to pay down bills."

Taylor stared at the trophy case across the room. "I'm not selling the jet; I will not fly on a commercial airline."

Paul shuffled some papers. "Get used to commercial. I recommend you sell a couple of your homes to pay a portion of your bills. Where will you be the next few weeks? I may need to discuss things with you."

"I'll be in Hawaii until the end of March. Don't bother me unless it's something important. Oh, one more thing. The next one who gives out my personal cell phone number will be fired. I've been getting threatening phone calls from subs and I'm tired of it. I may hire a personal bodyguard to protect me when I'm here in Sacramento, if this keeps up. If anybody tries to mess with me, I'll have them kicked up and down the street. All right, I'm late for my tee time." With that, Taylor got up, left his office, and headed out the door.

TWENTY-FOUR

A smug look of satisfaction crossed Janet's face. This money is just too easy, she thought. Taylor is so pleased I closed twelve loans for him that he's sending me twenty more. All I had to do was make a few small changes to a document or two and convince Worldwide Funding to make the loans. Piece of cake.

She opened her desk drawer out and fiddled for a pen. I'll do the same thing to these files—a little White-Out here, a new document there, and presto: a better loan package. No one will ever be the wiser. Worldwide Funding will sell the mortgage after six months to a New York hedge fund, and the loan will become someone else's problem.

Janet called to her assistant and waited for her to enter. "Carol, I'm taking a flight to Hawaii next week on the tenth and won't be back until the nineteenth."

"Is there anything else, Ms. Waller?" Carol asked.

"No." Janet waved her away. I hope Taylor can settle his divorce with Monica quickly, she thought. I've got some big plans for Taylor and me. She doesn't deserve the life she's living, but I certainly do.

She looked at her desk and saw a note that Barbara Whiteside had called. Janet had no doubt why she was calling. They need to get out from under that lousy loan I put them in a year and a half ago, she thought. It continued to amaze her that so many borrowers could be so dumb. All they had to do was look around their neighborhood to realize it would take a miracle to get their house to appraise for what they needed to get out from under their loan.

She raised a pen to her lips. Of course, I will assure Barbara I can probably help her, but she'll have to pay a five-hundred-dollar processing fee, upfront.

She leaned back in her chair, letting her mind wander. It's been quite a journey from the first time I met Taylor to where we are today, she thought. I know how to work men. Taylor's no different from the rest of them, other than the fact that he's rich.

She started doodling on her weekly planner. The wife issue is tricky, but I know ways to expedite that process. A couple of well-written love letters and a couple of racy pictures somehow get into Monica's hands, and it will be over.

She mused, I can't wait to move into his mansion and do a little redecorating. I'll remove all vestiges of Monica. Oh, the parties I'm gonna throw.

She knew Taylor wanted everyone he knew—and even people he didn't know—to come to his house and see how rich he was. Janet could make that happen for him and would relish the role. She wondered if he would give her the Mercedes that was parked in the garage. That'll send Monica into a screaming rage when she gets wind that I'm driving that car. Note to self: Bring that to front burner with Taylor the next time we get intimate.

She giggled. Her cell phone rang, snapping her out of her daydream. She looked at the number and recognized it as Taylor's. "Hello, darling."

"Do you want to meet for a drink at the Capri?"

"Sure, what time were you thinking?"

"Let's see, it's about four now, how about around five?"

"That works. You know I'm always excited to see you. I can rock your world later on." She hung up the phone and smiled. Sometimes this man thing is just too easy. Taylor thinks he's Don Juan in bed, but he's more like Don Knotts.

❖

Sometime after five, Janet pulled into the parking lot and spotted Taylor's Bentley taking up two parking stalls by the end of the build- ing. Janet parked her Mercedes, and turned off the engine. Pulling her visor mirror down, she adjusted her makeup. A couple of tune-ups on her lips and she was ready to go. She unbuttoned the top button of her blouse and adjusted her cleavage. No sense leaving those babies hiding.

Inside the restaurant, she saw Taylor and walked over to greet him. He gave her a quick nod and continued talking to a couple of men.

"You know this housing downturn is just a crock cooked up by the media. Everyone says this market is in a nosedive, but I'm selling my houses as fast as I can build them. I'm going to make forty million this year. I build the best house in town, bar none."

"How in the hell can you be the only builder in town that's making any money?" Angelo, the restaurant owner, asked. "Everyone else says they're losing their shirts. What the hell's your secret?"

Taylor puffed up his chest. "I told you. People want to buy a Whitney Home. They will pay a premium for that. I have people calling me all the time asking where my next subdivision will be so they can be first in line to buy a Whitney Home. I've been in business a long time and many people won't buy anything but one of my homes."

"Taylor, you're doing no better than the rest of us." Taylor turned his head and Preston Carson came into view. "People are not particular who builds their home. As long as they think it's a steal, they'll buy it. Donald Trump couldn't compete here on his name alone, and you're no Donald Trump."

Taylor looked at Preston contemptuously. "How would you know what's going on? You only build twenty homes a year. I sell that in one day. But it's good to know that you're still in business and slugging it out. At least I assume you're still in business, aren't you?"

"Of course I'm still in business. I saw you laid off half your staff a couple of months ago. You're feeling the same slowdown as the rest of us."

"I laid off my staff because I wanted to get rid of the deadbeats lying around my office. Now that we're down to a leaner company, we can be much more competitive." Taylor lifted his drink from the bar. "Did I tell you I'm working on building plans for a new place in Maui? I bought a lot and it only cost ten mil. It has a beautiful hundred-and-eighty-degree view of the ocean." He made a sweeping motion with his hand. "A forty-second walk down the pathway and you're on the beach."

"No, you hadn't mentioned it." Preston made a tipping gesture. "I'm sorry, I didn't notice you there, Janet. How are you?"

Janet nodded. "I'm fine, Preston."

Preston looked back at Taylor. "You paid ten million for a lot in Maui and you're building a huge home? In this market? Have you lost your senses?"

"I figure I'll probably spend about fifteen million to build it, and it'll take me about fourteen months to build. I've got to do it right—this lot is first-class and it deserves a statement house. That's what I'm going to build. Whoever sees that house will know that Taylor Whitney owns it."

"Good luck, because you'll be needing it. I've got to run. Taylor, I'll see you at the meeting I set up with you, myself, and Matt Whiteside next Tuesday."

Taylor rolled his eyes. "Don't worry. I can't wait."

"See you later. Good to see you, too, Angelo." He waved and headed toward the door. Taylor shouted at him as he left, "Hope you manage to stay in business. If you ever need a superintendent's job, give me a call." He turned to Janet. "That poor Preston is so jealous of me it's not funny."

Janet looked up. "Thanks for those new loan apps your office sent me. I might be able to close them by next Friday."

"If you close them by next Friday, I'll get you twenty more. This is like printing money, Janet. I'll keep feeding you buyers and you keep stuffing them in homes. I'm looking forward to getting over to Hawaii and out of this town. Everything around here is doom and gloom." He twisted the diamond ring on his pinkie. "It seems like every hour there's a big emergency at the office and I have to rush over there to sign something. Every day I have subcontractors calling me and threatening me with bodily harm if I don't pay them."

"You know what the problem is Taylor? You're just too available for them. If you're in the area, they know they can track you down to help them out. It's time you weaned them off you so they can stand on their own two feet and make their own decisions. Either that or you might think of replacing them with more competent people. Hey, I could run your company if you want."

He put his arm around her and gave her a squeeze. "You'd do a better job than Paul, that lazy weasel. But then you couldn't join me in Hawaii."

"I get spoiled going over there in your jet."

"I'm going to have to sell the Citation to get Paul off my back, but I'll get a new one next year. I can't stand flying commercial. Too many smelly people in one small space. Oh, well. My next jet will be bigger and better." Angelo came up and set a bowl of peanuts in front of Taylor. "Forget the jet; you haven't seen my new Ferrari yet. It's gorgeous. I just have to make sure I don't drive it too fast or I'll kill myself. That sucker looks fast standing still."

"I can't wait to get over there," Janet said. "How long has it been, three months since we were there? I'm bored with Sacramento. I need to get to the tanning salon for some color before we leave."

She looked at him seductively. "Order us another drink, will you, Taylor? Let's have one more and head back to your place."

He placed his glass on the bar. "You're on."

TWENTY-FIVE

The sound of Don Henley singing "The End of the Innocence" floated around Preston's office. He was sitting behind his desk, staring intently at the computer screen. His secretary came to the door. "There's a Matt Whiteside here to see you."

Preston looked up. "I'll be out front in a second. We're heading to a meeting and I'll be back in an hour or two."

She nodded. He turned his computer off, grabbed his briefcase, and headed to the lobby. "Hey, Matt, how are you?"

Matt got up from a chair and extended his hand. "I'm great, Preston, how about yourself?"

"I'm good. You ready to meet the infamous Taylor Whitney?"

"I am. Thanks for setting up this meeting. My parents had no luck getting Whitney Homes to respond to their requests."

"Sometimes face-to-face meetings work better. Any problems getting off work?" Preston opened the office door. "I tried to do this on a Friday, but Taylor had a golf game set up. You can see his priorities."

"I took a vacation day. My boss is less than pleased with me lately. I've been struggling to purchase large loan packages and with this market being in the tank, it's been tough. I have the feeling I'm in the dog house."

"That's not good. Let's take my car. I know where Taylor's office is."

"So how is Stephanie? You make such a good couple—any long-term plans?"

"I've thought of marriage, but can't seem to convince myself to take it to the next level. I'm still trying to figure out what I feel."

"You mean she's thinking that way—marriage?"

"Yeah, but I have this fear I'll get burned down the road." Matt looked at a new BMW stopped next to them at the stoplight.

"Look, Matt. With any relationship there has to be faith that the other party is in as deep as you are. Do all relationships last forever? Of course not; that's why there are so many divorces." Preston turned the radio volume down. "You can't worry that you and Stephanie are not going to make it down the road and base a decision on your fears of bad things that might happen in the future. You love this woman, don't you?"

"Yes, I think I love her."

"You miss her when she's not around, don't you?"

"I miss her terribly. I'm just not sure I want to get married." I also don't know that I fully trust her, he thought.

"No one ever has a 100% guarantee about marriage. But sometimes you have to go with your feelings. There are no guarantees in life, but don't use that as an excuse for not living your life to its fullest." Preston pointed out the window. "There's Whitney's office on the left. Let's see what old Taylor has to say for himself." Preston drove the car into the driveway and parked near the entrance. Matt got out and surveyed the two-story office.

"Nice building."

Preston opened a glass door with a Whitney Homes logo etched on it, and motioned for Matt to enter. They approached the receptionist.

"Hi, I'm Preston Carson with Matt Whiteside to see Taylor Whitney."

"I'll let Mr. Whitney's secretary know you're here. Have a seat." She picked up the phone.

Two minutes later, a heavyset woman came out. She took them down a hallway adorned with framed pictures of houses built by Whitney

Homes, then stopped at a large conference room and gestured for them to enter. Matt and Preston walked in and seated themselves at an enormous oak conference table. Matt looked around the room at the awards sitting on built-in bookcases.

Taylor came through the door. "Preston Carson, my favorite little builder. Have you sold more than one house this month?"

Preston ignored his remarks. "Taylor, this is Matt Whiteside. His parents bought a house from you a year and a half ago."

"Good for them." Taylor sat down at the conference table and made no attempt to shake either Matt's or Preston's hand.

"Well, Preston, what's up?"

"I set up this meeting as a favor to Matt, here, who's a friend of mine. He has been unable to get any response regarding service warranty issues at his parents' home."

"If he's such a good friend of yours, why didn't he buy one of your homes?"

"Mr. Whitney, my parents liked your house and the neighborhood it's located in," Matt said. "For the most part, they like the house you've built, but they have real issues that need to be addressed. We are here to get those problems solved."

"Look, I have a service warranty department that take care those kinds of things. We've sold a lot of houses over the years and because of the volume, it takes time to get to everyone. Tell your parents to chill out; we'll get to them eventually."

Matt's face did a slow burn. "My parents don't need to chill out. They have legitimate problems that need fixing and soon."

Preston looked at Taylor. "Is this how you treat your customers—insulting them? Matt came here to ask you politely to correct problems that Whitney Homes created. I don't think it's too much to ask."

"That's why you build twenty houses a year and I build four hundred. We'll get to your parents' house when we're ready and not before." Taylor leaned back in his chair, looked at Preston, and pointed at Matt. "Why is this joker coming here? He didn't buy the house. Are his mommy and daddy scared of me?"

Matt's voice started to rise. "Let me explain something to you, sir. It has been over a year and a half since my parents bought their home. Since then, they have heard nothing but empty promises from your warranty department. I shouldn't have to come down to your office and beg you to do what you're supposed to do. How you manage to stay in business the way you treat your customers is beyond me."

"You know what? I've got better things to do with my time than listen to you whine about your parents' home," Taylor said. "I can't say it's been a pleasure to meet you, because it hasn't."

Matt slowly rose from his chair. "Listen, if you don't get someone over to my folks' home within a week, they are prepared to start legal action. I didn't come here to be insulted. If you don't respond, you will be sued."

Preston stood up. "Calm down, Matt. He's not worth getting excited over."

Taylor flipped his hand in the air. "Yeah, calm down. I'm not worried about your threats. Your parents want to sue me? Tell them to get in line."

"You better watch your back, Taylor. I will not let up on you until you have your people correct the problems at the house. These are your obligations." Matt headed toward the door. "Preston, let's get out here."

"Good riddance. Both of you get out of my office."

When they got to Preston's car, Matt paused as he pulled on the door handle. "What an unbelievably rude, arrogant ass. I'd love to chase him around, whacking him in the head with a heavy two-by-four."

"He wouldn't be hard to catch. He's a flabby, out-of-shape moron," Preston agreed. "I've seen Taylor act like an ass many times, but this takes the cake. I'm stunned." He opened the car's door, as did Matt.

Preston flipped on the car stereo. "If you could give me your parents' fix-up list, I could send over one of my crews. What would really help is if you could break out the stucco where that upstairs window is leaking, so we can see where the water is coming from."

"That's really nice of you, Preston. My parents would appreciate it. I won't be able to get to it for a couple of weeks, but my folks have waited this long. A little longer won't kill them."

"I still can't get over what a jerk Taylor is," Matt said. "Do you have his cell phone number? I'm going to call that donkey every week and bug him to death."

"I have his number at my office. Your parents can also file a complaint with the state contractor's board. They won't do much, but at least it will get his attention."

Matt adjusted his seat belt. "There is one other thing I have been thinking about. My mom told me there are least four homes, maybe more, that Taylor personally signed up to buy in her neighborhood. All four of the houses ended up in foreclosure."

"You would think the media would have gotten wind if Taylor were the owner, wouldn't you?" Preston asked.

"That's what I thought. Why would he buy houses from his company in his own name and then let them go back to the bank?" asked Matt.

"I don't know, but it doesn't make sense. If you can get me the addresses I can get one of my title reps to check on it. We can figure out who was on the title when the houses were foreclosed. We can also find out who made the loan to whom and for how much."

Matt's cell phone went off and he fished around for it in his pocket. He looked at the number on the screen. "Not now, Steph." He hit a button on the phone and sent the caller to voicemail.

"Any problems?"

"No, that was Stephanie. I'm just not in the mood to talk with her right now. Maybe later when I calm down."

Preston turned down the air. "Give some thought to what I said about your relationship with Stephanie. You can't be worried about making a mistake in love, because all you'll do is succeed in being alone all your life." He turned left at the signal. "When I married Karen, there was no guarantee that our marriage would work. But I had a good feeling about her. It's been one of the best decisions I've ever made. You can do the same."

"Thanks, Preston. I'll do that."

"Better yet, why don't you call Stephanie and bring her to dinner at our place tonight? I'll make a meal you won't forget."

Matt looked at his phone. "All right, I'll give her a call."

As they were driving home, Stephanie turned down the volume on the radio. "Thank you for asking me to come tonight, Matt. I had a great time. Preston is a great cook." She looked out her window at the traffic speeding by. "What's your next step with Taylor?"

Matt turned the car onto the freeway. "I wish you could have been with us today. Taylor is a piece of work. I think he's heading to Hawaii next week. I don't know how I'm going to do this, but I need to get inside his personal residence. I don't think he would leave records that would implicate him at his office."

"Matt, how are you going to get into his house? Are you thinking of breaking in?"

Matt winced. "I don't know yet. I'll let you know once I figure it out."

TWENTY-SIX

Monica stretched out over the living room floor. Tuffy nuzzled her face into the folds of her loose, draping bathrobe. Monica's younger brother, Jake, sat on the floor across from her, setting up lines of cocaine on the glass coffee table. He had been anticipating getting high the entire way on his flight from LA to Palm Springs, and the party was on.

Monica leaned back. "I'm not sure I want to start this early after last night." Pushing Tuffy off her lap, Monica leaned forward and plucked a cigarette from the pack on the table. Taking a big drag, she fell back and exhaled, blowing the blue smoke up toward the ceiling. "I didn't smoke for eight years because of that control freak." She took another drag. "Too bad, Taylor, you can't stop me now."

A loud gunshot-like sound made both of them jump. Monica leaped up, ran to the sliding door, and yanked it open, running onto a deck that cantilevered out about twenty feet from the house. Leaning over the railing, she screamed at two men who were driving a cart toward the house. "Can't you idiots keep your golf balls on the course? This is the fifth time today one of you hackers has hit my house!"

The men stopped the cart, looked at each other, and then turned and drove down the course.

"Why don't you go take some lessons?" Monica came back in the house and plopped down on the couch. "I find so many golf balls in my yard every day and I'm getting sick of it."

Jake looked up, white powder on his nostrils, like he had sneezed into a bowl of powdered sugar. "Hello, sis. You live on a golf course, near a tee box. What did you expect to find, volleyballs?"

"I don't know. I never wanted this house. It was Taylor's idea. It's a monster."

"I wouldn't mind waking up here every day."

"Yeah, well, it's like a prison to me. Taylor is fighting to keep money from me. My attorney thinks she can get a fair monthly allowance, but that doesn't help my situation right now. I have to take things into my own hands, before he makes good on his threat to throw me out on the street."

Jake sat up and shook his head, trying to clear it. "Yeah, I get it." Head cocked, he stared at his sister though half-opened eyes. "Hey, man, you look terrible. Have you looked in a mirror lately?"

Monica walked to the front door, where a floor-to-ceiling mirror was attached to the wall. "You're right—my eyes are bloodshot, and I could wash my hair. I should slow down on partying." She turned and walked back to the couch. "I just need a shower." She poured another drink, lit another cigarette, exhaled, and eyed her brother. "So, are you sure your friend is up for the task? No clues left behind? I want it done clean and professional, and it can't be traced back to me."

"Don't worry, this guy is good. He worked for the Chicago mafia. I'm gonna need the deposit upfront, and he'll want the balance immediately afterward. He'll be impatient for the final payment, so you better have it ready. Does it matter to you whether he does it here or in Hawaii?"

"I don't care if it's done in Paris, Jake, as long as it gets done. If I can't have Taylor, nobody will. I want him to pay for cheating on me. Besides, I want what's rightfully mine and I won't let him squeeze me out because he has better attorneys." She tugged a cigarette out of the pack. "How do you know this guy? How can you be sure he can do this without any mistakes?"

"I told you, he used to be with the mafia. I know him from my dealer in LA. He's a bad hombre. My dealer tells me he's involved with the drug cartels. Those guys take things personally. You don't live long if you mess up on them."

Monica took a big drag on the cigarette. "The deposit money is in that envelope on the kitchen counter. Tell him I'll be ready with the balance when it's done."

"Okay, I'll take care of it. Want to do a line with me?"

"Sure—let's celebrate."

TWENTY-SEVEN

Matt sat at his computer, concentrating on the numbers on his screen. He was trying to wrap up a mortgage-backed security purchase from Citiloan before the end of the month, and to finish all his work for the week so he could take off early on Friday.

His mind wandered. *I need to figure out how to get into Taylor's house. Breaking in is probably not the best option—of course he must have alarms. There's has to be a better way.*

He didn't notice that John Ramsey had stepped into his office and Matt jumped when the man spoke to him. "Matt, have you seen the commitment letter from First Interstate regarding the seven hundred million in loans you were promised? I thought you said we should have received it three weeks ago."

Matt looked up. "Mr. Ramsey, you startled me. No, I haven't seen a commitment letter. Normally, it would have gone to the legal department for their review before sending it to me."

Ramsey looked concerned. "Nobody from legal or anywhere else has heard or seen anything from them in months. You'd better check with them to see what's going on. It would be a real blow to us if that deal isn't made."

Matt fumbled for his phone and stammered, "I'll find out right away, sir. My contact, Ben Johnson, said we had a deal and promised to send the letter right out. But you're right, that was weeks ago. I'll see what I can find out."

Matt's felt his pulse increasing. Something wasn't right. That deal was all but signed, sealed, and delivered. His jaw clenched. I've got to have that deal, he thought. My job is already in jeopardy. I don't need outside help from two-faced people like Johnson who say one thing, then do another.

Ben answered the phone on the second ring. "First Interstate, Ben Johnson speaking, how can I help you?"

Matt wanted to scream at him, but said calmly, "Hi, Ben, it's Matt Whiteside. I'm calling regarding the commitment letter you were sending me regarding the seven hundred million in loans we discussed. No one in my office has seen it."

Ben answered nonchalantly, "Oh, hi, Matt. I've been meaning to call you. I've been dealing with your colleague, Pete Ramsey. He said you were buried and he was taking over the deal for you. The letter went out to him yesterday, didn't he tell you?"

Matt tried to control his voice. "Is that so? Pete told you he was taking over for me? That's news to me. Do me a favor, Ben. In the future, if I'm working with you on a deal and someone tells you he's taking over for me, would you confirm that with me?"

"Sure, Matt." He paused. "Is there something wrong? Were you and Pete not working on that deal together? I apologize if I made any problems for you."

"No, don't worry. We work for the same firm, so as long as Franklin gets it we're good. But check with me next time, if you would."

"No problem. You take care."

"You too, Ben."

Matt put the phone down and spun his chair around to look out at the San Francisco Bay. How long will I be enjoying this view? he wondered. Pete could very well get me fired.

He could see in the distance a ferryboat from the Gold and Blue Fleet filled with tourists, heading out to Alcatraz Island. At the rate I'm losing deals, it won't be long before they throw me out of here.

Matt took a deep breath, gathered his strength, and headed to Mr. Ramsey's office. Mr. Ramsey looked up from his computer. "Come in, Matt. What did you find out?"

"Your nephew, Pete, has the commitment letter. The deal should close either next week or the week after."

Ramsey stood up. "They went through Pete? Why? I thought that was your client. Is there a reason they would be dissatisfied working with you?"

Matt spoke defensively. "Honestly, Mr. Ramsey, I've bent over backwards for them. I've taken their reps to sporting events, and wined and dined them. I've been nothing but helpful to them."

Ramsey looked skeptical. "I know Ben's boss, Fred Jackson at First Interstate. I'm going to give him a call and see if he knows what's going on."

"I made sure Johnson had everything he needed to complete the transaction. I was a step ahead of him the entire time."

"So, what's going on with Citiloan? Will you be able to make the deal, or is that going south, too?"

"I'm just putting the finishing touches on the commitment letter. Corporate counsel has already signed off with a couple of minor tweaks, which I've addressed, and it should close next week."

Ramsey sat back down in his chair and looked at Matt sternly. "I hope for your sake that the deal closes. I'm sorry this market has changed, but I can't help you if you can't improve the amount of mortgage-backed securities you purchase. There is a quota we need to hit and you are right on the bubble. If you don't hit your quota, I can't save your job." He pointed the pen he was holding at Matt. "Make that Citiloan deal. All right, that's it. I've got work to do." With a wave of his hand, he dismissed Matt.

Matt shuffled out of the office and mumbled, "Yes, sir."

He stopped at Pete's office on his way back. Pete sat at his computer, and he looked up. "Hey, Matt. Why the long face?"

"You know exactly what's happening." He took a step into the office. "I haven't told your uncle what you're up to, but I guarantee you one thing. You try this again and I will make sure he knows about this, and I will let New York know also."

"Relax, Matt. I've told you the deal's not done until the check clears. Your check hasn't cleared. It's nothing personal."

"That's where you're wrong. It's personal." Matt turned and left.

He went back to his office, sat at his desk, and stared at his computer screen. He needed to get his condominium on the market soon. His future at Franklin wasn't looking so bright. That big promotion was probably out the window.

He ran his hands through his hair. This has been a real roller coaster ride, he thought. He glanced down and looked at his watch. Still no Rolex. Maybe Kathy Ann was right: He was no Joe Montana and no Warren Buffet.

His phone rang. He recognized the number.

"Hi, Mattie, how are you?"

"All right, Mom. I'm coming home in a couple of days."

"Great, honey. Now, I don't want you to worry, but your dad has been admitted to the hospital. He has a terrible cough and has been having respiratory problems. I'm sure he will be okay, but they're running a series of tests."

"Make sure you call me after you get the test results, and if need be I'll drive right up if you need me."

"Okay, Mattie. There's a lot of pressure on your dad right now. Perhaps when you're up we can get discuss with you about how to deal with the house issues. Since my hours have been cut, and your dad's sickness, we've been struggling."

"I'll be glad to help any way I can. Are you all right, Mom? You sound tired."

His mother sighed. "I am tired. We're constantly hounded by our mortgage company and they won't help us. Oh, I almost forgot. Remember that neighbor we met, the Hispanic man, Manuel Garcia, who said he was a flipper?"

"Yeah, I remember him."

"I read in the newspaper a couple of days ago that he was murdered and his body was found in a ditch in West Sacramento. There wasn't much detail about the crime."

"That's strange. I wonder what the rest of the story is. Tell Dad I hope he gets well soon and call me if anything changes. I'll see you in a couple of days."

Matt rubbed his temples and took a deep breath. Damn, this was getting squirrelly. Could the murder be tied to the Worldwide scam? He'd better let Stephanie know. He checked his watch and realized he'd almost forgotten he was meeting Drew downstairs.

One minute later, he was sitting at the bar of the 13 Views, looking out at the Port of San Francisco building. He watched a couple of sailboats as they maneuvered toward the safety of their moorings.

Drew came up and slid onto a bar stool. "So, what's new with you, sonny boy?"

"I lost that deal I was working on with First Interstate. Pete Ramsey stole it from me. At least Franklin made the deal, but I didn't get the credit."

"No way! Pete did that to you again?"

"Yes he did. I'd love to come up with a creative way to get even with him."

"So, things aren't all rosy at Franklin, I take it?"

Matt took a sip of his beer. "No, they're not rosy at all. What are you seeing out there?"

"I'm seeing an ugly situation that is about to get uglier. My hedge fund is pretty strong financially, but there are other funds out there just starting to find out how deep they are involved in the housing market. Nationwide, delinquencies doubled last month, and foreclosures more than tripled. Many of these funds are starting to lose their liquidity." He turned in his seat to look down the bar. "Remember I was telling you a couple of months back that one hundred percent stated incomes would go away? Well, they're gone. Subprime lenders can't sell their mortgages because funds like yours and mine are refusing to purchase them. They're stuck with them, and a lot of their borrowers are defaulting on their loans. Bel Air Mortgage and Carson Investments, two of the largest subprime lenders in the country, are in real trouble and may go under."

Matt was surprised. "No joking—Carson Credit and Bel Air? I've bought at least ten mortgage-backed securities from them. I haven't done a deal with either of them since February, when things started to go sour."

Drew stared straight ahead. "You better hope for Franklin's sake that those mortgages you bought from Bel Air and Carson have refinanced and paid you off. Many of those are probably bad loans."

"I never know what happens to the mortgages after we buy them. They go into another department and I never hear about them again."

Drew cleared his throat. "Carson and Bel Air are just the tip of the iceberg. Santa Clara, Beverly Credit, FloridaMac—they all have liquidity problems. Unfortunately, since we don't buy from those lenders anymore, they are forced to restrict their lending. Money won't be available like before. If regular homeowners can't afford to pay their mortgages and can't refinance, they'll default and the cycle repeats itself." He looked at Matt through the mirror behind the bar. "Have you put your condo on the market?"

Matt waved at the bartender to order another round. "No, not yet, but I plan to list it soon. I'm probably going to take a hundred and seventy-five thousand hit on it."

"You're doing a smart thing, Matt, by selling your condo now. We're not near the bottom of this market and the worst is yet to come. Instead of losing a hundred seventy-five thousand, you could be losing two seventy-five."

"Yeah, I know. I'm trying to accept the fact that I'll lose money and will have to move. I don't know what else to do."

Drew watched an attractive woman come into the bar and sit at a booth across the bar. "Wow, that gal is hot."

Matt looked up and spotted the woman through the mirror. "She is attractive."

"So your parents are struggling with their house?" Drew asked, turning back.

The woman caught Matt's eye in the mirror and smiled. He smiled back. "Yeah, their payment goes up again in a couple of months. They can't afford it, and they can't refinance. Big surprise, the house has lost its value. They're putting it on the market and will try to do a short sale."

"That's tough. I hate to see that happen. Just keep your head up, Matt. You'll pull through this. I know you're probably feeling overwhelmed, but hang in there. Things will work out."

"I wish I could share your optimism."

By the time Matt arrived at his parents' house on Friday afternoon, his mother had brought Stan back from another trip to the emergency room where he had been admitted and released the next day. She was making chicken soup in the kitchen when Matt walked through the front door.

"Hi, Mom, how's the patient?"

Barbara gave Matt a big hug and kiss. "He feels better today. The doctors gave him some antibiotics and steroids and he has ongoing breathing treatments every three or four hours, but they just don't know what the problem is. He's still very weak. He just went up to his room; go up and say hi. He'll be happy to see you."

When Matt turned and started toward the stairway, a scratching at the sliding door caught his attention. Markus was bounding up and down on all fours. "Hold on, little doggie. I'll come out later and play with you."

The bedroom curtains were drawn back and the room was bright from the afternoon sun. Stan was propped up on a couple of pillows, the TV remote in his hand. He looked up and smiled. "How you doin', Matt?"

"I'm doing fine, Dad. The question is how are you doing?"

"I'm okay. I'm feeling a little weak. Wednesday, I couldn't catch my breath. Your mom, God bless her, had to physically help me to the car to take me to the hospital. It's just so strange—I come up here and after a day or so, I feel fine. I can get up and walk around. Then, I go to my office downstairs to try and get work done and after a couple hours, I start getting nauseous and short of breath. I was knocked down for a couple of days. Wednesday was the worst."

"But you're feeling better today?"

He picked up his inhaler that was sitting on the dresser. Nodding, he took a deep breath and exhaled. "Yeah, my doctor can't figure out what's ailing me. They keep running more tests, but so far nothing. We've got bills to pay, so I need to keep going to work, but it's been tough. I hate having to have your mother drag me around to hospitals. She never complains, but I know it's wearing on her."

"Man, I sure hope they find what the problem is and cure it. I'll let you get some rest while I work on fixing the window and that plumbing leak. If I can get everything torn apart this weekend, Preston's crews can come in and fix everything next week."

Matt climbed a ladder to the second-story window directly above the home office. He had torn a foot and a half of stucco off the bottom corner of the window. From inside the house, the sheetrock was damp from the window leak. Matt was trying to find the source of the water penetration.

The ladder moved. He looked down. "Markus, get off that step. You can't climb this ladder." Markus stood at the base of the ladder, front paw on the bottom rung, tail wagging furiously. Matt spotted a large cut in the sheet metal and could see bare wood through the cut. He yanked the sheet metal back and saw the wood was soaking wet.

"That's odd, Markus; it's summer. There hasn't been a rainstorm in a month, yet this wood is soaked. I better open up this wall further to dry it out, whadda ya think?"

Matt continued to tear the stucco off the wall until he had torn off two feet on either side of the window down to the ground. He was about halfway up the ladder, just above the second floor, when he noticed a plumbing pipe with a nail going through it. Water was squirting past the nail down the wall.

Matt felt the insulation that was stuffed into the wall. "Man, this stuff is soaking wet. I wonder how long this pipe has been leaking. The leak from the inside of the house seemed minor, but this is more serious."

Matt jumped off the ladder and dragged the wet insulation out of the framing bays. After he had taken out most of it, he moved to get a closer look at the wood framing. A foul smell came at him as he stared at a thick, black, mossy-looking blob with mushroom-like pods sprouting all over. He looked down at the dog. "Markus, the sheetrock is almost black." He yanked out his cell phone. Preston answered it on the second ring.

"Preston, it's Matt. I'm at my parents' house and I found the source of the leaks. The plumbing leak was inside the wall and there is something growing all over the studs and the sheetrock. It looks nasty. Can you come over here and take a look?"

"I'm on my way. It might be mold you're looking at. I'll have someone from Airborne Solutions meet me there."

Two hours later, Preston's crew had torn the stucco completely off the exterior wall and all the sheetrock off the interior wall in Stan's office. An inspector from Airborne Solutions took samples of the mold and put them in jars to take back to the lab. Matt and Preston stood watching him as he put the last of the samples away in a large box.

The inspector turned to Preston and Matt. "I don't think I've ever seen that much mold on a house this new. Not everyone is allergic to it, but if you are, it can kill you. I'll test the samples back to my lab, but I can tell it's Stachybotrys atra mold, one of the most toxic around. In the meantime, I'll treat the studs with a few chemicals that will kill what's left on the wall." He peeled off a thick piece of mold. "Leave these walls open so they can air out and dry. Everything in that office will need to be treated or thrown out. After that, the house can be repaired."

"I wonder if the mold is what has been making my dad sick."

"Your dad could have had a bad reaction to the mold," the inspector said. "The sooner you get him out of this house the better. For some people, it can be lethal."

"How long will it take to dry out? Should my mom move out as well?"

"As long as it doesn't rain, which it shouldn't, those walls will dry out in about a month." Mike looked up at the torn-up wall. "As far as your mother is concerned, it's totally up to her. She doesn't seem to react to the mold, so if she wants to stay here, I don't see any reason for her to leave."

Matt turned to Preston, his faced flushed. "That damned Taylor Whitney. He's the cause of this. If they would have come out here and fixed the leak, Dad wouldn't be sick."

"Easy, Matt. Taylor seems to be involved in a lot of bad news lately."

Matt bent down and petted Markus, lying at his feet.

"A lot of buyers of Whitney Homes have filed complaints with the Department of Real Estate," Preston said. "They'll probably fine him heavily."

"Good, I hope they fine him and make it hurt. I wish someone would come along and break his legs or something. He deserves it."

"You know your parents could sue Whitney Homes for damages."

Matt looked calmly at Preston. "I know they could, but right now they don't have the money to hire an attorney, and I've given them as much as I can. The way the market has turned, my income has gone down the drain. I can't put up much more."

TWENTY-EIGHT

Stan and Barbara sat at her mother's kitchen table with Mindy Olsen, a real estate agent from Coldwell Banker who had sold the house down the street from them. Stan was staying with Barbara's mother at her house in Rio Linda until repairs on the house were completed. Since moving to his mother-in-law's, Stan was slowing gaining his strength back, feeling better each day.

A grandfather clock in the hallway began to chime. Mindy looked over at it briefly, then back to Stan and Barbara. "Thanks for the coffee, Barbara. I have a list of every sale in the immediate vicinity of your home in the last six months, and a list of all the houses that are listed for sale." She spread them out on the table. A lawn mower started up somewhere outside. Mindy brought out a Whitney Homes price list. "Here is the price Whitney is selling your floor plan for. If we go through all the sales and listings, the price to move the house should be three hundred and forty thousand."

Stan looked at Barbara. "Our loan on this house is for four hundred twenty-five thousand. How do we get the bank on board?"

Mindy pulled out a piece of paper from her briefcase. She handed the paper to Stan. "I wrote down some tips on how to approach your lender to do a short sale. I suggest you call your lender tomorrow morning and tell them what you are doing. If you'll sign the listing, I'll be on my way." She handed the papers across the table. Stan and Barbara signed the listing and then walked Mindy to the door. "Thanks for all your help."

"It's no problem, Barbara. Stan, I hope you have a speedy recovery." She waved. "I'll talk to you both later."

Barbara shut the door. "I guess there isn't anything else we can do." Stan held her tightly. "No, babe, I don't think there is."

The next morning, Barbara sat at the breakfast bar, the phone up to her ear. She sipped on a cup of coffee. Finally, after forty minutes on hold, a live voice came on. "This is Sonya, may I help you?"

"Yes, hi, Sonya, I need to talk to you about doing a short sale on my house."

"I'll have to transfer you to our special assets division. Please hold the line."

Barbara was transferred to another department, where she waited on hold for another twenty minutes. Finally, someone came on the line again. "Hello, this is Gina, how can I help you?"

"Gina, this is Barbara Whiteside. We have a loan with you, number 02356. We have listed our house for sale and we want to do a short sale with you as we can no longer afford the payments."

"Let me look up your loan. Bear with me a minute. Okay, here you are. Mrs. Whiteside, I show you current on your payment. Our policy at Citiloan is we will not discuss short sales with borrowers until you are sixty days delinquent."

"You mean we have to go into foreclosure and ruin our credit before the bank will even consider accepting a short sale?" she asked incredulously.

"That is correct. We won't do anything until you're two months behind on your mortgage payments."

Barbara hung up in amazement. She called Stan at her mother's to tell him what she had learned.

"That doesn't make a lot of sense. Look, Barb, if that's what it takes to do this, then we'll quit paying the mortgage."

"I guess we can look at the bright side. We just saved ourselves about thirty-five hundred dollars by not making this month's payment."

Barbara continued working while Stan recovered. Several days later, the phone rang. She picked it up and answered, "Hello?"

A young woman's voice asked on the other end, "Can I speak to either Barbara or Stan Whiteside?"

"This is Barbara Whiteside speaking."

"This is Alicia from Citiloan and this phone call is being placed to collect a debt. We have not received your June mortgage payment. Have you sent it out in the mail yet?"

"No, we have not sent it. We can no longer afford this house and we're trying to work with your bank to sell it."

"I'm sorry, Mrs. Whiteside; did you say you sent the payment in?"

"No, ma'am. I said we're not sending it in."

"Your payment is late and therefore you must include the late payment. Will you be putting the payment in the mail tomorrow?"

"Alicia, I've told you I'm not making the payment." Barbara was exasperated.

"You realize that if we don't receive your payment soon, we will start foreclosure proceedings and that you could lose your house and jeopardize your credit? Can we expect your payment this week, Mrs. Whiteside?"

Barbara almost screamed into the phone, "Haven't you heard a word I've said? We are not making our payments this month or next. We've stopped paying you."

Alicia read the next line from her prepared text. "We need to receive your payment by next Friday. Will you be putting your check in the mail by tomorrow?"

Barbara hung up the phone. This is something out of the Twilight Zone, she thought.

Later that night, Stan arrived home to have dinner with Barbara. The phone rang and this time he answered it. "Hello?"

"Yes, may I speak to either Barbara or Stan Whiteside?"

"This is Stan Whiteside."

"This is Andrew from Citiloan. This call is to collect a debt. We have not received your June payment yet. Will you be putting it in the mail tomorrow?"

"No, I'm not putting a payment in the mail tomorrow. We've notified your bank we want to do a short sale. Someone from your office already called today. My wife explained we're not sending in our payment."

"If you don't have your payment to us by Friday, it will affect your credit."

"We're not sending in this month's payment—didn't you hear me?"

"If you don't send in your payment, Citiloan could start foreclosure proceedings. Can I expect the payment by Friday?"

"No!" Stan slammed the phone down.

Barbara said to him, "See what I'm saying? You can't get through to them. It's like they're in a zombie trance and can only repeat the same line. 'Will you be sending your check in tomorrow?'"

"I imagine that Citiloan has a group of people making call after call and who have very little to say other than 'Send us your money.' What a colossal waste of time."

Barbara came home from work and found her message machine blinking with seven messages. She hit the play button. Call one, hang-up. Call two, hang-up. All seven were hang-ups. That's weird, she thought. She called Stan at her mom's. "Were you trying to reach me at home today?"

"No, I wasn't, why?"

"When I got home from work we had seven messages and they were all hang-ups."

Just as she hung up with Stan, the phone rang. Barbara answered, "Hello?"

The person on the other line asked, "Can I speak to Barbara or Stan Whiteside?"

"This is Barbara speaking."

"Mrs. Whiteside, this is John from Citiloan. I'm calling to collect a debt. We have not received your March mortgage payment yet. Have you made this payment to us?"

Barbara rolled her eyes. "Listen, John, we told the last two people who called yesterday we're not making any more payments. You calling and harassing us won't change that."

"But can we expect your payment by this Friday?"

Barbara hung up on him. She shook her head. This was not going to be easy. Every day for the next three weeks, Barbara came home to multiple hang-up calls on the answering machine. She received at least three calls a day from Citiloan, and each time the representative would start going through the debt collection speech. Eventually, Barbara quit answering as she recognized the number on caller ID. It got to the point where they turned off the phone altogether.

Within a few weeks, the house repairs had been completed and Stan moved back in. He was still not out of the woods medically, since he had been exposed to the mold for such an extended period of time, and his recovery would take a long time.

Each week, Barbara's work schedule was cut further. She was down to just over twenty hours the last two weeks, and even though she tried to make it up by volunteering for the worst shifts, she couldn't make up the money she had lost. She requested a meeting with her manager, but that went nowhere. It was obvious he didn't care what was happening in her personal life, or if he did, she was not his top priority.

Barbara sat with Stan in the kitchen. "I don't know what to do next, Stan. I've placed my résumé online and have gotten no requests for interviews. I've inquired around town at other grocery chains, but no one is hiring." Coming home didn't help, as she couldn't help but think that her home was the source of all their problems.

"Maybe we should burn the house to the ground and collect the insurance," she said with a smirk. "Speaking of insurance, have you heard anything from America Insurance regarding our mold claim? We can't expect Preston to repair our house for free."

"I haven't heard or seen anything, Barb. We should call them tomorrow to check on the claim."

At that moment, the phone started ringing.

Barbara and Stan had done what the loan agent had told them and withheld her March and April house payments. Their mailbox was filled daily with threatening letters and urgent messages. The number of phone calls they received from Citiloan per day had increased to six.

Why can't somebody at Citiloan mark down in their computers that the Whitesides are trying to do a short sale and quit bothering us? Barbara wondered.

She finally managed to talk to someone who knew what they were doing at Citiloan. "Mrs. Whiteside, I need you to send the following items to me: a financial statement, W-2s for both you and your husband for the last two years, and your last two months' bank statements. You need to write a hardship letter explaining why you are behind on your mortgage."

This is like in grammar school, Barbara thought, when you did something wrong and the teacher made you write an essay detailing your indiscretion, and why you were sorry for doing it. "All right, I'll get those things together and send them off to the bank tomorrow."

"It will take at least two weeks before you can expect an answer."

Stan came through the front door, looking grim-faced. Barbara saw him walk into the house and go directly to the refrigerator and grab a beer. He slipped into a seat by the breakfast bar and let out a big sigh.

She walked over and put her hand on his shoulder. "Is everything all right?"

He looked up and said stoically, "I just got the mail. Our insurance company is denying the claim for our repairs. It appears we had a mold exclusion clause in our policy."

Barbara slowly sank down on the bar stool next to him. "Wasn't that the insurance firm that was recommended by Janet Waller?" She buried her face in her hands and lamented, "We can barely make ends meet now. How will we pay Preston Carson?"

Stan slowly sipped his beer. "We have to get out from under this place. We should have a garage sale soon. We won't have room for all this furniture when we move."

"You're right. I hadn't really thought about moving. We can't afford another big house and we've got a lot of stuff here. It's hard to believe we had such high hopes and dreams for our lives when we bought this house. Now we're losing everything."

The next morning Stan got up and made his way to the kitchen to make a pot of coffee. He shuffled out the front door and searched for the newspaper that had been tossed toward his porch, but ended up in the magnolia tree by the walk. He came back inside, poured a steaming cup of coffee, added in Mocha Mix, and sat down at the breakfast bar. He opened the paper to the big, bold headline, "Whitney Homes' Money Woes Continue; Bank Files for Foreclosure."

He had read the article and was skimming through the balance of the paper when Barbara came into the kitchen. She went over to the coffee pot and poured herself a cup. Stan held up the front page. "Look what's happening with Whitney Homes."

She looked at the headline and put her hand to her mouth. "I thought Whitney Homes was the strongest homebuilder around."

"It looks like they have so much debt, there's no way of getting out from under it. They may have to file for bankruptcy and the courts may liquidate the whole company."

"So they could liquidate the company just like that?"

"It hasn't come to liquidation yet but the news isn't good. Taylor owes a lot of people a lot of money. I wonder if he's skipped town," Stan said. "I wouldn't want to be in his shoes."

TWENTY-NINE

Taylor sat at the head of the conference table, a cup of coffee to his left and the morning edition of the *Sacramento Bee* in front of him. The headline seemed to mock him. The newspaper article quoted several subcontractors who had initially filed liens and now had filed lawsuits against Whitney for non-payment of bills, and who had no trouble venting their anger to the *Bee*. In addition, there were quotes from angry homeowners who had no qualms about venting their feelings to the paper. A picture of Taylor accompanied the article, the same picture the *Bee* always used when writing an article about Whitney Homes. Taylor hadn't read the article and had no intention of ever doing so. He was only here because Cooper Harding, Whitney's new president since Paul Bayless resigned, demanded he show up. Cooper was a slender man, well-dressed, looking very corporate with his well-groomed silver hair and charcoal-gray suit.

Also in the conference room with Cooper was Blake Wilson, Whitney Homes' corporate counsel. Blake, a former basketball star at Pepperdine, kept himself trim and fit, even though he was approaching fifty. His receding hairline and wire-rimmed glasses gave him the distinguished look of a business professional.

Taylor looked around the room. I'd rather be having a root canal than be here, he thought. Look at all these worthless empty suits.

He broke the silence. "Well, what's the crisis for today? Did Bank of the Northwest wake up out of their stupor and meet our demands?"

Cooper looked at Taylor and said, "No, Taylor, Bank of the Northwest has not met your demands. As a matter of fact, as of yesterday they have shut off funding. National Pacific stopped funding two days ago. They also filed a notice of foreclosure. The only bank still giving us money is Security National, and we don't know how long that will last. We set up a meeting today with Royal Bank of Toronto to see if they'll work with us." He pulled out a list from his briefcase and held it up. "We are defending two hundred separate lawsuits from subcontractors demanding payment, and our payables are reaching two hundred million dollars. We can no longer operate like this. I wanted Blake here to start discussing options so we can figure out what to do next."

Taylor exploded, "What is wrong with you wussies? These banks need to be slapped across the face with a sledgehammer. You let them jerk us around. Why haven't we sued Bank of the Northwest yet, those blood-suckers? They need to start releasing funds to us and do it now."

Blake's face turned scarlet. He stood up, all six feet five inches of his physique towering over the table, took his glasses off, squinted at Taylor, and spoke through clenched teeth. "Taylor, don't ever address me in that manner. We have been busting our tails trying to keep this company afloat while you've been out gallivanting and spending company money like a junkie at a shooting gallery." He stood up and turned his back to Taylor. "Instead of paying your subs, you've been out buying lots in Maui and chasing golf balls in Florida. Whitney Homes has very few arrows left in their quiver. We all have discussed this at length, and because you were absent, you weren't in on the conversation. It is our unanimous opinion that the only reasonable option left to Whitney is to file for bankruptcy protection."

Taylor was indignant. "That's the best you can come up with, bankruptcy? Any mental midget can file bankruptcy and throw in the towel. I'm not ready to do that. I've been through this before, but this is your first rodeo."

Blake turned around. "It's time to start thinking about whether the banks will come after you personally for spending their money on things other than the projects they lent money on."

Taylor stood and screamed, "These banks have no choice but to work with me and do as I say. They are in too deep with me. They're afraid of bad press and non-performing loans. They'll get both if they squeeze me too hard."

Cooper jumped into the fray. "What's your suggestion, Taylor? We go back to Bank of the Northwest and say, 'Hey, guys, we were just kidding the last time around. Lend us more money and we swear we'll spend the money where it's supposed to be spent. We'll pay our subs this time around, we promise.' They'd call their security and throw us out of their offices." He picked up his briefcase and threw some documents inside. "Blake is right. You'd better hope they don't start digging through our books, because there have been funds shifted to places they shouldn't have been."

He pointed at Taylor. "You know that Bank of the Northwest did not subpoena our checking accounts for exercise. They're trying to figure out where their money went, and why it didn't go to the projects they lent it for."

Blake shuffled the papers around in front of him. "Taylor, this is your call. But as your counsel, and from all of us who are close to this situation and have looked at this company from all angles to try and figure out a way to salvage it, we feel that bankruptcy is your only choice. If we thought there was another way, we would suggest it. Also, I want you to be aware that if you do file bankruptcy, this company will no longer be able to withdraw funds for your personal use." He put his hands on the conference table and leaned forward. "There will be a receiver put in place to oversee the operations, and you will be put on a salary that is commensurate with your position. And you aren't going to be able to call Cooper here and have him send $500,000 to your personal checking account."

Taylor's face was twisted. "Whose name is on this building? Does it say Blake Homes? Does it say Cooper Homes? No, it says Whitney

Homes, and in case you forgot, I'm Taylor Whitney. I call the shots around here, not you two. I'll decide if I can make it through this downturn or not, and nobody here will tell me how much I can take out of my own business. However, I'll give you the benefit of the doubt and think about your suggestions."

Blake got up and gathered his things together. "I think you'd better think about it, Taylor, because if you don't, I can guarantee this place will be liquidated in less than six months. We've done the best we could. The fate of this company lies in your hands. Call me when the bankers arrive."

Cooper followed him.

Taylor sat there fuming. These guys are idiots, he thought. All the money I pay them and this is the best they can come up with? There is no way I'm going to let a pinheaded bean counter tell me what to do with my money.

He went to the window and stared at his Bentley that was parked in a handicapped space. These ignorant fools don't have my experience, nor are they as smart. I'll be vindicated, just wait and see. I'll get with Janet and step up our endeavors. We'll close another forty homes in the next few months.

An hour later, Taylor was back in the conference room with Cooper and Blake. The representatives present from the bank were James Marshall, chief credit officer, and Mark Parker, attorney for the bank. They sat down across from each other and Taylor was in his usual position at the head of the conference table. After a few minutes of small talk, James Marshall spoke to the group.

"We are all aware what a tough market you homebuilders are going through. We would like to talk about things we might do to prevent an absolute meltdown of your company and the deterioration of the assets that are securing our loans. We have seven loans with you." He looked down at a sheet of paper that he had pulled out of his briefcase. "You have an outstanding balance of one hundred forty-five million dollars on those loans. You are scheduled to make payments of eight million dollars a month, starting next month. Will you be able to keep the loans current?"

Steve Cooper spoke first. "We currently have about four million in the bank and anticipate another four to five million after sales close this month. We have been liquidating any non-essential equipment and are trying to unload projects that we haven't started. I can't say as we sit here today that we will have eight million dollars within the next thirty days, but we should be close."

Marshall then asked, "How about the month after that, and then the following month? Will you be able to service eight million a month until the debt is retired?"

"It depends on how many houses we sell and close," Cooper answered. "The way things stand, there is no way for us to service that debt. We are going to need some help from you."

Marshall asked him, "What specifically do you have in mind when you say you need some help? What kind of help can the bank give you?"

Taylor leaned back in his chair and said, "I'll tell you what the bank can do. Give us an unsecured line of credit for seventy-five million and give us a year to get it back to you. Give us relief of interest payments for eight months and reduce the amount of your payoff demands as each of our houses close. That will keep us afloat and will save you from losing your shirts if you have to foreclose on these subdivisions."

The bankers looked at each other and then looked back at Taylor. A long silence hung over the table before Marshall spoke. "Sir, even if we wanted to do something like that, it would be against the law. We can't just suspend your interest payments with the flick of a pen. If you don't keep the loan current, we have to file a notice of default and then set aside reserves to write down a potential loss. We can't just arbitrarily forgive your debt. Given the economic climate for homebuilders and your depressed financial condition, we couldn't give you an unsecured line of credit for any amount. Can't you liquidate a couple of your large land holdings?"

Taylor leaned forward. "I've sold as much vacant land as I'm going to sell. I'm not going to give my land away just to appease you people.

You need to be more creative and help us out of this jam. Just sitting there and telling me I need to pay you off is not helpful."

Mark Parker, the bank's attorney, looked directly at Taylor and said sternly, "Mr. Whitney, the bank is all for working with their borrowers on a 'reasonable' level to help alleviate their problems." He put his hands up and held his fingers like quotation marks. "We're not asking you to appease us." He swept his arm around the table. "We're saying you owe the bank over a hundred and forty-five million dollars and we want a reasonable effort from Whitney Homes to reduce that debt. Asking the bank to throw more money at you is not reasonable. We don't care how you accomplish paying us off, just that you do."

Taylor stared down at the business cards in front of him. "Look, Mr. Parker, whether the bank likes it or not they are now partners with Whitney Homes. We owe too much money for you to let us fail. Failure would only send your shareholders searching for someone's head to roll and all of you boys in this room will be the first casualties. You better put your minds together and come up with new ideas."

"I hate to pop your bubble," said Mark, "but the bank is not your partner and we have plenty of remedies at our disposal to protect our assets. Sure, we are not developers or homebuilders, and the last thing we want to do is to take over your projects. But if you don't reduce your debt to us, we will take the appropriate steps to save our assets. I agree with Mr. Wilson. Given your financial condition, getting more money from the bank is not an option, nor is forgiveness of interest. If you think we will sit on our hands and do nothing, you are obviously mistaken."

Taylor stood. "Well, I guess, then, this meeting is over. Gentlemen, thanks for coming. I'll give your suggestions some thought."

Steve Cooper meekly shook their hands. "We understand the severity of the situation." He lowered his voice. "I will approach Taylor about unloading the land holdings. We've already downsized on personnel and equipment."

Mark Parker shook Steve's hand. "Thanks for your time. I hope you can pull it off."

THIRTY

Janet sat stiffly in her chair at Ruth's Chris Steak House. Taylor seemed his usual self. After examining the wine list, he looked up. "How about a '98 Silver Oak? That's a great year."

"Silver Oak sounds yummy." Overall, Taylor seemed in a good mood. She didn't understand how he could take the pounding he'd been taking in the press and still function. Recently, one of Taylor's subcontractors threatened to physically assault him in the parking lot of his office for not paying a bill. Taylor told Janet he'd calmed the man down by assuring him there would be a check for him at his office in the morning. After the sub left Taylor laughed at him, called him a chump, and swore he'd never pay him a dime.

While they were enjoying a steak dinner Janet said, "I received three letters from the California Department of Real Estate today. Worldwide Funding has filed three complaints against me to revoke my real estate license. They're opening up an investigation, demanding I turn over my Worldwide Funding files from 2003, 2004, and 2005."

"What do you think they're looking for?"

"Since the loans in question were three of the ones I placed for you personally, they're probably trying to find a connection between us."

"Don't worry, Janet. The government is great at investigating things but better at doing nothing about them. If anything comes of those loans, I'll vouch for you. Is there anyone at your office who could be blamed?"

That got her to thinking. Who in her office could she make be the patsy for this complaint? The perfect candidate was Becky Brown, a young loan officer who had been with Janet for nine months. She was a sweet woman, about thirty-two, with two young children at home. She worked hard and was dependable, but she was prone to make small mistakes and Janet inevitably caught them. Janet had made Becky cry on many occasions, and knew she'd be the perfect person to lay the blame on. "I believe I do have someone who could take the heat off me."

Taylor leaned closer to her. "Let's step up our program, Janet. I want to move standing inventory and prop up sales prices. I'll send you more new sales in the next few weeks, but they need to close quickly." He winked. "There will be plenty of money for all of us."

"Including your mystery partners?" Janet asked sarcastically.

"If I'm feeling generous, they might get some cash." Taylor slid his hand into his pocket and pulled out a small white-velvet box. "I saw this and knew you should have it." He handed the box to Janet.

Janet couldn't hide her excitement as she opened the box slowly. She put her hand to her heart. "Oh my god, Taylor, it's beautiful." She held up a thin gold chain with a blue sapphire the size of a dime, surrounded by diamonds. She turned it to the light and watched it shimmer. "I...I can't believe this—it's so exquisite." She was beaming as she planted a long kiss on Taylor's lips. "Thank you so much. I'll never take it off. What is the occasion?"

Taylor looked pleased with himself. "Hey, it's the middle of 2006. I don't need an occasion. I knew you would like it."

Janet rubbed the stone as it hung from her neck. "Like it—I love it!"

The next morning when Janet arrived at her office, she went through the mail and came across five more envelopes from the California Department of Real Estate. She recognized the logo on the envelopes and didn't need to open them to know what the letters inside said. She opened them anyway, and after glancing at the addresses on each complaint, she recognized a pattern.

The department wanted everything involved with the five files mentioned in the letters she held in her hand. She hadn't heard anything back on the first three complaints, so she guessed that was good.

She lifted up the land phone and dialed the code to listen to her voicemail messages. The third one made her sit straight up. "Ms. Waller, this is Bill Lawrence with the State of California Department of Real Estate. We've received the files you sent to us regarding the complaint from Worldwide Funding. There appears to be intentional tampering with documents connected to these files. We would like to meet with you here at our office no later than ten days from when you receive this message. If you feel you need to have counsel present, feel free to do so. I look forward to hearing from you and setting up a time to meet. Thank you." He then left a phone number for her to call to set up the meeting.

Damn, she thought. With her heart pounding, she spun through her Rolodex and looked up the phone number of her attorney. She dialed a number and waited to be connected.

"Hello? This is Carl O'Conner."

"Carl, it's Janet Waller. Hey, I need to meet with you. It's pretty important."

"How about two o'clock in my office tomorrow?"

"Sounds good to me, Carl. I'll be there."

She hung up and stared at the letters on her desk. The more she thought about it, the more angry she became. "After all the deals I've given Worldwide, they turn on me because of a few bad loans?"

The next afternoon, Janet sat in Carl O'Conner's office. Carl was an attorney with McCormick, Bressner, and Williams, one of the most prestigious law firms in Sacramento. A small man with a rumpled look, he looked more like a funeral parlor director than a highly respected lawyer. Carl's office stood in the northeast corner of the building, and he had a scenic view of Old Town Sacramento to the east and the Sacramento River to the north. Janet looked down out of the window at a couple of fishermen in a small skiff who were trolling for salmon in the river below her.

Carl looked up from the files he'd been studying. "Did you make the changes that this complaint asserts, or do you know who did?"

Janet nervously cleared her throat. "I don't remember making any changes to the documents, but there obviously have been changes made. There are ten other people in my office and any one of them could have done this."

"What would be the motivation for anyone in your office to change the documents?"

"They're jealous, or they dislike me, or they are being bribed, of course. Everyone knows that if I, or anyone else for that matter, were caught tampering with loan documents, there would be serious consequences. One might even lose their license."

"Yes, one might even end up in jail."

Janet gasped. "Jail? Why would the government send someone to jail over this silly complaint? No one was hurt, and it was probably an innocent mistake."

Carl put his hands together and leaned forward, his brows furrowed. "Let me explain something to you, Janet. These charges are not to be taken lightly. Whether or not you think the charges are 'silly' or 'innocent' is irrelevant. The government takes it serious when people play around with a bank's money. Did you change any documents in your loan files?"

"I'm not sure I did, but the only reason I would have done that is if I saw a glaring error, and rather than send the file back to processing to correct the error, I did it myself."

"That will not be acceptable to the government." Carl lifted up a file and thumbed through it. "As far as you are concerned, you do not know how any of these changes came about. You just worked up the file, sent it to the lender, and closed the loan. These government investigators will try to press you to admit you made the changes. Keep your head and don't let them anger you. They have to prove that you authorized these changes or you had a hand in the changes." He placed the file on his desk. "Once I get a time and a date, I'll call you and go with you. If you can find any evidence that either the appraiser or someone in your office tampered with these documents, let me know immediately. Don't go to the Department of Real Estate or anyone else. You call me."

Janet was rattled. "Just out of curiosity, if the government did find something, how would you make this go away?"

"It doesn't go away, Janet. If there was any involvement on your part in this tampering, I would suggest you come clean. Tell everything you know about the operation and turn state's evidence on whomever is behind this, and then hope you'll get leniency."

"Okay, Carl, you let me know as soon as you get a date firmed up." Carl escorted her through the office and to the elevator. "I'm sorry if I scared you, Janet, but we have to be very careful how we deal with the government and these files." Just then, the elevator arrived and opened. "I'll see you in a day or so."

Janet waved at Carl as the elevator door shut. As she walked out of the building to the parking garage, heading toward her car, Janet's mind was racing in a thousand different directions. There is no way I'm going to end up in jail! she told herself. I'd sell my mother out before I'd go to jail.

Before she had gotten back to her office, Janet's phone rang. "Hello?"

Carl's voice came on. "The Department of Real Estate is demanding we be at their office Monday morning at ten a.m. I want you to spend the weekend going through your files and getting familiar with them again."

"That's just great."

Janet sat with Carl in the lobby of the offices of the California Department of Real Estate, rubbing her hands nervously and eying the people who were coming and going. A door burst open and Bill Lawrence exited and introduced himself. He led them to a conference room on the second floor. It was similar to every government office in California: dull, plain, and nondescript. Janet felt as if every person in the building was watching her.

Once they settled into their chairs, Bill laid out a stack of files and spoke to Janet. "As you are aware, we are investigating a complaint by Worldwide Funding regarding some loans that originated out of the Sunset Mortgage offices. Ms. Waller, are you the sole owner of Sunset Mortgage?"

"Yes, I am."

"Have you always been the owner?"

"No, I've been the owner of Sunset Mortgage since 2001."

"When was the company started?"

"It started it in 1996, here in Sacramento."

"Do you have any partners or do you own one hundred percent of it?"

"I own one hundred percent; I don't have any partners."

Bill pulled two files from the stack and handed them to Janet. "Ms. Waller, would you look at this file I'm holding and compare it to this file right here? Tell me if you see any discrepancies."

Janet took the two files and slowly thumbed through them. "I see that there have been changes made. The appraisals have different values and the bank accounts have different amounts in them."

"Do you recognize these loan files? Do you know who in your office was working on these files?"

"Yes, I recognize the files. These were my files but one of my assistants, Becky Brown, helped me with them."

"Do you think Ms. Brown would have changed the files?"

"I'm not saying she did anything; I'm just saying she helped me with some of my loans. I have no idea if she was the person who changed the documents."

"Is there anyone other than yourself or Ms. Brown who would have had access to these files prior to your sending them to Worldwide Funding?"

"I don't think there was anyone else, but my office is not security-proof. I have an assistant named Carol, but she only files and answers phones. I've never had any issues with stolen or forged documents before."

"So, to the best of your knowledge you don't know who might have changed the documents?"

Janet stared at Bill, stone-faced. "I have no idea who could have done this."

Bill picked up another set of files and handed them to her. He asked, "Would you mind going through these files and let me know if you see any discrepancies?"

Janet looked through the files slowly and then handed them to Carl to review. "It appears that these files have also been changed."

"Do you recognize these files?"

"Yes, I do. I worked on those files and then sent them to Worldwide for their approval."

"I have seven other files I'd like you to go through. Take your time."

Janet's hands shook under Bill's watchful eye. After Janet and Carl had gone through every file, she handed them back. Bill asked her, "Did you recognize those files?"

"Yes, I did."

"Were they all files that were generated out of your office?"

"Yes, they were."

"And you worked on them personally?"

"Yes, I did."

"Now, Ms. Waller, when you were working on these loans, didn't it seem strange that many of these houses were sixty to seventy thousand dollars higher in price than similar houses in the immediate neighborhood?"

"I really didn't pay that much attention to the sales price. That was a very busy time and I was handling a lot of loans at the time."

"I understand you might have been busy. Didn't it seem odd that these loans were made against either brand-new or recently finished Whitney Homes?"

"I don't know. I just missed it, I guess." Janet shifted anxiously in her chair.

"Didn't anything in these files arouse your suspicions? I mean, all of these loans are stated-income, one hundred percent financed loans. If you look at some of the documentation you'd have to be suspicious about the borrowers, wouldn't you?"

"Not really. They were just another loan to me."

"Do you still keep in contact with these particular buyers?"

"No, I haven't been in contact with them since their houses closed."

"Well, you're in good company as Worldwide hasn't been in contact with them, either. All of your borrowers disappeared right after their loans were closed and never made a payment. How did you come to get these people as clients?"

"I don't remember how they came to me. They may have come from the sales people at Whitney or somewhere else. I just don't remember."

Bill kept taking notes. Carl was busy doing the same. "You know, Ms. Waller, I'm sorry to say that your denials are somewhat unbelievable. We are in possession of fifteen files that were generated by you. Each of these fifteen borrowers was buying brand-new Whitney Homes, which were way overpriced. Once the loans closed, the buyers disappeared. You're saying that you knew nothing about this?"

Janet's face turned scarlet. "Are you saying that I'm the one who is behind this?" Her voice was starting to rise. "Are you accusing me of tampering with these loan files?"

Carl put his hand on hers. "Relax, Janet. He's merely trying to get some answers from you."

She turned to Carl and snarled, "He's accusing me." She flipped a file back at Bill. "Look here, I pay my taxes and you work for me. I came down here voluntarily and now I have to listen to you accuse me of bank fraud. Why don't you do a little investigating yourself? Why don't you talk to that dumb appraiser, Stephanie? Her handwriting is all over these files."

Carl tugged her arm. "Janet, calm down."

She glared at him. "Shut up, Carl. I know a frame job when I see one."

Bill looked at Janet and said calmly, "I'm not accusing you of any-thing, Ms. Waller. All I'm pointing out is there were clear signs that something is amiss here and you say you never noticed anything wrong. You were the person who was directly involved in making these loans. You have the most intimate knowledge about them."

Janet scowled at him. "I've answered all the questions you've asked. If you're not going to charge me with anything, I'd like to go now."

Bill stared at her for a second. Finally, he said, "Yes, I think that will be all for now, Ms. Waller. Please be aware that this is an ongoing investigation, and if we determine that you had a role in this scheme—any role—your license will be suspended or revoked. Additionally, Worldwide may be looking to press civil action."

Janet stood up and hissed at him, "Well, good luck. Try looking at someone other than me. You might be able to justify your salary, but I doubt it." With that, she turned and headed for the door.

Carl put his notepad in his briefcase and shook Bill's hand. "I'm sorry for my client's behavior. She sometimes gets a little emotional."

Bill stood up and walked him out of the conference room. "Yeah, I can see that. Can you find your way outside?"

"Yes, I can. Thanks for your time."

THIRTY-ONE

The TV in the corner of the bar was showing a Brazil versus Venezuela soccer match for a chance to advance to the World Cup. Smoke hung around the room from the half dozen cigarettes either hanging from patrons' mouths or burning in a dirty ashtray on the well-used wooden bar. The concrete floor was sprinkled with sawdust. Lights from six neon beer logos, along with a few dirty stained glass fixtures, barely lit the place. Five men lined the bar speaking to each other in Spanish as they watched the game. A heavyset woman in a colorful apron leaned against the bar, listening to their conversations.

José sat in the corner booth with faded, torn-leather seats, his head facing the door. Stephanie and Matt sat across from him, each nursing a Corona. A few heads had turned when they walked into the bar—two gringos who obviously didn't belong—but when José motioned them to his table, they turned back to the TV.

"I really appreciate you meeting us," Stephanie said. "The information you gave me was very helpful. But I need a little more to push this case forward and José, you are the key." She took a sip of her beer and waited for a response.

José took a drag of his cigarette and looked first at Matt, then Stephanie. "Like I said to you on the phone, this information is not free. You brought the money with you?"

Stephanie nodded and pulled her purse up to the table.

"Good, because this is very dangerous. You are looking for buyers who disappeared after they buy the houses. I only know that two are dead. Shot in the head, then left in a ditch in West Sacramento. This is our last meeting, last."

"Who were they and do the police have any leads?" asked Matt.

"Their names were Juan Gonzales and Manuel Garcia, and the police have nothing. They think it was a drug deal gone bad."

"They both bought a Whitney Home. I saw their files," Stephanie said.

"I met Mr. Garcia," Matt said. "He bought the house across the street from my parents. My mom saw something about it in the paper and told me. At the time, I asked myself if this could be connected, but I dismissed it." He took a long sip of his beer. Someone had put a quarter in the jukebox, and a Mexican singer belted out a sad ballad.

"Any idea who might have killed them, José? Is this related to Taylor and his partners at the apartment?" Stephanie asked.

José slowly scanned the bar, never taking his eyes off the front door for any long length of time. A couple of the men at the bar rocked back and forth to the sway of the music. He almost squinted at Matt. "It might be a, how do you say, coincidence. If they did not do as they were told to and came back, this might be the reason they were killed. I have names of two buyers that are hiding in Southern California. You can talk to them. I told them about you and they are expecting your call." He crushed out his cigarette. "Of course, they will want money, too."

"I'll get them some money. José, you mentioned something about Taylor's house in your message. What were you referring to?" Stephanie asked.

José signaled the bartender to send another round. "You are trying to find a way into Taylor's house, no? I have a way." He pulled a Titan house key out of his pocket and set it on the table, along with a slip of paper with numbers written on it.

Matt looked at the items, then at José. "What are those?"

José drew another cigarette from his pocket and fumbled for his lighter. He lit the cigarette, took a drag, and spoke through smoky breath. "It's the key and alarm code to Taylor's home." Noting the quizzical looks on their faces, he continued, "Taylor's maid lives in the apartment complex where I am the manager. I made a copy of her key. Of course, she is expecting payment for this, and do not take or touch anything valuable."

Matt could barely contain his excitement. "Don't worry, we only want to look for some files, or check his computer. We won't touch anything and we'll be in and out quick. Did she say which was the best way in?"

"Go through the gate on the left side of the house when you look at the front. The neighbor to the right has a dog. The lots are big, so if you are careful, it will not hear you." José thanked the bartender, who had brought him another drink. "Use the back door. When you are in you will see a keypad to the alarm on the wall at the left. Taylor's office is close by the kitchen. Here," he took a piece of paper from his pocket, unfolded it, and laid it on the table. "This is a rough drawing of the inside of the house."

Matt studied the drawing for a second. "I'll say it's rough." He pointed to a spot on the drawing. "This is the back door and this is the kitchen, right? Where is the office?"

José turned the drawing around, then pointed. "Here, next to the kitchen. Here is the alarm pad on this wall." He pushed the drawing back to Matt.

Stephanie gathered the key, the house code, and the phone numbers of the other buyers and stuck them in her purse. She handed José an envelope. "I can't thank you enough for all your help. We don't want to see anyone else hurt; we won't bother you again."

José picked up the envelope and cautiously stuck it in his jacket. He nodded at them and indicated it was time to leave. "Be very careful, my friends. These people are not nice, as you can see."

They thanked him and left the bar, hopped in Matt's car, and raced away. They drove in silence for about a mile before Stephanie spoke. "Oh my, my heart is just beginning to slow down. Is anybody following us?"

"I don't think so." Matt looked into the rearview mirror again. "Should we go there tonight, get this over with? I could be in and out of there in ten minutes."

Stephanie rubbed her hands together. "I don't know, Matt, this is making me nervous. Do we know if Taylor is even in town, and how are we going to get past the guard shack?"

Matt turned the car onto the freeway and sped up. "I'll call Preston and tell him we might stop by and see him. When we get to the gate, the guard can check with him to let us through. Once we get into the subdivision, we can stop by Preston's, then go into the house around midnight. Why don't you call Janet's assistant. Didn't you say Janet and Taylor would be in Hawaii until the end of May?"

Stephanie rummaged through her purse for her cell phone. "Yeah, I'm sure that's what she said."

THIRTY-TWO

Winchester Country Club was quiet for a Saturday afternoon. Taylor and Guy had the course to themselves for most of their round. Lining up a putt on the eighteenth hole, Taylor stroked the ball and watched in dismay as it scooted five feet past the hole. He tossed his putter in disgust. "Damn it! I make that putt, I win. Guy, you are so lucky."

Leaning on his putter a foot away, Guy laughed. "Taylor, I almost feel bad taking your money again. But not really." Guy looked over at Taylor and sensed something other than the golf match was bothering him. "Taylor, what's wrong? You look like you just met with the wife's attorney." Then he remembered the Kentucky Derby had run earlier in the day. "Don't tell me you had a big bet on the derby."

Taylor looked down. "I had that stinkin' horse, Bluegrass Cat, to win and he came in second. Barbaro beat him. I just can't catch a break."

"How much money did you have on the race?"

"Two hundred and fifty thousand."

Guy whistled softly. "Taylor, that is insane."

"Guy, I told you, I do it all the time. This just wasn't my day to win."

"How can you get your hands on money like that with the problems you're having?"

"I snag money from any account where I can find it. We get bank draws in almost every week." Taylor leaned down and yanked up his putter.

"Taylor, that is illegal. You can't continue to spend money like you used to. Things have changed and you have to change, too."

"Guy, you worry too much. I know what I'm doing. I tell the banks to go pound sand. All the money in Whitney's accounts is my money." He walked over to their golf cart and stuffed his putter in his bag. "As for all the rest of the people I owe money to, I don't care about them. Their money problems are not mine."

Guy slid into the driver's side of the cart. "Well, I can only say one thing. You've got a lot of balls doing what you're doing."

At around six-thirty, Taylor left Guy and the country club. He was driving to meet Janet when his cell phone went off. "Hello?"

"Hello, Taylor, it's Artie Tennelli. Sorry about your horse today; he almost won."

"Almost doesn't do much for me, does it?"

"No, it doesn't. I just wanted to make sure you don't forget to send the two hundred and fifty thousand dollars to me tomorrow. My clients don't like waiting for their money. Given your problems, they are nervous about you. They also are wondering where their money is for the last closings on our real estate deals. They know they've supplied you the buyers for your houses, but you haven't sent the money. That's not sitting well."

"Artie, tell them to relax. I'll get them their money. There have been some complications with my banks. They've been getting greedy lately."

"My clients don't care about your problems with your banks. They want their money."

"They'll get it, Artie—tell them to stop worrying. I want to lay a bet down on the Preakness coming up. I like that Barbaro nag."

"Hold on there. Let's take care of your last bet before we start making new ones. They don't want to chase you again like the last time. I'll be looking for your check on Tuesday. This time, don't be late."

Taylor hung up and shouted, "Don't you know who you're talking to, Artie? I'll pay you when I feel like it. I've been betting with you for over three years and haven't missed a bet yet. You'll get your money when I decide you will."

Taylor turned into Carver's parking lot and parked his Bentley. He strode up to the front door and went inside the restaurant, walking past the hostess and right into the bar. Janet sat by herself. He walked up to her, gave her a squeeze, and sat down.

"Hey, Janet, how's it going?"

"Good, how about you? How was your golf game?"

"Ah, it was all right. I'm torqued about the Kentucky Derby. The horse I bet on ended up coming in second." He adjusted the collar of his shirt. "The jockey wouldn't use his whip on the horse. He should have beat that horse harder and he would have won. I hope they send that nag to a glue factory tomorrow."

"Sorry to hear about that, darling. You'll win the next time. Have you had any inquiries from the Department of Real Estate? I haven't heard from them for two months and their silence worries me."

"I haven't heard a thing. Those people are low-rent government employees. This will all blow away."

"I wish I shared your optimism. I just can't believe the Department of Real Estate would toss in the towel so quickly." She sipped a martini. "Are you going back to Hawaii? I'd like to go with you and get out of this city for a few days."

"I want to get out of here, too. I can't run to the grocery without being hassled by subcontractors. I've even received death threats from subs, can you believe that? I ran into this homeowner's son named Matt at a stoplight in Roseville. He starts giving me grief about finishing some warranty issues at his parents' place. I told him to take a hike. Between Monica, my bookie, subcontractors, and these homeowners, I need a break."

"There are a lot of crazy people around here," Janet said.

"I'll book a flight and we can leave for Hawaii next week."

"Darling, that sounds like a plan," Janet said as she toyed with her necklace. She leaned down and rubbed his thigh, cooing seductively.

THIRTY-THREE

The quarter moon, high in the sky, gave off an eerie light across the mansions in the gated community. Soft landscape lights added illumination to the yards. Carriage lights, hanging off the front of the houses every thirty feet or so, increased the glow. Hundreds of crickets chirped in the bushes, and an occasional dog barked in the distance. Matt parked a block from Taylor's house in front of a vacant lot. Standing outside his car, he used Stephanie's penlight and felt around in the trunk for his briefcase with the portable disk drive. Finding it, he held it up to Stephanie and slid it into his pants pocket.

She took his hand. "Please be careful, and don't stay in there long. Carol said she thought they were in Hawaii till next week, but I don't know about her. Put your cell phone on vibrate, and I'll text you if anyone comes along."

Matt gave Stephanie a hug, looking at the soft silhouette of her face in the glow of the moon. "I don't mind admitting this, but I'm scared to death."

"That makes two of us. Don't forget to put on the gloves and cap. You can't leave any evidence."

Matt let her go. He felt his pocket for the disk and sprinted to the house, half bent over, dodging from oak tree to oak tree, until he hit the corner of Taylor's property. He rested briefly by a large plum tree to slow his breathing. He still had at least 30 yards of landscape to cover before he would be at the backyard gate. He looked around the yard and down the street. Seeing all was empty, he took a step out from under the tree. A flock of starlings exploded from the top, squawking and screeching at the top of their lungs, their wings making as much noise as their shrieks. Matt dove back behind the trunk, scrambling on all fours, his heart racing a mile a minute.

Just birds, he thought, trying to catch his breath and clutching his chest. He listened intently, waiting for his heart to stop racing. Hearing nothing other than the crickets who were soon joined by frogs croaking from a nearby pond, he crept along the bushes that surrounded the expansive lawn. Looking down at his watch, he saw that what seemed like an eternity had only taken five minutes.

He slipped through the gate and came around the house to the back door. There were a few lights on in the house, and he could see the keypad to the alarm on the wall. Matt took the key out of his pocket along with the alarm code, put it in the slot, and slowly turned the doorknob. Hearing the lock disengage, he pushed the door gently until it opened and the alarm beeped methodically. He ran over to the pad, hit the five numbers, and sighed deeply when the green light came on and the beeping stopped.

I'm not sure I'm ready for this line of work, he thought, rubbing his neck.

He put the key and code back into his pocket, pulled out the penlight, and headed to a room just off the kitchen.

He felt his phone vibrate. Stephanie had texted him, "u ok?"

He texted back, "im in."

Matt peeled the latex gloves off, rubbed his hands on his jeans to wipe off the sweat, then put them back on. The office was large, as was the desk where he sat. With the penlight he checked out the room. On one side was what looked like a huge stuffed moose's head protruding out of the wall. He scanned the opposite wall with the light and saw a blue marlin running its length. Hmm, he mused. I didn't know Taylor was a great white hunter. He wiped his forehead with a handkerchief and turned on the computer. The whirling of its engine as it started was the only sound coming from the house. Matt concentrated on the screen as it ran through its checklist to boot up. A loud *bong* followed by a second *bong* made Matt jump out of his seat. The *bongs* continued and he realized it was a grandfather clock outside in the hallway. "I've got to hurry; this is killin' me," he said aloud.

Sitting back down, he saw that the computer had successfully booted up and Matt set the mouse to the "My Documents" icon. Opening the folder revealed about two hundred files. He started searching for the right file, not sure what the right one would look like. He wondered, after looking for a minute or so, if he'd find what he was looking for. Then, right dead in the middle a file jumped out at him: "Taylor's escrows." Bingo! With the penlight Matt found the port for the removable disk, stuck it in, and began downloading all the files.

He was down to the last two files when his cell phone began to vibrate. Pulling it out, Stephanie had texted, "GET OUT NOW." Just then, he heard the unmistakable sound of a garage door opener's motor.

"Oh, crap!" He yanked the disk out of the computer, turned the computer off, and sprinted to the back door. He closed the door just as he heard a car door shutting and voices coming into the house. Matt ran around the side of the house, stopped at the gate, and listened, barely hearing anything over his heavy breathing. Hearing the garage door shut, he drew back the latch on the gate, squeezed out, then bolted across the yard, staying close to the bushes, back to where Stephanie and the car were parked. Stephanie saw him coming and started the car. He flung himself into the car and she sped off.

"Man, that was close," he said, gasping for air as he pulled off the gloves and cap. "I barely got out of there. I don't think anyone saw me."

"I was so scared, Matt. When that car turned into the driveway, I almost fainted. I was fumbling with my phone so much that I could barely hit the right key. Did you get the files?"

"Oh, yeah," he said, patting his pants pocket, his breathing finally slowing down. "I've got everything right here." He pointed up the road. "Let's take a lap around this place slowly. I don't want to raise any suspicion."

"Good idea."

THIRTY-FOUR

Taylor drove the Bentley onto the long, wide driveway leading to the house. He hit the garage opener and pulled up to the door. Nothing happened. "Damn it." He tried another button. Nothing. On the third try, the garage door started to open. He eased the car into the garage next to the Porsche and shut off the engine.

Janet stepped out. "You know, Taylor, you ought to drive that Porsche once in awhile. It's a great-looking ride. You look good in it."

"Yes, you might be right—I should drive it more often." He stuck his key into the lock and opened the door. Janet followed right behind. Taylor headed to the alarm pad and stopped. He stared at the pad a second. "That's weird. I thought I set the alarm before we left, but it's not armed. I must be losing it."

Janet came up behind him and gave him a hug. "You're not losing it, Sweetie; you just have a lot on your mind." She headed into the family room. "I need to get off my feet."

Picking up a *People* magazine from a stack on the coffee table, she curled up on the couch. Taylor sat down across from her in a recliner. He turned on the TV and started watching a *Simpsons* rerun. Janet looked up. "What time did you say our flight leaves Friday?"

"Eleven o'clock. The limo will be here at 10:30." Taylor turned his head. "Did you hear a car pull up?"

"No, I didn't hear any—"

Janet was interrupted by four loud explosions that shattered the front window in the living room behind them. Before either of them could move, four bullets had ripped through the house, tearing up walls and shattering furniture. Janet screamed. Taylor yelled, "Get down on the floor!" He dove down to the carpet and crawled behind a large bookcase. Janet crawled over and clung to him, shaking like a leaf. Two more shots rang out and a vase on the bookcase above them exploded into a thousand pieces, raining bits of glass down on them.

Janet screamed, "Taylor, who is that? Why are they shooting at us?"

"I have no idea," he shouted. "Stop screaming. Wait a minute." He held his hand out. "I hear a car pulling away." Wheels screeched and gravel flew as a vehicle peeled out of the driveway. Taylor crawled on his belly to the broken front window and carefully looked out into the darkness. He saw a car that looked like a BMW pass the house and head down the street. "I know that car!" The landscape lighting illuminated his yard sufficiently for him to see that no one else was around. Taylor scrambled for a phone, fumbled with it, and finally managed to dial 911.

"This is 911, do you have an emergency?"

Taylor's hands were shaking and he barely could hold onto the phone. He spoke excitedly. "This is Taylor Whitney. Someone just shot into my house."

"Is anyone hurt? Do you need an ambulance?"

"No, we don't need an ambulance, but send someone from the sheriff's office right away."

"All right, sir, I will send help over immediately." Taylor hung up, then dialed another number. A male voice came on the line. "Hello?"

"Ron, this is Taylor Whitney. Somebody just shot up my house. One of your deputies is supposed to be on their way here."

"Calm down, Taylor, you're talking too fast. Are you hurt?"

Taylor took a deep breath. "No, I'm okay. But I know who did this. I want you to arrest him."

"I can't just arrest a person without evidence. How do you know who did this?"

Taylor's voice was rising. "Look, Ron, you're the damned sheriff. I'm telling you I know who did this. His name is Matt Whiteside; I saw him driving away from here—I recognized his car. He's been harassing me for months and now he's shot at me in my own house. I saw him. I want him arrested." Taylor screamed into the phone, "If you don't have him arrested, I will fund your opponent's next campaign and put you out of office!"

"Slow down, Taylor. I'll come over there right now and you can explain what you know."

"All right, Ron, but get here immediately!" Taylor hung up.

"Taylor, I'm scared," Janet said, her voice quaking. "What if he comes back? Is he going to kill us?"

Taylor plopped on the couch, visibly shaken. "I don't think he wanted to kill me. That was done to scare me, but it only made me mad." He pounded his fist into the couch. "I know it was Matt who was behind this, and I'll make him pay. Nobody takes a shot at me without payback, nobody!"

THIRTY-FIVE

The headlights illuminated the empty street as Stephanie drove slowly through the neighborhood of moonlit houses set back behind expansive lawns and manicured landscaping. Stephanie kept a firm grip on the wheel as she navigated through the subdivision.

"You know, Steph, this was a little too close for comfort. I don't think I've been that scared before in my life, and after that episode, I think I'm retiring from the private investigator role."

"I'm with you. I thought Carol said Taylor and Janet were out of town until next week. Lesson one in burglary: Make sure the occupant is not anywhere near the home."

Stephanie stared straight ahead. "I need to have a heart-to-heart talk with Carol about the info she gave me on Janet's whereabouts."

"I bet the disk contains enough information to help Justin figure out what Taylor and Janet have been up to. I'll call him in a little while so we can get it to him, and he can take it from there."

Suddenly, four loud pops broke up the night, followed by two more. Stephanie jumped. "What was that?"

"That sounded like gunshots, really close by. We better get out of here."

"The fastest way is gonna take us right by Taylor's house," Stephanie said. "What should I do?"

"Get out of here now, the quickest way."

She gunned the engine and drove past Taylor's house. Rounding the corner and heading toward the entry gate, they noticed a dark pickup ahead of them with its lights off, waiting as the gate slowly opened. The guard was sticking his head out of the shack, looking at the truck. As the truck exited, Stephanie and Matt were on its tail, spinning tires and spraying gravel as they sped out of the subdivision.

"As soon as you can, let's take a side street and let that truck get away from us," Matt said, pointing down the road. "I don't know if they had anything to do with that shooting, but I don't want to find out."

Stephanie nodded and took a right at the next street. She steered the car over to the side of the road about a hundred yards from the intersection. "We probably should have gotten that truck's license number."

"You're right. Pull over and let's wait here a minute," Matt said. "Wait, do you hear that?" He rolled down his window. "Oh great, sirens! In a few minutes there'll be cops everywhere. Let's get out of here and head to your house. Drive carefully, so we don't attract attention. I've had enough excitement for one night. Go to your house—we'll drop you off and then I'll head to the city. I can give Greg the disk in the morning. He'll get it to Justin."

Stephanie accelerated and the car sped up. "I can't get out of this area soon enough. Do you think they're looking for us?"

"I don't know, but I don't want to hang around any longer."

THIRTY-SIX

Putting the phone down, Monica put her hand to her mouth. She had just spoken with her attorney, who broke the news about the shooting. She grabbed the phone, dialing it furiously. Her brother answered after the second ring. "Hello?"

"Jake," she spoke breathlessly. "Why didn't you tell me your buddy would go after Taylor so soon? He didn't get him. Your incompetent friend missed!"

"What time is it?" he asked groggily. "What are you talking about?"

"It's nine o'clock in the morning and I'm talking about what happened last night at Taylor's. Someone fired shots through the front window of the house, but they missed. He's still alive."

"No way! I haven't talked to my friend in a week. I didn't know he was going to move so fast. Where are you?"

"I'm still in Palm Springs." Monica walked over to the couch and sat down. Tuffy jumped on her lap. "Tell your pal he won't be paid until he completes the job. What a moron. How do you miss six times?"

"They shot at Taylor six times and missed?"

"That's what the papers are reporting."

"Let me call my friend and ask him what's going on. I had no idea he was moving this fast. What if it wasn't him? What if someone else shot at Taylor?"

"Honestly, I don't care who kills him as long as he's dead. Tell your friend to do it right this time and don't fail."

Monica put the phone down and stroked Tuffy. The cat responded by purring loudly. She thought, Wouldn't that be something if somebody else beats me to the punch? Oh, I wish I could get that lucky.

THIRTY-SEVEN

Barbara sat in the family room, waiting on hold for someone to help her at Citiloan Bank. It had been five months since she and Stan sent a mortgage payment, and their mailbox was stuffed daily with legal notices warning them of impending foreclosure. Every day, Barbara fielded at least seven phone calls from Citiloan's debt collection department demanding payment. The same script was read to her, asking when the bank could expect payment. Barbara had given up trying to explain their short sale attempt and just hung up.

Barbara had sent all the information the bank had requested for the short sale: listing agreement, comparable sales, financial statement, hardship letter, and eventually, their first offer. So far, she had been unable to get anyone to approve the sale.

After twenty-five minutes of waiting, a voice came on the line. "This is Shirley, how can I help you?"

"Shirley, this is Barbara Whiteside. I'm calling regarding loan number 02356."

"Okay, Barbara, I need to verify it is you I am speaking with. What's your social security number?" Barbara gave it along with her birth date and her mother's maiden name. Satisfied, Shirley asked, "What can I do for you, Mrs. Whiteside?"

"I've been trying to sell my house with a short sale and have been unable to get a hold of anybody who can help. I've sent everything that was requested of me, but when I've called to confirm the information was received, no one at your office can find what I've sent."

"I have to put you on hold for a second." After a thirty-second pause, Shirley came back on the line. "Mrs. Whiteside, I don't see that we have received anything from you. When did you send it?"

"I sent everything but the purchase contract a month ago. I sent the purchase contract to you two weeks ago." Barbara stared at a form on the table. "I'm holding a UPS bill that says your office received my package two weeks ago and Aretha Smith signed for it."

"Well, that might explain it. Aretha quit working here last week. I don't know who took over her files, but I can check. In the meantime, I would suggest you resend everything and address it to me, Shirley Thompson."

"Everything has been lost?"

"I apologize for the inconvenience, Mrs. Whiteside. We have thousands of short sale approval requests. We don't have the staff to handle them all."

"That doesn't make me feel any better. Thanks for your help." Barbara slammed the phone down. She looked up at the ceiling. "Will this nightmare ever end?"

Barbara picked up the phone, dialing Mindy Olsen's phone. "Mindy, it's Barbara Whiteside. I was just calling to let you know Citiloan still does not have an answer for us about the short sale. I have to resend everything I previously sent to them because they lost everything again."

"Jeez, Barbara, that offer was submitted two weeks ago. I don't know how long these buyers will wait for an answer."

"I know, Mindy, I apologize, but I can only do what Citiloan lets me do. They can't seem to get their act together, but I will try again. Please let the buyers know we are doing everything we can. We really want to sell this house."

"I'll try, Barbara, but they're getting really antsy. Keep trying with Citiloan and I'll try to hang onto the buyers."

"Thanks, Mindy, I'll do my best."

Stan wandered into the room holding the morning newspaper. Barbara looked at him.

"How are you feeling today?"

"I'm about the same. I just have no energy." He sat down on the couch and opened up the paper and read the headlines. It read in bold type, "Local Builder's House Shot in Drive-By Shooting." Stan turned the paper toward Barbara. "Look at this."

Barbara saw the headline. "Taylor Whitney, right? Wow, did he get hurt?"

"Apparently not. Sounds like he was very lucky. It says the sheriff has a suspect but they don't name him."

"We have our own problems, Stan. We need to figure out what we're going to do about living arrangements. The foreclosure date is coming up in less than a week. Four of our rental applications have been turned down because our credit is so bad. Do you have any ideas?"

Stan put down the paper. "Do you think we could stay with your mother? Maybe she'd like some company for awhile."

"I was thinking the same thing and mentioned it to her last week. She was excited about having us stay with her. I just don't want to impose."

"We're running out of options at this point, Barb. Why don't you give her a call and go over the details. If she's agreeable, we might as well start packing our things."

Barbara buried her head in her hands. "I can't believe it's come down to this. We're being forced to move back into my mom's house to make ends meet. I just can't believe this is happening to us." She started to weep quietly as she stared at the floor. "Dear God, help us out of this mess. Help me find someone who can make a decision at the bank. I'll go crazy if I have to keep doing this. Give me the strength to carry on." Stan hugged her tightly.

Thirty-eight

The San Francisco office of the FBI was located outside the financial district in an old, drab two-story building by the airport. Every thirty seconds or so, the building was rattled as a 737 jet flew overhead. Justin Miller, counsel for Worldwide Funding, and Brian Ferry, counsel for Beverly Credit, sat with special agent Steve Olson going over loan files generated by Sunset Mortgage. Steve had been with the FBI for eight years, specializing in bank and credit fraud. All three had their coats off, their ties loosened, and their shirt sleeves rolled up.

Having reviewed the files before the meeting, Steve spoke first. "I received these loan files from Bill Lawrence at the Department of Real Estate. He's handling an investigation of a complaint by your firm, Justin. He thought we should be brought in. It's clear these loans are fraudulent and Sunset Mortgage appears to be at the center of everything. Have any of you had any luck tracking these people down?"

Brian Ferry was looking at a file and said, "We've made contact with three of the borrowers. None of them are being cooperative with us. We've sent them multiple letters, but it's been to no avail."

Justin said, "Our people have tracked down four of the borrowers and have run into the same problems. None of these people want to cooperate. But we know where they live and in two cases, where they work. We've been doing our own investigation and we feel we're close to obtaining enough proof to prove what's taken place. We'll need to subpoena both Taylor and Janet's records."

Steve said, "I can do that for you and if this is as you've explained it to me, I can issue an arrest warrant once we verify what transpired. Let's review what you think went on with these loans."

Brian spoke first. "We know Janet Waller would qualify a straw buyer borrower for a home loan that was around seventy to eighty thousand higher than needed."

"What's a straw buyer?" asked Steve.

"It's a phony buyer—one who has no intent on living in or making payments on the home. We believe Taylor sent Janet these buyers and that they were people who lived in a rental apartment complex Taylor owns. Janet has said they just came to her out of the blue, but that's nonsense. She would underwrite these loans as stated-income, 100% loans. All her documentation is in order." He flipped through the file. "The borrowers had clean credit. They appeared to be employed. There were no red flags with these files. She would get an appraisal for a house, submit the package to our underwriters, and get the loan approved. What we don't know yet is how she managed to get the houses under contract for seventy thousand dollars more than they were worth. The other thing we haven't determined is where did the extra money go? Who benefited from this plot? We have some evidence to show where it went, but we need more."

Steve lifted up a file. "All these homes were purchased from Whitney Homes, correct?"

"That's correct."

"Did the extra money go to Whitney Homes?"

"There is a second title company which no one has heard of called New Federal Title, and we think it's owned by Taylor Whitney," Justin answered. "We don't have the closing statements from that title company yet, as we speak. Once we get them we can determine where the money went and who benefited from these loans. Usually, in a scam like this there are three people involved: the mortgage broker, the borrower, and an appraiser."

"This constitutes mail fraud and money laundering. Whoever is behind this is looking at major jail time. What about the appraisers?" Steve held up his hand as a jet passed overhead. "Has anyone spoken with them?"

"So far, from what we have determined the appraisers who did the appraisals on the houses are clean. Brian and I have copies of the original appraisals, and the ones in our loan files have been altered from the originals."

"Is it possible the appraiser made the changes?" Brian asked.

Brian scratched his head. "I guess they could have done that. But why go to all that trouble when they could have appraised the house at a high value to begin with?"

Steve turned to Justin. "How about your appraisers? Could they have been involved with this deal?"

"Two different appraisers worked on these loans. One of them is working with us more or less undercover, and has been helpful in finding information about Janet and Taylor. The other one remembers some of these particular houses, and he questioned Janet Waller after their first appraisals came in low. Janet gave them several comps that were close to where the value needed to be, and to do her a favor they stretched the value a bit." He handed Steve an appraisal. "If you look at this appraisal the comps are in order. So in answer to your question, I don't think the appraisers on our loans were involved. I think they might have stretched the values at the beginning, but after that they were legitimate."

Steve closed the file and put it on the pile. "We're looking at a big-time fraud ring for which we've obtained a lot of good evidence. I still need you to try to get as much information about these borrowers as you can. I'll get a few of my agents out to interview these people and see what we can find." He pulled a pair of business cards off his desk and handed them out. "Someone out there is the puppet master pulling all the strings, and I don't believe it's Janet Waller. She's involved deeply, but she's not the mastermind. Secondly, we need those escrow files from New Federal Title, fast. They'll help us figure out who was the benefactor of these inflated loans. I want you to call me when you find anything new. Is there anything else you can think of that we might need?"

"What about Whitney Homes?" Brian asked. "It's strange that all these loans are against brand-new Whitney Homes. Steve, don't you think someone there might have a hand in this?"

"I'll try to get an interview with one of the executives, but I hear they're pretty tight-mouthed. Didn't I read somewhere that the president of Whitney Homes stepped down earlier this year?"

"Yeah, it was Paul Bayless." Brian nodded his head. "He resigned at the end of last year. He's just started a consulting business. I can get you his address and phone number."

Justin wrote a note on his file folder. "Great. He'd be a good source of information since I'm sure he's probably not as loyal as he once was to Whitney Homes." He put his pen down and looked at Steve. "I can't tell you how I obtained this information, but Taylor left a virtual map of what this enterprise is all about on his home computer. I suggest you get a search warrant and start there."

Steve sat up. "Really?" He paused and chewed the tip of his pen. "Okay, let's break this up. I'll get a judge to sign a warrant for Taylor's residence and office. As soon as those files come in from the title company, get them to me and we'll meet in another week." Steve got up and they shook hands. The bankers left his office and headed out of the building.

THIRTY-NINE

Preston left early in the morning to review working drawings at his engineer's office for a subdivision he was working on. He wanted to get as much done in the morning as possible to avoid the heat. With temperatures of 100 degrees or hotter the past three days, he wanted to be close to his pool when the heat rose in the afternoon.

He turned into his favorite coffee place, Donut King, to get a cup of coffee. As he walked to the entrance, he passed a newspaper rack, glanced down at the headlines, and stopped dead in his tracks. The headlines screamed, "Local Builder Indicted by Grand Jury."

He fumbled around in his pocket for a couple of quarters, put them into the machine, and pulled out a paper. He scanned the article as he walked into the donut shop. Charlie, the owner, and his wife Kim were behind the counter. Charlie called out, "Hey, Preston, long time no see! You want one or two cups of coffee?"

"Just one for me today, Charlie." Charlie took a Styrofoam cup off a stack and poured the cup of coffee. Preston paid him, then tucked the newspaper under his arm, his coffee in his hand, and headed out the door. "See you, Charlie. See you, Kim."

Preston got to his car and hopped in. He closed the door and unfolded the paper. As he read the article he shook his head. The Bank of the Northwest and Royal Bank of Toronto had filed complaints with the district attorney, and a grand jury had handed down indictments for diversion of loan proceeds. The total amount allegedly diverted was close to a hundred and fifty million dollars. Preston whistled softly. Taylor's attorney, Jeremy Stephens, was quoted in the article. "It was all a misunderstanding. Taylor looks forward to clearing this up."

When he arrived at the engineer's office, Bill O'Brian greeted him. "Hey there, Preston, how are you?" They shook hands.

"I'm doing fine, Bill. How are you doing?"

"Not well. Business is way down. We've had to lay off almost half our staff this year." Preston pointed to the *Sacramento Bee* sitting on a coffee table. "Can you believe that? Taylor Whitney indicted, with a warrant for his arrest. That's incredible."

Bill turned and stared at the newspaper. "It couldn't happen to a bigger dope. I hope they throw him in jail forever."

"I take it Whitney Homes owes you money."

"You got that right. We've been trying to collect a hundred and fifty thousand dollars he owes us for over a year and a half. They kept stalling us off. We filed a couple of liens, but now we'll be lucky to get a few crumbs of what's left over. Taylor's hurt a lot of subcontractors and if I was him, I'd be looking over my shoulder. I wouldn't show my face in this town. It might be dangerous."

"Well, somebody already took a few shots at him," Preston said. "Next time they might improve their aim."

Preston drove to his office, and as he was parking his car his cell phone rang.

"Preston, it's Deputy Hunter."

"Hey, Billy, how are you?"

"I'm fine. I know you're friends with a kid named Matt Whiteside. Sheriff Turner has issued an arrest warrant for him for attempted murder and illegal discharge of a firearm in the shooting of Taylor Whitney's house. The sheriff thought you might want contact Matt and ask him to come down to the jail and surrender."

"Wait a minute! Matt Whiteside? There must be some kind of mistake!"

"Taylor Whitney swears he saw Matt's car drive by his house at the time of the shooting."

Preston ran his hand through his hair. "Billy, thanks for calling me. I'll contact Matt and ask him to turn himself in."

He sat in his car for a minute. Something is horribly wrong here, he thought. He dialed his phone.

Matt answered after the first ring.

"Matt, it's Preston. Where are you? Did you know there is an arrest warrant out for you?"

"What are you talking about? I'm at my office in San Francisco. I don't know anything about it. What was the crime I supposedly committed?"

Preston leaned forward and picked the coffee cup out of the holder. "Taylor Whitney's house was shot at Sunday night. According to the deputy I received a call from, Taylor swears he saw you in your car in front of his house at the time of the shooting. They're charging you with attempted murder and illegal discharge of a firearm."

"This is all I need. I'll get fired over this, all because of that idiot Taylor. You saw me—I was at your house Sunday night. After I left your place, I dropped Stephanie off at her home and drove to the city. I don't even own a gun."

Preston sipped his coffee. "Unfortunately, that puts you in the area on the night in question."

"What do I do now?"

"Let me call Sheriff Turner and see if I can find out what's going on. In the meantime, I'll help you get an attorney to represent you. You need to drive back to Sacramento to surrender. If your alibi is as you say it is, I can't see them holding you long."

"You mean I'm going to jail?"

"You might have to go there until you post bail. Don't worry. We'll get you out quickly."

"All right, I'll leave here within the hour and should arrive in a few hours. If you find out anything new, let me know right away."

"Be careful, Matt. Taylor has a lot of friends in law enforcement. Don't give them an excuse to do something to you."

Preston set his phone down and sipped his coffee. There's no way Matt was involved in this, he thought, but if he isn't, who is?

FORTY

Matt came to the doorway of John Ramsey's office and rapped on the door. John looked up from his computer screen. "I've been expecting you, Matt."

"Can I come in, John? I need to talk to you."

"Sure, Matt. Have a seat. I heard about your problems. Pete saw an article about you on the internet and told me all about it."

Of course Pete told you, Matt thought. That's just perfect. He sat in the chair. "I wish the article was wrong." Matt squirmed in his seat and wrung his hands together.

"What are the authorities charging you for?"

"I've been accused of attempted murder and discharging a firearm. I'm driving to Sacramento to surrender to the authorities."

John sat up and leaned on his desk. "What happened, Matt? How could you be involved in something like that? You know what? It doesn't matter. I'm sorry to hear about this." John stood up. "You know I have to let you go. Franklin Smith's corporate people have zero tolerance for their employees being arrested. If Pete knows about this, I guarantee you he's told our people in New York about it. I really feel sorry you have to go through this."

Matt hung his head. "I know you have no choice, John. I want to thank you for the opportunity you gave me here."

"Good luck, Matt. If what you say is true you don't have much to worry about." John stuck his hand out to Matt. "Please keep in touch."

"I will, John, I will." He went back to his office and gathered his personal belongings. Five minutes later, he was in his car driving home for some extra clothes. After a quick stop he was back on the road again. He dialed the phone. "Drew, it's Matt. I've got to tell you something." Matt proceeded to tell him what had transpired in the last 48 hours. He finally finished.

"Wow, Matt. Is there anything you need me to do? Do you need any money?"

"I'll be okay for now, but thanks for offering. I'll keep you posted as best I can."

"Good luck, bro."

"Thanks."

He hung up, then thought, How can I tell my parents about this?

He dialed his phone. "Preston, it's Matt. I'm on my way. I'll be at your house in an hour and a half."

"Okay, Matt. Your attorney will be here. I contacted Sheriff Turner and talked to him about your case. Since it's an ongoing investigation, he wouldn't say much, other than that Taylor swears it was you who fired the shots. I told the sheriff he's rushing to judgment, but that you'd surrender this afternoon. Taylor owns Sheriff Turner and he'll do whatever Taylor demands. However, he was okay with you coming in on your own."

"Thanks, Preston. I'll see you in a while."

Matt noticed a California Highway Patrol car in his rearview mirror about five vehicles lengths behind him. His heart beat faster and faster as he tried to concentrate on driving. Suddenly, the CHP accelerated and began to close the gap between himself and Matt. Matt started perspiring profusely, his sweaty hands shaking so violently that his car almost swerved into the next lane. Matt quickly corrected the steering, but not before the CHP came into the lane next to his and started to accelerate more. The CHP was barely two car lengths back when he turned on his lights and siren.

The CHP was coming closer and closer, his siren screaming in Matt's ears. Matt could see through the side mirror that he was almost directly behind him. Matt hit his blinker to indicate he was pulling over when the CHP blew past him and screamed up the highway.

Matt took a deep breath. He slowed the car down and waited for his breathing to slow to a regular pace. He reached into the back seat, pulled a towel out of his gym bag, and wiped his face. "I can't believe this. I feel like a fugitive."

When he arrived at Preston's, Matt was introduced to Johnnie Gibson, a local defense attorney. Johnnie was a forty-something, bald black man dressed in an impeccable gray suit with a white-and-blue tie. He had a look that said he didn't back down from much. Preston introduced them. "Matt, Johnnie is one of the best attorneys in the area. He'll take care of you."

Matt flopped down in one of the kitchen chairs.

Johnnie faced Matt. "I want you to explain everything to me—where you were, who was with you, and will swear to it. Also, I don't want you speaking to anyone without me being present."

Matt replied wearily, "Okay, Mr. Gibson."

"What we're going to do is go down to the sheriff's office and you'll turn yourself in. They will fingerprint you, photograph you, and interrogate you. We should be given a bail amount. Once you post that, you can go free."

Matt stood up and nodded to Johnnie. "I'm ready to go."

FORTY-ONE

An hour later, Matt was in the Sacramento County Jail being fingerprinted, photographed, and booked. A deputy handed Matt a Kleenex to clean his hands. "Please follow me."

He was led to an interview room down the hall from the front desk. The deputy opened the door and let Matt pass.

Johnnie sat in the center of the room at a rectangular table surrounded by six folding chairs, and motioned at one of the chairs. "Have a seat, Matt." Matt looked around the room, noticing the paint peeling from its walls.

The door to the interview room opened up and a burly, middle-aged man entered. "Hi, I'm Detective Bill Watson. I'd like to ask you a few questions if you don't mind."

Matt and Johnnie sat next to each other and the detective sat across the table from them. "I'll answer anything you ask, Mr. Watson."

"Okay, Mr. Whiteside. Do you have any objection to taping our conversation?"

Matt looked at Johnnie, who shrugged his shoulders. "No, I don't."

"Do you know Taylor Whitney?"

"Yes, I met him once at his office."

"Have you spoken with him recently?"

"I had a phone conversation with Taylor about four weeks ago. I asked him when he was planning on either fixing my parents' home or reimbursing them for the repairs."

"Was it a long conversation?"

"No, it was short. He swore at me a few times and hung up."

"Have you seen him since?"

"I stopped next to him at a stoplight a few weeks ago. I had a few choice words for him about my parents' house."

"So he knows what kind of car you drive?" Watson was scribbling notes.

"I would assume he knows what I drive."

"Did you ever threaten him?"

"No, I never threatened him physically." Matt shifted in his seat. "I threatened to have my parents sue him, but that was all."

"Isn't that a threat, Mr. Whiteside?"

Johnnie jumped in. "Detective, he just said he didn't threaten him physically."

Watson continued in his monotone voice. "Do you know where Mr. Whitney lives?"

"Yes."

"You've never been there?"

Matt was getting agitated. "I've driven by his house as he lives in the same subdivision as a friend of mine, Preston Carson." He couldn't help thinking about the break-in. Did they have any evidence? Did he leave something in Taylor's house? Everything had happened so fast that night.

Watson put his pen on the table. "Mr. Whitney says he saw you in your car in front of his house immediately after the shooting. Was that you?"

Matt tried to stay calm. He rubbed his hands under the table. "It could have been. I left Preston's house and we heard four loud pops from somewhere, followed by two more. I wasn't sure what the sound was; my windows were up and the stereo was on. Taylor's house is on the way out of the subdivision, so I had to pass it on my way out."

"Did you see anyone else as you left?"

"There was a dark pickup ahead of us at the gate, and the guard seemed to be checking it out. Once the gate opened, they flew out of there. The truck was too far ahead to identify whoever it was."

"Do you own a gun?"

"No, I don't." Matt swallowed hard.

"Did you borrow one that Sunday night of the shooting?"

Matt slammed his hands on the table. "I don't have a gun, I didn't borrow a gun, and I didn't shoot at Taylor's house."

Johnnie put his hands over Matt's. "Calm down. Just answer his question. He's just doing his job."

After three hours of questioning, Watson turned off the tape recorder, shut his notebook, and stood up. "I'll be back. Stay put."

He left the room and Matt turned to Johnnie. "What do you think?"

"Matt, this is the flimsiest case I've ever seen. The only thing they have is Taylor's testimony, and that makes no sense."

Matt breathed deeply and tried not to show the anxiety he was feeling. Watson had said nothing about being inside Taylor's house, and only questioned him about driving by the house the night of the shooting and his whereabouts before the event. If he knew about the break-in, he hadn't said anything.

The door opened and Watson returned with Sheriff Turner. Turner nodded. "Hi, Johnnie. How are you?"

"I'm fine, Sheriff, but I'm not here to discuss my health. You have booked my client on bogus information." He pointed at Matt. "I demand you drop the charges and free this man."

"I'm afraid I can't do that, Johnnie. These are serious charges. Taylor Whitney is an upstanding citizen of this community. We have to check out Mr. Whiteside's alibi before we make any decisions. Right now, it's Taylor's word versus his." He nodded at Matt. "I know Mr. Whitney personally. I don't know your client."

"Everyone knows you know Mr. Taylor personally." Johnnie glared at the sheriff. "Will you release my client on his own recognizance?"

"I've discussed this case with the district attorney and we've requested bail be set at two hundred thousand dollars."

Johnnie jumped out of his chair. He screamed, "Two hundred thousand for this case? There's no way! This is garbage." He pointed at Matt again. "That means this young man has to come up with ten percent of the bail money, which is twenty thousand dollars, to post a bond, just because your buddy thinks he saw him that night."

Sheriff Turner's face turned red, and he raised his voice to Johnnie. "We haven't checked out all the facts yet, and if you start giving me more trouble, I'll see to it that we raise his bail higher." He turned and went out the door.

"I'll give you a few minutes with your client and then I need to take him to his cell," Detective Watson said. He turned and left the room.

"Matt, I'm sorry. The sheriff is normally a stand-up guy."

"Johnnie, tell Preston what happened and see if he will contact my parents and let them know what's going on. I don't know what I'm going to do. I can't turn to them for money. They're not in a position to help me. I don't know where I'll get the bond money."

"I'll see what I can do. I know people in the bail bond business. Stephanie mentioned something about someone named Justin getting some money for you. Try to keep composed and we'll get you through this."

"Thanks, Johnnie."

Detective Watson came back in the room and asked Matt, "Are you ready, Mr. Whiteside?"

Matt nodded and the detective led him out of the room.

Matt found himself in a jail cell with a young, scrawny man with tattoos up and down his arms. His had a crew cut and his eyes were almost black. He paced the cell, scratching himself constantly. Matt lay down on the bottom bunk since the top had already been claimed by his cellmate. He stared up at the ceiling and listened to noises coming from the adjacent cells. Men were screaming, singing rap songs, or rattling cups on the metal bars. A combination of disinfectant and body odor permeated the cell.

After an awkward period of silence, Matt's cellmate asked, "What you in here for? You beat up your wife?"

Matt sat up and rubbed his temples. "No, nothing like that. I'm accused of shooting a gun at a house."

"No kiddin'? Ya'll hit anybody?"

"I didn't do it, but no one was hit."

"Damn, that happens all the time where I come from. The cops, they never catch nobody, though. You must be pretty dumb to get caught."

Matt rolled his eyes upward. He lay on his back. This is going to be a long night, he thought.

A deputy sheriff came up to the cell. He ran his baton across the jail bars, making an enormous racket. "Hey, college boy." Matt turned his head toward the deputy. "I hear you're the one that went Rambo on Taylor Whitney's house. Taylor's a good friend to the sheriff's department, and we don't take kindly to punks like you messin' with him. You better watch your back while you're here." He sneered at Matt as he beat his baton in his hand and slowly walked away.

FORTY-TWO

The Sacramento Courthouse was bustling with people going in and out of the building. Heat from the sun rose off the cement and added ten degrees to the already hot day. Barbara and Stan stood about twenty feet off to the side of a man standing at a podium outside the courthouse. He had a stack of files at his feet.

"How does this work?" Stan asked.

Barbara looked at him. "A friend of mine from the title company gave me a quick little history lesson. Foreclosure sales are usually executed on the steps of a courthouse of the city or county which the foreclosed property is located in. Usually, an agent for the city or county 'cries the sale'—this is a term used from before the American Revolution—in which the address, debt, and opening bid are cried out to the public." Barbara pointed at the man behind the podium. "That's the crier. Sacramento County is similar to other jurisdictions in that they hold their foreclosure actions on their courthouse steps."

She watched the man flip through pages of a six-inch binder of documents. A dozen or so people milled around him. Three young men dressed casually were circling the man on the podium, constantly talking into their cell phones, seeking directions from persons on the other end of the line.

"I'll bet those guys are here to pick at the bones of the dead car-casses," Stan said, looking at the men. "What happens if no one bids on our house?"

Barbara reached for his hand. "The house sells back to the beneficiary."

"Who's the beneficiary?"

"The bank."

The crier read out addresses as one property after another was foreclosed. After about the fiftieth property, they heard, "3452 Amber Court, Antelope, California, case number 3457223."

"That's us," Barbara said softly.

"The minimum bid for this property is four hundred forty-five thousand dollars." Without looking up he said, "Do I hear a minimum bid of four hundred forty-five thousand for this property? Going once, going twice…" he paused for a second, looked up and around "sold to the beneficiary for the minimum bid."

Barbara looked down at her feet. "Well, it's done. We can leave now." Tears welled up in her eyes.

Stan put his arm around her shoulders and squeezed her. "It will be okay, don't cry."

Barbara plucked a tissue out of her purse and dabbed her eyes. "We've lost everything, Stan. We have to start all over again with nothing."

They walked back to their car, and then drove in silence to Barbara's mother's house in Rio Linda.

FORTY-THREE

Sounds carried through the building. Up until a few days ago, metal doors clanging shut, raised voices, and shouting guards were foreign sounds to Matt. He sat in a visiting room on the first floor of the Sacramento County Jail. He had been unable to post a bond for his bail, and this was his second day in jail since his arrest.

He had been brought to this room by one of his jailors, where he sat waiting nervously. The door opened and Preston, his attorney, and Stephanie walked in. Stephanie rushed over to Matt, gave him a hug, and kissed him on the lips. "Are you okay?"

Matt hugged her back. "It would be better if I was out of here. I'm scared to death of this place." He looked at Johnnie. "They treat me like I'm Charles Manson."

Stephanie looked around. "This place gives me the creeps."

"I have some good news Matt," said Preston. "Justin sent Stephanie the money to post your bail, so you are being released. You should be freed within the hour."

Matt sat back in the chair. "Thank you." He leaned forward and slapped his attorney on the back. "I can't get out of here soon enough. Did you have a chance to talk to your friend the sheriff? You were here when I was grilled yesterday by that detective for three hours—he wanted to know if I would let them search my condo. You heard me. I told him to go ahead; I've nothing to hide. Did they conduct the search?"

Johnnie nodded at the door. "Yes, and if your condo checks out, they will drop the charges. I also think the sheriff is beginning to realize you had nothing to do with the shooting that night."

Preston walked over and looked at the solid metal door. "I forgot to ask you, Matt. How did it go with your boss when you told him about the arrest?"

"It went just perfect, Preston. He fired me. Not only did I get to languish in jail for two days, I lost my job over this bogus charge. If I ever see Taylor on the street, I'm—"

"Matt, don't talk like that. Especially here," Johnnie said, looking at the door. "This is what landed you here in the first place. The only person who will suffer if you harm Taylor is you. Don't let him goad you into that position."

"You're right, Johnnie. It's just that what he's put me and my family through is unforgivable."

The door to the reception room opened and a deputy stuck his head inside. "If you come with me to the front desk and sign release papers, you'll be free to go, Mr. Whiteside."

Matt jumped up, pulled Stephanie by the hand, and headed out the door. Preston followed a few steps behind. After signing the necessary documents, they found themselves outside walking to Preston's car.

"Where do you want me to take you, Matt? Where your parents are staying?"

"That would be great, thanks." They found Preston's car and piled in. Matt sat in the passenger seat and Stephanie rode in back. She leaned against him and stroked his neck as they were driving.

"Okay, we know I didn't shoot at Taylor's place, so who did? There is somebody still out there who has unfinished business to attend to." He looked at Preston. "Do you have any ideas?"

"Taylor has a lot of enemies." Preston turned down the radio. "I'm sure he must have offended a lot of people over the years. I don't know who would go after him, but I would bet it has to be over money. Taylor probably owes someone a lot of money and that someone wants it paid, bad."

FORTY-FOUR

Taylor and Janet were having dinner at the Four Seasons in Maui. They had left town a month ago, the day after the shooting. They had been keeping a low profile ever since the story hit the *Sacramento Bee* about their indictment and impending arrest warrants. The Associated Press had picked up the story and it was all over the national media and the internet. Reporters had been combing Maui and Palm Springs looking for them. Things died down when Taylor's and Janet's respective attorneys informed the FBI and the press that Taylor and Janet would turn themselves in to the appropriate authorities in two days.

Janet played with her food and constantly looked around the room, as if the FBI were about to jump out of a nearby planter and arrest her. She turned to Taylor and said rather sharply, "I can't believe you talked me into this fiasco. I knew this would eventually turn out badly."

"Look, Janet. I didn't hear you complain when you pocketed ten thousand dollars with each sale we made. This won't be a big deal other than the harassment from the media. The FBI will make a big scene reporting that they broke up a major ring, and they will fine us and slap us on the wrist."

"How much do you think they'll fine us?"

"Probably around fifty thousand each. Then they'll put us on probation for a couple of years, and they'll move on to their next targets. This is a white-collar crime." Taylor pushed his food around with his fork. "No one was physically hurt, and so what—Worldwide and Beverly Credit lost a little money. Big deal. The real criminals are out there shooting and killing people. That's who they want to put in jail, not people like us."

"But why are the district attorney and the FBI making such a fuss? You'd think they recaptured Bonnie and Clyde."

"These guys are government workers. They punch a clock. They need to justify to the taxpayers—who are their real bosses—that they're doing their jobs. If the FBI didn't arrest people once in awhile and make a big deal out of it, who would even pay attention to them? These government people are jealous of anyone who makes big money. They can't stand that. That's why they make such a ruckus over these cases."

"What does your attorney tell you? Does he think the same way you do about what will happen to us?"

"Blake Wilson is a worrywart. He's always thinking everything is a crisis. I don't pay a whole lot of attention to what he says. I just tell him to get through this as soon as possible so I can move out of Sacramento."

"Taylor, that's not what my attorney is saying. He's not sure I can get out of jail right away. He's negotiating to allow me to post bond for bail."

Taylor reached for her hand. "Janet, they're not going to hold you long. You're not a flight risk. They don't think you'd flee the country. The only way we could run into trouble is if one of us talks. You can bet I'm not talking."

She pulled her hand away and forced a smile. "I won't say a thing, either. But let me tell you something. If I am ever convicted of a crime and I have to do any jail time, the district attorney can kiss my ass goodbye—I'll be in France. I won't sit in a jail cell."

"Nothing's going to happen. This is our last night here. Let's talk about something else. I'm tired of this all this government garbage."

She narrowed her eyes. "It's not easy to think about pleasant things when we have this hanging over our heads."

"Next weekend is one of the best weekends of the year—Labor Day weekend."

"Why is that?"

"Because football season starts, that's why. College football officially gets going this Saturday, and the following Sunday the NFL starts up. I like the Dallas Cowboys this year, and I want to bet a bundle on them."

"You and your betting. I don't know how you do it."

"It takes years of practice." Taylor glanced down at his watch. "It's almost nine-thirty, and we've got an early flight tomorrow. Shall we head back to the house?"

Taylor paid the bill with his credit card, and they headed for the house. They walked into the courtyard and up the steps to the balcony overlooking the ocean. Taylor opened the door and Janet entered. She took two steps in and stopped. "Taylor! Someone's been in the house. I smell cigarette smoke, and strange cologne."

"I smell it, too." He flipped on the light to the kitchen. He hauled a knife out of the drawer and slowly edged down the hall.

"Taylor, you can't go down there!" she hissed. "What if they've got a gun? Let me call the police."

"Shhhh. Be quiet. Go ahead and call."

Janet picked up the phone and put it to her ear. She looked at Taylor. "It's dead. The phone is dead." Her hands shook as she held the phone. "This is scaring me, Taylor."

Taylor put a finger to his lips. He slowly crept down the hallway, turning lights on as he went. "I think whoever was here has left." He came to the master bedroom and paused. He felt around the corner and flipped the switch. "The house is empty."

"Well, I know very well someone has been here." Janet entered the hall bath. "Look! There's a cigarette butt in the toilet. We need to get out of here. Someone is looking for you. Is it the same person who fired shots at your house?"

Taylor walked into the bathroom, looked down, and then flushed the toilet. "It was probably one of the maids."

Janet shrieked, "The maids? You can't be serious! Maids don't smoke in people's houses. Maids don't wear cheap men's cologne. Somebody deliberately cut the phone lines. I don't like this."

"Calm down, Janet. Nobody's here now. Get your things and we'll spend the night at the Four Seasons. Hurry up."

Taylor laid his head back against the seat in first class and closed his eyes. "That was quite a night. I didn't get much sleep."

Janet adjusted a pillow behind her head. "I'm still shaking. The two martinis I had haven't calmed my nerves. I need another drink." She reached up and hit the call button above her head. When nothing happened after a couple minutes, she hit it again.

A hostess showed up. "I'm sorry for the delay, ma'am. This flight is overbooked, and we're trying to get everybody seated."

Janet stared at her. "You need to take care of the people in first class. I don't really give a damn about what happens behind me. That's your problem. I need a martini and I don't like waiting."

The hostess leaned back. "Sure, ma'am. Be careful with your alcohol. When you get to high altitude, it can affect you more than at sea level."

Janet leaned forward. "Just get me the drink and save the moral lectures for your AA meetings."

The hostess turned and left. Taylor was already snoring.

When they arrived at Taylor's house in Granite Bay, it was dark. The limousine drove up to the front door and let them out. The driver took all their suitcases in through the door and then left.

"It's good to be back home," Taylor said. "I want to get all this legal stuff behind me so I can move on. I'm tired of this investigative harassment." He walked into the kitchen and looked out toward the back yard. "Wow, I left the back French door keys in the deadbolt before we left. Somebody could have broken that glass and opened the door with the keys."

"Did you set the burglar alarm, Taylor? I'm scared. I don't like spending time here anymore."

Taylor pulled the keys out of the door and set them on the breakfast bar. "Yeah, I'll set it. I usually don't do that while I'm here, but tonight it's a good idea." He punched the keypad on the wall. "2-4-2-4." He laughed. "That code is so simple nobody would guess it."

Janet turned and headed up the stairway toward the master bedroom. "I'm tired." She yawned. "I'm headed to bed."

"I'm gonna make myself a stiff drink," Taylor said as he watched her walk up the stairs. He wandered over to the bar and pulled out a glass.

Janet entered the bedroom, turned the corner, and her body immediately stiffened. "I know that scent," she muttered. She reached to turn on the light, but a gloved hand clamped down across her mouth. As she was hauled further into the bedroom, the back of her head and body slammed into the chest of the intruder. Janet felt a cold metal object pressed against her head. She tried to scream, but it was stifled.

"Don't struggle or yell," he whispered in her ear, "and I won't hurt you."

She could smell cigarettes and whiskey on his breath. She raised her right arm and elbowed the intruder in the ribs. Using every muscle in her body, she lifted her leg and kicked him in the shin with her heel. He grunted and held her tighter. She bit down as hard as she could on the finger nearest her mouth, tasting the dirty leather glove on his hand. The intruder yelped and relaxed his grip.

Janet screamed and started toward the door. She never saw the flash from the muzzle, heard the explosion from the gun, or felt the bullet crash through her skull into her brain. Her momentum, and the force of the bullet, propelled her face first into the blood-splattered wall beside the door. Her head bounced backward, and she fell lifelessly to the floor.

The intruder bent down and rolled her on her back. Her wide-open eyes stared vacantly at the ceiling, her face forever frozen in a frightened look. The gaping wound above her right eyebrow oozed blood.

"Sorry, lady. You didn't listen."

Taylor jumped at the sound of the scream and dropped his drink. He sprinted toward the French door that led to the back yard. The gunshot caused him to slip, and he fell against the door. Clumsily, he jerked the handle. Where did I leave the keys to the deadbolt? he thought. He turned and saw them setting on the breakfast bar. Taylor lunged at the bar and fell to his knees. He snatched the keys and crawled to the door. Out of the corner of his eye, he saw a dark figure coming down the stairs. "Which key is it?" He fumbled with the keys and then dropped them to the floor. "Damn it!" He turned as he reached for the keys and saw the stranger was at the foot of the stairs and was coming toward him. "C'mon, which key is it?" he screamed. He inserted the key and had turned it halfway when he felt the gun at his temple.

He heard a voice say, "You don't need to open that."

Taylor turned and put his hands in the air. "Please don't shoot me! Please! Tell Artie I'll wire him the money tomorrow, I swear."

"I don't know no Artie."

Taylor pleaded as he unclasped his watch, "Here, please take this. It's a diamond Rolex. It's worth a hundred grand." He twisted his pinkie ring off his finger. "Take this—it's worth eight grand. Don't shoot me!"

The intruder took the watch and the ring and held them up. He placed them in his coat pocket.

"My girlfriend has a sapphire necklace. Take it; it's worth at least seventy-five grand."

Taylor covered his face. "Take any of my cars. I've got a Ferrari, a Bentley. The keys are over there." His hands shook violently as he pointed to the kitchen, where the keys were hanging. A wet spot started to grow around Taylor's crotch.

"That's gross, man. I don't need no ride."

Taylor looked up, perspiration beading on his forehead. His lips quivered as he spoke in a squeaky voice. He clasped his hands in a praying position. "Please don't shoot me. I'll give you anything. I don't want to die."

The stranger stuck the gun on Taylor's forehead. "That's not for you to decide. What did you say was the code to unarm the alarm? Don't worry; I already know it—2-4-2-4, right?" He laughed, and sqeezed the trigger twice. The shots exploded and reverberated throughout the house. Taylor's head snapped back, and his body slumped to the floor, convulsing and twitching, as smoke and the smell of gunpowder filled the kitchen. The intruder walked over to the wall and pushed four numbers on the alarm keypad. He stepped over Taylor, careful not to step in the expanding pool of blood flowing from his head, and left the house.

FORTY-FIVE

Matt sat at the kitchen table, licking an envelope containing the last résumé to be mailed out. None of the twenty job ads he had responded to were offering close to the money he had made at Franklin. He looked at his watch and yawned. "Done for the day." His mind started to wander as he pondered the uncertainties of his future. I don't have a job, and my chances of getting one look bleak. Where will I live? What about Stephanie? What woman in her right mind would want to be with me?

It had been a long day, and Matt's head hurt. He grabbed a coat and headed for the door. Twelve minutes later, as he sat sipping a cold beer at the bar, Drew arrived.

"What's up, dog? Any new job search leads? Have you updated your résumé?"

"I updated it a few months ago and I started hitting the pavement this week."

"Your old boss, Diane Amory, is working at General Technology. She was always happy with your performance at Sun Systems. You should give her a call."

"Diane works for General? That's awesome, Drew, thanks. I'll definitely give her a call."

"Any bites on your condominium?"

"There's been an offer for six hundred thirty thousand. I sent the offer to the bank, but haven't heard if they'll accept it. I swear these banks are half the problem with this real estate market. I must get ten calls a day regarding my mortgage payment from Ameribank. Each person asks me the same question, 'When can we expect a payment?'" Matt shifted in his seat. "I try to tell them I'm trying to work with the bank to do a short sale, but it's like talking to a wall. You can't get them to understand what I'm saying. For some reason, these employees of Ameribank are like robots and only know one script: 'When can we expect your payment?' Do these companies really think it's effective to call people every day to harass them?"

"Apparently so. Borrowers are frustrated with banks and financial institutions' unresponsiveness. You'd think the last thing the bank would want is to take over problem houses through foreclosure."

Matt sipped from his beer. "My parents went through the same thing, and in the end they lost their house. It has really devastated them. I hope the same thing doesn't happen to me. I don't know how long this buyer is willing to wait for an answer. Two weeks seems like a long time to mull over a contract."

The next morning Matt awoke early, made a pot of coffee, and searched the internet. Around eight, he dialed Ameribank to see if he could get the short sale resolved. He was placed on hold for twenty-five minutes before finally talking to a live person. Naturally, that person was in the wrong department, so Matt was transferred to the loss mitigation section of the bank. After another twenty minutes, Matt spoke to a bank representative. "My name is Matt Whiteside, the last four digits of my social security number are 7774, and my mother's maiden name is Randall."

"Okay, Matt, my name is John. How can I help you?"

"I'm trying to facilitate a short sale on my condominium," Matt replied. "I sent all the paperwork to the bank two weeks ago and I'm following up on it."

Matt could hear John fumbling around with some papers. "I don't show us having received those documents, Mr. Whiteside. Could you resend everything?"

"I can do that, but can I send them to someone specifically? The last time I just sent it to the address I was given and I have no way of knowing if it ever arrived."

"Send it to my attention, Mr. Whiteside, and I'll work on your file."

"Can you call me tomorrow when you receive the package? I'm going to overnight it to you. I have a sale pending and time is of the essence. I need an answer on this sale quickly."

"Yes, Mr. Whiteside. I will call you when I receive your package. I'll try to expedite your file."

"Thank you."

Matt hung up and shook his head. He thought, I can't sell my home without their permission, but they can't figure out how to give their permission. How many other homeowners are going through this debacle? How many just throw their hands up and walk away?

Matt called Diane's direct line at General Technologies. "Diane Amory, how can I help you?"

"Diane, hi, this is Matt Whiteside."

"Matt Whiteside! How have you been? It's been so long since we've talked. It's great to hear from you."

"I'm doing well, Diane, thanks for asking. Since the housing market has cooled off, I've been laid off. I thought I'd call you and see what you've got going."

"Matt, I'm so glad you called. General Technology is an expanding firm. There are a few job openings that might be a nice fit for you. The only problem will be that I don't think we can match what you were making at Franklin. Our positions don't warrant that kind of income."

"That's okay. I realize I'm going to have to take a pay cut to land a good job and I'm willing to do that. I just want a position that is steady and reliable."

"Do you have any free time to come by my office this afternoon?"

"Absolutely. How about two o'clock?"

"Two o'clock looks good to me. I'll see you then."

Matt arrived ten minutes early for his interview with Diane.

Diane burst through the door that led to the main office area. "Matt Whiteside, it is so good to see you. You look great, as usual. Follow me." She took him down a hallway to a conference room. She held the door for Matt and gestured for him to have a seat.

"So, Matt, fill me in on what you've been doing since you left Sun Systems."

He filled her in on his time at Franklin Smith, the trading, Wall Street, and the collapse of the mortgage-backed security market.

"You've done some interesting things and have gained a lot of experience," Diane said. "We can use you here at General Technologies. We have a position similar to the one you had at Sun Systems, running our pension plans and 401(k) plans. You'd be working with approximately the same amount of money as at Sun Systems. The salary starts at eighty-five thousand dollars per year, plus excellent benefits. You'll also need to find an assistant fairly soon. The one we currently have is on maternity leave and will not be coming back."

"Diane, eighty-five thousand a year will work for me. I have one question, though. You have an office in Sacramento, don't you? Would it be possible for me to work out of that office rather than here in San Francisco?"

"I don't see why you couldn't work there. If you accept the job, though, I'd like you to work here for at least a month to familiarize yourself with the people here."

"When do you want me to start?"

Diane grinned. "How about if you start a week from Monday?"

"A week from Monday would be perfect." He stood up to leave. "Thank you so much for giving me this opportunity. You don't know how much I appreciate it."

"You're very welcome, Matt. It will be great working with you again."

Matt got in his car, picked up his phone, and dialed. His mother answered.

"Hi, Mom. Guess what? I was offered a new job today."

"Oh, Mattie. That's great news. Is it General Technologies, the one you told me about?"

"Yes. I can't wait to start."

"Your dad is feeling better and the doctors have given him clearance to return to work. He is just elated."

"Tell him I wish him good luck, and thanks for your help this week. I'll let you know how it turns out."

"Matt, after all you've done for us, it was the least I could do."

That night, feeling nervous about the task he was about to undertake, Matt sat at a table across from Stephanie. "You don't know what a burden has been lifted by my getting this job, Stephanie." The dinner crowd at Il Fornaio was light on this particular evening. Matt had requested a table by the window looking out on Capitol Avenue. Dinner was superb, as usual.

"I can imagine, and you're going to end up working here Sacramento, too. I'm really happy for you."

The waiter came to their table with a bottle of Dom Perignon. He looked at Stephanie and said, "We heard today is a special day for you." With that, he produced a champagne glass out from behind his back and filled it for her. He set the glass in front of her and backed away. Inside the glass was a diamond ring shimmering in the bubbles.

Stephanie put her hands to her mouth and looked up at Matt, who was on a knee in front of her. He reached out and held her hand and asked softly, "Stephanie, will you marry me?"

Stephanie tried to compose herself and stammered, "Yes, yes, of course I will."

Matt got up, kissed her on the lips, and raised his arms in triumph. Several restaurant patrons applauded and then offered congratulatory wishes to Stephanie and Matt.

On the way home, Stephanie rested her head on Matt's shoulder. She couldn't take her eyes off the ring sparkling on her hand. "That was unbelievably romantic, Matt. I had no clue you were going to propose to me."

"I wanted it to be a surprise. Didn't you wonder why I was here for the day last week and then went back? I wanted to get your mother's permission before I asked you. I wasn't sure she would be able to keep the secret until I asked you."

"I wondered why you came and went so fast. It did seem odd to me. Now it makes sense. How did you decide on such a gorgeous ring? I didn't know you knew anything about diamonds."

"I don't know much about jewelry, so I got some feminine help—" he paused for a second "my mom. She knows all about carat, clarity, color, and cut, plus any other c's I forgot. She helped me pick the ring out. I thought it looked very pretty."

"Matt, I love you."

"I love you too, Stephanie."

That evening, Preston sat in a booth next to Karen at Café Bistro. Matt and Stephanie sat across from them, sipping a drink. Karen had Stephanie's hand in hers and was admiring her ring. "My, Stephanie, that is so gorgeous. You did a great job choosing this ring, Matt."

"Thanks, my mom helped. So, Preston, do you know if they figured out who killed Taylor and his girlfriend?"

"Several people had motives, but so far they haven't arrested anyone. Initially, there was some talk of a murder-suicide. The thinking there was that Janet was about to rat out Taylor on their straw buyer scheme, and he put an end to that. There was no break-in and the alarm was set. Then, there were stories that Taylor had a big gambling problem and welched on a few big bets with a drug cartel. Then, there was a subcontractor who they linked to the shell casings they found at Taylor's house here in town—" Preston pointed at Matt "the shooting you were arrested for. The guard at Taylor's subdivision identified him as a person he let into the place earlier in the day to do work on another house there. He waited all day and half the night for Taylor to show up at home. You just happened by at the same time."

Matt cast a quick glance at Stephanie, who was listening intently.

"The police also suspected Taylor's wife Monica and her brother." Preston took a sip of his drink. "After figuring out it may have not been a murder-suicide, the authorities looked to who would benefit the most from a dead Taylor. Monica was the logical candidate, and they started following the money. Those two were looking to hire a hit man from a mob in Los Angeles. Only problem was, Monica's hit man was a small-time druggie who couldn't spell mob if you spotted him the m and the b, and he spent all her deposit money on drugs. He was so spun he couldn't function for a week, let alone shoot a gun." Preston took a napkin and wiped at a wet spot on the table in front of him. "The cops started squeezing her brother and eventually he 'fessed up about their plan, but since nothing came of it, no charges have been filed. They're still looking for the supposed hit man."

"All I know is I'm glad they dropped the charges against me. It all seems like a bad dream." Matt gave a knowing glance at Stephanie, and she seemed to be stifling a grin. He thought, I would love admit that Steph and I were in fact at Taylor's house the night of the shooting, but I don't dare. I'm not sure anyone would believe it, anyway.

"Could it have been another subcontractor?" Stephanie asked.

"Maybe, but seemed too professional. They found no murder weapon, prints, or DNA evidence. The crime was well thought out. Nobody could figure out how the gunman got in and out without tripping the alarm. It could have been someone close to Taylor, like an employee or something. Who knows? The irony is, if Monica had just been patient, someone else would have gotten him for her and she could have gotten her hands on more of his money. As it is, she may find herself facing charges for attempted solicitation of murder, even though she didn't succeed."

Everyone just shook their heads.

"It's an amazing turn of events," Preston said. "But the sheriff says he's not sure if they will ever find the killer—there're so many pieces to the puzzle."

FORTY-SIX

Matt was sitting at his desk at General Technologies, making notes on the résumé of a prospective assistant he had just interviewed, when his cell phone rang. He answered it.

"Hello, Matt, it's Ming Sung. I have good news for you. Your condominium buyer's loan documents are ready and they were sent to the title company today to sign everything. We can close escrow on it by next Wednesday. I was worried we would have to wait many more months to get it approved. You did a great job of getting the short sale approved by Ameribank."

"I'll tell you, Ming, it wasn't easy. I had to make about fifty calls for that sale. I almost gave up, it was so discouraging."

"I know. I hear many bad short sale stories. Oh, before I forget, there will be a lease agreement in escrow for you to sign, giving you one month to lease the condo from the new buyers."

"That's great, Ming. Thanks for all your help."

He looked down at his watch and saw that it was almost four-thirty. He had done six interviews and had one more to go. After that, he was free to enjoy the weekend.

His secretary showed up in his doorway. "Matt, your four-thirty interview is here."

Matt looked up from his desk. "Thanks, Cindy. Would you mind bringing him back to my office?"

"Sure, I'll be right back." A couple minutes later, she was back at Matt's door with a middle-aged, balding man dressed in slacks, a white shirt, and a tie. Cindy gestured toward Matt's office and said to him, "This is Matt Whiteside."

Pete Ramsey walked into the office, looked at Matt, and his mouth dropped. "Matt...Matt Whiteside, it's good to see you." They shook hands. "I didn't know I was going to be interviewing with you. When did you start working for General Technologies?"

Matt nodded at his secretary. "Thank you, Cindy. That'll be all. Come in, Pete, and have a seat." Matt closed the door and sat down at his desk across from Pete. "I started work here about a month or so ago and I'm looking for an assistant to help me run the company's pension plan, as you are aware. What happened to your job at Franklin?"

Pete rolled the file folder he was holding into a scroll and squirmed in his seat. "I, uh, I got caught up in the collateral damage of the subprime mortgage mess. You know how Franklin had gotten very aggressive with their single-family lending in 2004 and 2005. We held out for a long time, but the market kept declining. My division was one of the first to get whacked. My uncle couldn't do anything for me. That was a while ago. I've been looking for work ever since. I really need this job, Matt."

"Tell me, Pete. How did you get out of the Worldwide Funding mess? What was their relationship with Whitney Homes and how did you avoid getting caught in the prosecution of those loan scams?"

Pete adjusted his tie nervously. "Uh, I knew some people at Worldwide who, I guess, had what you would call a business relationship with Taylor Whitney. They would turn a blind eye and make all of the questionable loans for Whitney, provided they were given a kickback, and provided Franklin Smith, through me, immediately took them off their hands." He wiped his forehead with a handkerchief. "I only knew that Worldwide was spooning me deals and I was making money off them legitimately. I helped Franklin unload those loans to Freddie Mac and Fannie Mae. Things only went sideways when New York decided to cut back on buying Worldwide's bundled loans."

Matt wrote some notes on a legal pad. "When the feds were looking for someone on the inside at Franklin, didn't they question you?"

"Yes, they interviewed me, a dozen times. But nothing came of it as I never underwrote the loans or approved them. I was innocent and everything I did was legal. All I did was buy the loans from Worldwide, then our group sold them off to Freddie Mac or Fannie Mae. What happened to them after they left my desk, and Franklin's portfolio, was someone else's problem. Besides, most of the banks and Wall Street firms that got into trouble, got bailed out by Congress. I say, no harm, no foul." He held up his hands and feinted washing them.

Matt chewed on the end of the eraser on his pen, leaning back in his chair. "What about the homeowners, and small businesses? Where was their bailout? Doesn't it bother you that many people lost their homes and were hurt because of this phony and inflated market? People lost their houses, all their savings, their credit— everything they had."

Pete's eyes narrowed. "Come on, Matt. You know Wall Street is all about money; all about the Benjamins. They and Congress could care less about homeowners or small business owners. Anyway, most of those people who lost out didn't deserve to be in a house, and all they wanted was to cash in on the bubble. Face it, they got what they deserved."

Matt raised an eyebrow and leaned forward. "Let's get back to the reason you came here."

Pete picked a couple of papers out of a file he was carrying. "Here's my updated version of my résumé." He leaned across the desk and handed the document to Matt, who glanced at it briefly and set it down.

"I don't need to look at your résumé to know you are qualified for this position," Matt said. "I know what you can do. You could easily handle the work required. The salary is seventy thousand per year with an annual bonus, which is subjective. The job comes with health benefits and a two-week vacation. You will be reporting directly to me. I am not a drill sergeant, but do require promptness and accuracy. Do you have any questions for me, Pete?"

"No, I don't have any questions for you. I just would like to tell you I really enjoyed working with you at Franklin. I'm sorry about the way some deals went down, but that's just business; it was never personal."

"Don't worry about that, Pete. I've moved on from Franklin Smith. I don't carry grudges. Well, like I said, you have what this position takes and if you don't have any more questions, this will conclude our interview. I'll get back to you next week about specifics." Matt stood up and they shook. "I assume you can find your way out?"

Pete stood up, smiling. "Yes, yes, I can find my way out. Thanks for seeing me, Matt. I look forward to working with you. Have a good day." Pete walked out of Matt's office and turned left toward the lobby. Matt sat down, leaned back in his chair, and put his hands behind his head. Then, he leaned forward and picked up his phone and dialed Drew's number.

"Hello?"

"Hey, Drew, it's Matt. What time are you wrapping it up for the day?"

Drew paused. "In about five minutes. Do you want to meet at 13 Views?"

"Yes I do! Give me about fifteen minutes. I'll meet you there."

"Sounds good to me. Hey, by the way, congratulations on your engagement to Stephanie."

"Thanks, Drew. I'll see you there." Matt hung up. He straightened up his desk and picked up Pete Ramsey's résumé. Holding it up to his eyes, he spoke out loud, "What was your favorite saying, Pete? The deal's not done until the check clears. Well, in your case, this check didn't clear." Matt crumpled up the résumé and tossed it off the wall into the corner trash can. He picked up his coat and walked out of the office.

FORTY-SEVEN

His dark, wrinkled eyes squinted through faux designer sunglasses into the pickup's rearview mirror, seeing the huge dust trail he was leaving on the dirt road. The truck rattled and creaked as it seemed to hit every pothole in the road. It was necessary to turn on the windshield wipers every mile or so to wipe the dust off as he sped toward his destination.

His crumpled, sweat-stained cowboy hat fit low on his head, and his shirt was wet from perspiration. He had driven more than five miles since he left the paved road, and the only view he had was of saguaro cacti, tumbleweeds, an occasional roadrunner, and the heat waves rising off the rock-infested landscape. At least the air conditioning worked...somewhat. As the truck came to the top of a rise in the road, he saw a sprawling Spanish-style ranch house with a red barrel-tiled roof. It was surrounded by a tall adobe wall, which stood about thirty feet away from the house.

He edged the truck up to the wrought-iron gates, which slowly opened inward, and he was waved through by an armed man. The gate was shut quickly behind him. Pulling in front of the path leading to the front door, he slowed down and stopped. Exiting the truck, he took off his hat and slammed it against his jeans, knocking off the dust. He wiped his forehead with his forearm.

A small, dark-haired man came out of the front door and rushed to greet him. "Welcome, cowboy; it has been a long time since we met," he said as he pumped the cowboy's hand furiously.

The man put his hat back on his head and glanced back down the dirt road as the gates closed completely. "It has."

"Follow me; he is waiting for you."

The cowboy followed the guide through the wooden front doors and into a large entry with tile floors and filtered light. A ceiling fan spun quietly overhead, throwing off cool air. A tall, dark-skinned man with a thin mustache and wearing a white shirt, designer jeans, and cowboy boots came around the corner and embraced him. "My friend, it has been too much time. How was your trip?"

"It was long, Carlos my friend, but everything was done as you wished."

The tall man grinned, showing off a gold tooth. "Everything? No problems?"

"No problems."

"Excellent. I can always count on you. Come, let's go to the back and have a cold drink by the pool." He nudged the cowboy in the ribs. "I have arranged for a little celebration for you and some pretty friends who want to meet you." He winked, and elbowed the cowboy playfully again. "Real pretty friends."

"Thank you for your hospitality, *amigo*. Before we go out there, I have a present for you." He felt into his left pocket and lifted out a bulky gold watch, its face surrounded with diamonds. He held it out, and with his other hand lifted out a blue sapphire necklace, also surrounded with diamonds, hanging on a gold chain. "I thought you might like these."

The tall man whistled softly as he slowly inspected the jewelry. "These are very beautiful." He looked up, his eyes wide. "They are real, no?"

The cowboy nodded. "A jeweler I know in San Diego assured me yes, they are real, and very expensive."

The tall man leaned his head back, held his belly with both hands, and laughed. "Maybe I didn't lose as much money as I thought after all." He slapped the cowboy on the back. "Come, my friend. We have drinks to drink, food to eat, women to love, and we can talk about your next assignment." Laughing, they walked across the tiled floor, their boots clicking noisily, and exited through the patio door.

CPSIA information can be obtained at www.ICGtesting.com
Printed in the USA
LVOW060325250612

287423LV00003B/2/P